THE
FLORIST
ON
Amelia Island

SEVEN SISTERS
BOOK FOUR

HOPE
HOLLOWAY

Hope Holloway

Seven Sisters Book 4

The Florist on Amelia Island

The Seven Daughters Of Rex Wingate

Born to Charlotte Wingate

Madeline Wingate, age 49
Victoria "Tori" Wingate, age 45
Rose Wingate D'Angelo, age 43
Raina Wingate, age 43

Born to Susannah Wingate

Sadie Wingate age 35
Grace Wingate Jenkins, age 33
Chloe Wingate, age 29

Chapter One

Raina

For once in her life, Raina couldn't wait to leave the office and go home at the end of the day. Maybe not the *official* end, since the clock was a good forty-five minutes from what any self-respecting workaholic would call "quittin' time."

Yes, she enjoyed every day of running Wingate Properties, her father's real estate company, but the truth was, the further along her pregnancy progressed, the less she wanted to sit behind that desk.

In fact, it had just occurred to her when she perused the latest update from the divorce attorney that her love affair with a long day's work was ending with the same speed as her love affair with the man she'd married sixteen years ago.

And honestly, she was just fine with that.

"You're leaving?" Dani Alvarez, her assistant, looked up from her desk as Raina breezed out of the office holding nothing but her purse.

At a desk across from Dani, Blake Youngblood,

Wingate Properties' newest agent and Raina's nephew, cocked a brow. "And not taking your laptop or briefcase?"

Her two best employees shared a look. "That's at least five nights in a row," Dani said in a stage whisper.

"Do you think she's sick?" Blake asked, fighting a smile that she now knew looked familiar because it was—he'd inherited the classic Wingate grin that looked exactly like Raina's father's, Blake's biological grandfather. She hadn't recognized it before—no one had—but now that they knew he was family, the similarity was obvious.

"Please." Raina rolled her eyes at them, but she had to laugh at the energy these two brought to this formerly lifeless office. "I'm not sick, but I am five months pregnant with twins, thank you very much." She turned one way and then the other, one hand on her ever-growing baby bump. "And, in case you missed it, we closed a million-and-a-half-dollar deal today."

"Oh, we didn't miss it," Dani said, fluttering a contract. "I'm filing the paperwork now."

"And I'm adding up my commission on that sale," Blake chimed in. "Which I thank you for handing me."

"You earned it," she assured him. "And thank you for handling the filing, Dani. I'd be lost without you two. But right now, I can't wait to get home to my dream beach house, where I will sit on my deck, stare at the ocean, and bask in the glow of elevated bare feet."

"I don't know what you love more, Raina," Blake mused, smiling at her. "That house or being pregnant."

"It's a tie." She rubbed her belly again, never tiring of

the thrill of that bump. "No, actually, pregnancy wins. I know most women hate this and, at forty-three and teetering on the edge of divorce with the baby daddy, I probably should complain, but..." She grinned like a little kid. "I have never been so happy."

"Aww!" Dani cooed. "You're the cutest, Raina. And what ever happened to Chase Madison? Wasn't he going to rent a room in your beach house for a few months when you bought the place from him? You never mention him."

Raina shrugged. "He said he had to go to Europe. That was the day I moved in a month ago, and I have not seen hide nor hair. Again, not complaining." She hadn't been overjoyed about the idea of sharing her house with the previous owner, despite the fact that he was paying a hefty rent that covered her mortgage payments. All she wanted to do was nest and enjoy her pregnancy. "I imagine he could be back at any time to take care of the boutique hotel he's building down by the Ritz. Do you know the status of that property, Blake?"

"I've heard through the rumor mill that things are on schedule for a soft opening soon. So he should be around at some point."

"Fingers crossed he'll stay there once it's open," she mused.

"Doubtful," Blake said. "It's already got bookings into next year, and there aren't that many rooms in the place. It's very high end."

"Oh, well. So far, so good, then." Raina glanced at the piles of paper on both their desks. "Yikes, we're busy these days. Should I stick around and help you guys get through this mountain of work?"

"No." Blake stood, coming around his desk. "You should go home and stay happy and have an early night, Aunt Raina."

She gave him a sly smile, always loving it when he called her that. She'd known Blake for months before she learned that his father was her half-brother, given up for adoption well over five decades ago. Although that man, Brad Young, refused any overtures to have a relationship with the Wingate family, Blake had finally accepted their love and was settling nicely into the clan.

Raina reached her hand to him, so grateful he'd made that decision. "Thank you, my dear nephew. And thank you for the assist on that deal today. You earned your commission through professionalism and tenacity."

"All right, all right," Dani groaned. "The kid's a natural. Don't feed his already inflated ego."

"Oh, please, feed it some more." He lifted his hands, flicking his fingers to encourage them.

"What I'm going to feed is my little brood." Raina patted her belly again. "Thing One is healthy and wants broccoli. Thing Two?" She grinned. "That baby is begging for french fries."

"Then make them both in an air fryer," Blake said, his expression turning serious. "You can't put greasy french fries on those precious heads."

Dani practically choked. "For the love of all that's holy, Blake, do you have *no* idea how babies are grown inside a woman? Raina can eat what she wants. In fact, give those babies a *Cubano*." She rolled the word off her Spanish-speaking tongue. "Roasted pork, swiss cheese, pickles and mustard on buttery bread smashed in a grill. *Delicioso!*"

"You will not put any of that in your baby vessel, Raina Wingate." Blake pointed at her, all kinds of serious. "Make yourself some steamed vegetables and clean protein."

She held up a hand, not wanting to get in the middle of their unending and contradictory nutritional advice. "I'll figure it out, on my own, at my home, with my feet up." Then she blew them a kiss and waved. "I'm off!"

They let her leave without any more discussion, but the smile stayed on her face as she drove from Wingate Way in downtown Fernandina Beach, traveling one mile east to the coast of Amelia Island.

Turning onto the beach road, she passed her parents' waterfront home where she'd lived for a few months after moving up here from Miami. Then she continued until she reached the cedar shake beach house that she'd so happily called home since she bought it a month ago.

As she pulled into the front drive off Fletcher Avenue, her heart soared, as it had since the day she'd stumbled upon the place while walking on the beach. From the moment she'd stepped inside the place called The Sanctuary, Raina had "home vibes" and knew she belonged here.

With the unexpected sale of her Miami company by her soon-to-be ex-husband, she could afford it. Sort of. She did have to take out a hefty loan while she waited for the sale and divorce papers to be finalized and signed, which would end what she'd thought had been a happy marriage to Jack Wallace.

As it turned out, she hadn't been so happy, she mused as she parked in the driveway, skipping the garage because there was nothing she enjoyed more than entering through the front door.

Everything that she thought made her happy in Miami—a handsome husband, a showplace house, a successful business—had been frighteningly fleeting.

But then her father had a stroke, bringing her back up to her family on Amelia Island. Not long after she arrived, she learned her husband had fallen in love with another woman. As fate would have it, he didn't reveal that ugly truth to her until *after* they'd had one last night together.

And that was how Raina Wingate became a forty-three-year-old about-to-be divorced pregnant woman carrying twins.

As she unlocked the front door, she actually laughed out loud, because if that wasn't proof that God had a sense of humor, then—

"Hey, honey, you're home."

She froze with a gasp at the sound of the man's voice, thinking for one horrifying second that it was Jack. That she'd come around the corner and see him holding a scotch on the rocks in one hand and a phone in the other, making reservations for wherever they'd have dinner.

The thought *shook* her.

But that wasn't Jack. It was...

She squinted into the late afternoon sunlight streaming into the house as a tall, broad-shouldered man walked from the kitchen toward the entry where she stood.

"Chase." She whispered his name as relief that it wasn't Jack mixed with a thud of disappointment in her chest. So much for solitude, nesting, putting her feet up, and wallowing in the comfort of her own home.

"I should have warned you," he said, stepping out of the sunlight, closer to her. "I'm back from my travels." He paused, searching her face, giving her a split second to remember his arresting features and the dark eyes that reminded her he was proudly half-Sicilian. "And how are you?"

"Oh, um, good. Wow, wasn't expecting you."

"I can see that," he said on a laugh, reading her reaction. "I should have called. Or not parked in the garage, but I meant to move the car before you got home. At least you'd have had some warning at the sight of my car. Sorry."

She took a breath, realizing somewhere in the back of her mind that she couldn't remember Jack ever saying he was sorry for anything, let alone about where he'd parked.

"No, no," she insisted, still a little shocked at his startling presence in her home. "I mean, you live here." Those words tasted like sand in her mouth, which was suddenly very dry. "You shouldn't have to call, I just..."

"Wasn't expecting me," he finished for her, tipping his head. "I get that."

"But you paid your rent," she said, digging for brightness and hoping it didn't sound false. "So, it's your home, too."

Dang, what was she thinking when she got roped into this arrangement? That he'd be fun to have around? Maybe for someone who wasn't... *a forty-three-year-old about-to-be divorced pregnant woman carrying twins.*

"Well, you're gracious and understanding," he said, a smile crinkling his eyes.

"And exhausted." She slipped off the heels that had grown tight throughout the day and dropped her bag on the entry table. "So I'm going to..."

Wait. She wasn't going to lounge in her soaker tub with him in the house, was she? Well, if he was living here, she'd have to eventually. And the main suite was upstairs, so...

"Chill and unwind," he suggested. "You should sit on the deck. Have a cocktail—er, mocktail, I suppose. Want me to whip you up a Virgin Mary? I'm making dinner."

Dinner? Well, that explained the tangy aroma of tomatoes and basil floating out from the kitchen, but... really? Someone else was cooking in her kitchen?

Although, based on that agreement and the hefty amount that had hit her account a day after closing, it was his kitchen, too. Temporarily, he'd said. Six months at the outside.

Six interminable months and somewhere around month four, she'd be having two babies.

Suddenly, she felt utterly overwhelmed and longed to regroup.

"I'm just going to go up to my room for a while," she said. "But thank you."

"Sure, sure. I'll be in the kitchen and you can have a little chicken parm if you want some. How are you feeling, by the way? Everything good?"

He asked like...like he really cared. Which touched and baffled her.

"I'm great, thanks, but...you made chicken parmesan?" For one second, she tried—and failed—to imagine coming home from work to a dinner that Jack had made. The very thought was laughable from a man who'd been challenged by the coffeemaker.

He gave a casual shrug. "I spent some time in Italy and that always inspires me."

She stared at him, still taking in his height of six feet or so, the silver hair at his temples highlighting dark good looks, and the obvious comfort he felt just being...him. A man who was inspired to cook and owned oodles of properties and had enough intelligence and moxie to build a boutique hotel just south of the most famous one on Amelia Island.

Was he even real?

Unfortunately, he was...and standing in her *sanctuary*. "As tempting as your dinner sounds—and smells— I'm going to rest."

He nodded and inched back to let her go by. "Absolutely, Raina."

Somehow, the use of her name sounded...personal. Intimate, even. Which meant she'd officially lost her mind, because what else would he call her? *The Soon-To-Be-Former Mrs. Wallace?*

With a quick smile, she slipped past him and darted up the stairs—as much as a woman five months pregnant with twins could *dart*—and turned the corner to enter her favorite room on Earth.

From the day she'd entered this ocean-facing haven, she'd been in love with the four-poster bed, the sunrise view, the soft splash of the waves, and the gentle salt-infused breeze.

She opened the French doors and stepped out on the balcony, taking slow, deep breaths that she suddenly seemed to crave. This was a haven *and* her heaven.

At night, she'd watch the moon paint a silver streak over the ocean and rub her growing belly, talking to her Things. She'd ask them what they wanted to be named and wonder if she could ever love anyone as much as she already loved these unborn babies.

But now...*he* was here. Cooking and being tall and charming and effortlessly attractive and...*here*. She resented that. She resented all of that. She really resented the attractive part because...she didn't ever plan to find another man attractive. *Ever*.

But it was hard not to give at least a nod of appreciation for someone who was kind and offered a mocktail and probably turned every female head in town when he walked by.

Fine. Props to him for all that. But she wanted to be alone.

Oh, well. Six months, he'd promised, and one had already come and gone.

That left five months, and most of the time would be spent at work during the day and resting for the babies in the evening. He would hardly even be here, she told herself, at least if the last month was any indication.

Feeling a little like her twin sister, Rose, who was famously capable of only seeing the best in every situation, Raina finally dropped onto the bed. With a long sigh, she put her feet up and scrutinized the slight swelling in her ankles.

She let her eyes close gently, inhaling a mix of sea air and something ridiculously delicious wafting up from downstairs. She heard the scrape of a pan on the burner, the pop of a wine cork.

Just make yourself at home, Chase. My home.

Pushing back the thought, she drifted off, letting sleep wash over her while the babies rumbled around and gave her tiny kicks of love.

When Raina opened her eyes, dusk had fallen hard over the island. The sky was purple and a few stars had come out over the ocean. Slightly disoriented, she looked around for her phone, only to remember it was in her purse downstairs.

Guessing it was around eight, she pushed up on one elbow, blinking off the nap and hoping she wouldn't have insomnia later because she'd rested so long. Then she shot straight up, remembering her roommate. She listened for sounds of life downstairs. But it was silent.

And she was *ravenous.*

Suddenly so hungry it actually hurt, Raina stood on bare feet, straightened her cotton dress, and decided that homemade chicken parm sounded like the greatest thing ever cooked.

She made her way down the steps, noticing that the entire downstairs was dark and quiet. The dinner aromas were even gone, replaced by the same sea scent that had filled her room. That was because one of the French doors was open, letting in the breeze and the last whispers of daylight.

From the deck she heard the soft ding of a phone and the sound of one of the deck chairs moving on the wood.

"Well, hello, beautiful," he said, his voice low and...tender.

For a moment, she didn't move, painfully aware that she was eavesdropping on a personal conversation. She took a step toward the door, planning to close it to give him privacy, when she saw him stand, the phone to his ear.

"You're alone? He's not there tonight? I'll be right over."

She turned to the sink and flipped on the faucet to make her presence known.

"Are you kidding?" he asked as he walked in, his face registering that he just realized Raina was there. He gave a quick smile, then switched the phone to the other ear. "Are you hungry? I made your favorite." As he asked the question, he opened the fridge and pulled out a plastic container. "You just give me ten minutes and, I promise, you won't be lonely anymore."

He ended the call and heat crawled up her cheeks as she imagined the woman on the other end, some lucky lady lounging in something sexy, waiting for this handsome man to arrive with homemade Italian food and... whatever else relieved her loneliness.

"Hey, sorry," he said to Raina as he snapped the top off the container and peered at what was inside. "Did you want some of this?"

"No, no. Take it...to your friend."

"I did promise you some. I'll put some on a plate and take the rest. But I have to leave."

Yeah, he wouldn't want to miss stolen time with someone who was...unexpectedly alone.

Her gut clenched and a bad feeling crawled up her spine. A married woman? Was he no better than Jack, her cheating ex?

"I don't need any," she said quickly. "I, um..." She put her hand on her belly. "Just want a little soup tonight."

He glanced at her with a hint of a question in his eyes and, for a moment, looked like he was going to say something. Then he nodded. "Of course."

"Please take it all." She eyed him, quiet while he replaced the lid and checked his phone again. He left and went toward the guest room, and she busied herself in the pantry looking for soup she didn't really want.

Honestly, she had no right to say or think anything about his personal life, and she certainly didn't expect a man as warm, charming, and great-looking as Chase not to have one. And she could be jumping to extreme and wrong conclusions.

She heard his voice again, in that low and intimate tone, too soft to make out the words but certain he was talking to the same person.

After a moment, he reappeared, keys in one hand, a small bag tucked under his arm as he grabbed the Tupperware.

"Are you coming back?" she asked and instantly regretted the intrusive question. "I mean, can I expect to hear the door late or..."

A sly smile threatened. "I don't know. It depends."

On whether or not her husband shows? Raina hated the thought but there it was.

"I'll use my own entrance." He angled his head toward the guest suite, reminding her that he didn't have to come in and out of any other door.

"Of course. Okay. Bye." She planted a smile and looked down at the can of chicken noodle soup in her hands.

"Are you sure?" He raised the container. "There's plenty."

"I'm fine." But for some reason, she wasn't. Her stomach felt sour and heavy. "Have fun."

He gave a nod and walked toward the garage door, and left.

Was he a cheater, too? Were all men?

Probably not, but she was so jaded, it could be

another lifetime before she ever believed one again, at least on a personal level.

She heard a noisy engine fire up and the garage door rumble. For some reason, she walked to the front of the house and looked out the window next to the door, just in time to catch sight of a two-seater convertible Mercedes turning onto Fletcher.

"Of course he drives Jack's dream car," she muttered, huffing out a breath.

She stood in the entry for a few seconds, holding the can of soup and really not liking...men. All men. Every single one of them.

She had to get out of here. Just by *being* he'd ruined her night.

Without giving herself time to second-guess the decision, she went back to the kitchen and locked the French door and put the soup back in the pantry. Then she got her bag and shoes and stepped out the front door, sucking in the evening air.

She'd go see Rose she decided, as she walked to her car. Her sister would welcome her, and she even had an air fryer. No doubt sweet, optimistic Rosebud would make her french fries and broccoli and remind Raina that not all men were cheaters.

Chapter Two

Rose

W aking up alone wasn't that unusual for Rose D'Angelo. But this morning, as the dawn sky slipped from midnight to silver, alone felt truly *lonely*. She'd tried to explain that to Raina last night, but in her usual fashion, Rose had glossed over how much she ached and painted a happy picture of her "new normal."

She was used to being alone, she'd insisted. And that was partially true. Her husband, Gabe, had been an EMT and firefighter for sixteen years and that meant plenty of overnight shifts that had her in an empty bed when the sun rose. But this kind of solitude was different. This made her ache.

She turned, the sheets sighing in harmony with her sad exhale as she stared at the empty pillow next to her.

Gabe wasn't ten minutes away at the Fernandina Beach Fire Department on Amelia Island. He wasn't cooking with his crew or waiting for the next call or expected home when his shift ended. He wasn't even covering for her at the flower shop, accepting early deliveries while she stayed home to get the kids off to school.

He was at the other end of the state, which might as well be the other end of the Earth.

But he's not gone for good, Rose! He's in Miami, not... heaven! Wasn't that always your fear?

She could still hear Raina's voice of reason, somehow sounding like Rose, pushing the positive of any situation.

And her sister had been right. The fear of Gabe having an accident, injury, or worse had always pressed a low-grade anxiety on Rose's usually happy heart. After all, it was Gabe's job to put his life on the line to save others.

And then he quit that job to follow his lifelong dream of finishing medical school and becoming Dr. Gabriel D'Angelo.

Another sigh threatened, but she swallowed her sadness and dug for her bone-deep optimism.

Her famous and frequently mocked "Rose-Colored Glasses" had gotten her through every family crisis, major or minor, every decision, every day. And this day— along with the next two or so years while Gabe finally earned the degree he'd partially completed before their first child was born—would be no different in that regard.

Rose was determined to stay strong in the face of this unexpected life change of having her husband live almost four hundred miles away, coming home only on the occasional weekend. She would stay supportive as Gabe followed his heart, regardless of the fact that, at forty-three, he was as old as some of his professors at the University of Miami's Miller School of Medicine. She would stay cheerful as she managed the deliveries, orders, and staff at Coming Up Roses, her lively flower shop on Wingate Way.

But most important, she would be present and loving and twice the parent to her four wonderful kids as they navigated their lives without their beloved father around on a daily basis.

She flipped the comforter back and sat up, pressing her fingers to her temples to ward off a headache at the thought of doing all that...alone.

"But you're not alone," she whispered as her feet hit the floor, once again remembering all Raina had said last night.

Rose had four of her six sisters living right here in town, the two greatest parents down the road, and a thriving business. Best of all, she had Zach, Ethan, Alyson, and Avery, kids who were as close to perfect as humanly possible.

Right now, they were all consumed with the start of a new school year. Their father's big goodbye a few days ago hadn't really hit them yet. To them, it was no different than Dad doing a couple of back-to-back shifts at the station.

But when enough time passed that this house felt the absence of the rock-solid leader of their family, she would have to fill those shoes.

She stared down at her feet as they touched the wide-planked wood of the nearly hundred-year-old Victorian where she'd been raised and now raised her own family. How could she fill his big Size 12s with these woefully small...

She sniffed, straightening at the scent of...was that *bacon*? Or was the house on fire?

Grabbing her robe, she rushed to the hall and took a deep inhale of...Gabe. At least that's what it smelled like. The aroma of a day when her husband didn't have a shift, so he'd start them off with his signature breakfast of bacon, eggs, and pancakes, cooked with love for the kids before school.

So far this year, there'd been a lot of oatmeal and— she cringed in shame—Pop-Tarts.

Tiptoeing down the stairs, she heard the ding of dishes, the scrape of a spatula, and the sound of water running. Coming around the corner, she opened her mouth in surprise at the sight of her oldest son moving around the kitchen like a whirling dervish, dishes and bowls and utensils everywhere.

"Zach?" she murmured. "What are you—"

"Oh, Mom! You're early. I'm not ready for customers yet."

She smiled, because Gabe always called the family his customers when he made breakfast, but also because Zach had put an apron on over his school clothes of khaki shorts and a T-shirt, and it was kind of the cutest thing she'd ever seen.

She took a few steps closer. "Honey, what are you doing? It's a school day."

"Exactly, so I'm making breakfast but don't the girls have, like, another twenty minutes? Ethan's up but he's still struggling with that pre-algebra. I didn't make him finish it last night because he was zoned-out tired. I don't remember doing those kinds of equations in eighth grade."

She almost laughed at the way he said it, like eighth grade was twenty years ago, not three. "You did his homework with him last night?"

"Aunt Raina was here." He shrugged. "Mine was done and the little dude was on the struggle bus."

"Oh!" She pressed her hand to her heart. "How much do I love you, Zachary D'Angelo?"

He broke into a wide smile. "Decide after you taste my eggs. I'm not Dad in that department."

"But in every other you are." She scooted around the counter and wrapped her arms around his back—which she could have sworn was broader than the last time she'd hugged him—and turned her face to press her cheek against his shoulder, which seemed a little higher and broader every time she hugged him. "You have the same good heart."

As he chuckled, she opened her eyes and her gaze landed on the weekly calendar she kept on the fridge, divided by each child's name, with a section for her own important meetings. It used to also include Gabe's firefighting schedule, but now...those days were gone.

Looking at it, she studied today's date under Zach's name.

"Hey, wait a second," she said, leaning back. "You have a National Honor Society meeting this morning and it starts in..." She squinted at the microwave clock. "Ten minutes?"

"Nah. I'm skipping that."

"Zach, you were going to put your name in to run for secretary. Didn't you tell me a few weeks ago that this was the day you had to file to be in the election?"

He made a face, tipping his head as he lifted an egg. "I'm thinking scrambled, because there's no way I could replicate Dad's over-easies. Those things are next level."

"Zach." She put a hand on his arm, stopping him before he cracked the egg. "You don't have to do this."

"What happened to all the love?" he joked.

"I do love you, but you don't have to miss important activities at school."

"It's fine, Mom. And no, I don't want to be secretary, and there's no other reason to go to this morning's meeting. Oh, dang it! I forgot to turn on the griddle for the pancakes."

"We don't need pancakes and eggs and toast," she said, pulling at the tie of her robe as she regarded him carefully. "What brought this on? Are my Pop-Tart breakfasts too awful? I can make these—"

"*And* lunches for the girls and Ethan? *And* get dressed and out the door to get the morning deliveries going at Coming Up Roses?" He gave her a "get real" look. "I got this, Mom."

"Zach, you don't have to—"

"Mommy!" Avery burst into the kitchen, her wispy golden hair as wild as her blue eyes, a Barbie nightgown fluttering around her six-year-old body. "Aly locked the bathroom door and won't let me in!"

"Oh, that's not good."

"And I can't find my Little Mermaid T-shirt and that's what I want to wear today."

"It's in the laundry, which"—she rolled her eyes—"I forgot to do because Aunt Raina came over."

"Want me to put a load in?" Zach asked, and she almost laughed but Avery hung on her robe sleeve.

"I have to go to the bathroom and I can't get in there!"

"Go tell her—"

"Mom, please." Zach gestured toward the stairs. "Go deal with the girls. I got this."

She honestly wanted to laugh at that, but Ethan came marching down the steps before she could react.

"I cannot do that problem!" he called out to the world. "Pre-algebra sucks!"

Rose opened her mouth to reprimand the language but Zach barked louder. "Hey, pottymouth! Cool it!"

She whipped around and looked at him. What was happening here?

"What?" he asked. "Dad told him not to use that word and Dad told me..."

When his voice faded out, she narrowed her eyes at him. "Dad told you what?"

"Mommy!" Avery tugged at her arm. "Please get her out of the bathroom."

Ethan rolled in, his dark blond hair a curly mess, his impish smile missing. "I'm not doing that homework," he said, the comment directed at Zach.

"Then you better go in early and talk to Mrs. Coleman." Zach tapped another egg on the side of a bowl. "I had her in middle school. She'll...oh, *crap*!" Raw egg splattered all over the counter and a chunk of shell dropped into the bowl.

"Oh, now who's the pottymouth?" Ethan countered. "Maybe *I* should get on the phone with Dad until midnight telling him what's going on around here."

"What?" Rose looked from one son to the other. "You were on the phone with Dad until midnight?"

"Not...midnight. Just while you were talking to Aunt Raina."

"Mommy!" Avery pulled at her again.

"And does Dad know you're not going to run for secretary of the National Honor Society?" she demanded, knowing that Gabe would *not* approve of that decision.

Zach looked up from the egg mess, his whole expression so very much like his father's that she nearly melted. "Take care of the girls, Mom. I got this."

She started to argue, not appreciating the fact that he not only didn't answer the question, he told her what to do, but Avery yanked.

She let herself be led away and the subject dropped...for now.

As they neared the steps, Avery whispered, "He *was* on until midnight, because I got up to tinkle and heard him through the bathroom vent. Also, Ethan said 'sucks' about twenty times."

Fighting a smile, she reached down and picked up her smallest child, clearly as needy as the rest of them. But this one could still fit on her hip as they climbed the stairs together, and Rose liked that.

"What other offenses were committed on the overnight shift, Officer D'Angelo?" she teased.

Avery giggled and wrapped her legs around Rose's waist. "I didn't say my prayers last night."

"Excuse me?"

"'Cause Daddy always comes in and says them with me after you tuck me in."

Rose fought a grunt of frustration, because she had promised Avery she'd be back to pray when the doorbell rang to interrupt the nightly routine. "I'm sorry, baby girl. Aunt Raina came over and we got to—"

"Blabbing," she supplied.

"Blabbing? No, we were talking."

"Daddy said you and Aunt Raina can blab until the sun comes up."

And he wasn't wrong. They had *blabbed* for a long time while Rose made her pregnant sister a weird combination of french fries and broccoli. Blabbing had included Rose whining about Gabe being gone and just getting the pure adult and sister time she craved.

By the time Raina had left, the girls were sound asleep. And Zach, she assumed, was off the phone, because Gabe had called her at midnight just to say he loved her.

As they reached the closed door of the bathroom the two youngest D'Angelos shared, Avery dropped her head on Rose's shoulder and sneaked her thumb into her mouth, a bad habit that had returned lately.

"I miss Daddy," she murmured.

Easing the thumb out, Rose hugged her. "Me, too, Ave. Me, too."

"Will he come home soon?"

Define "soon," she thought glumly as she lowered Avery to the floor. "A few weeks, I think." Before Avery could answer, Rose held up her hand to quiet her and listen to a noise coming from the other side of the door.

"Aly?" she called after hearing another loud sniff. "Are you okay?"

She reached for the knob, but the door whipped open before she got it, revealing the red, teary, swollen face of a little girl who rarely cried.

"Alyson!" Instantly, Rose reached for her, not used to tears from her famously undramatic daughter. In fact, on her ninth birthday a few weeks ago, Aly had announced she would never cry again. "Oh, honey. I know you miss Daddy, too."

She shook her head and backed away, holding something behind her back. "I can't go to school, Mommy."

"Why?"

"I can't go anywhere." She swiped at her tear-stained cheeks, blinking her smoky gray-blue eyes. "I did a bad thing."

And that would be as rare as her tears. Alyson was easily the most well-behaved of the four kids, and that bar was high. She didn't break rules, she didn't test boundaries, and most of the time, she was so mature, it was easy to forget she was a kid.

"What happened, honey?"

She took a noisy swallow and tugged Rose closer,

then brought her other hand around to show what she was hiding. Her precious purple glasses were bent beyond recognition.

"I put them on in bed and fell asleep."

Guilt punched. Rose should have noticed the glasses in her bed when she did her last check after Raina left. She could have prevented this accident.

"Oh, Aly." She took the broken frame and tried to fix the arm, but it snapped off. "Yikes, and you just got these a few weeks ago. You'll have to wear the old ones until we get—"

"No."

Rose drew back. "Excuse me?"

"I can't see with those."

"But they'll get you through until we can order a new pair."

She shook her head. "They'll just get broken, too."

Cocking her head, Rose searched the little face she knew so well, seeing something she rarely—if ever—saw in this child. She was hiding something. She looked...guilty.

"Alyson," she said slowly. "Are you not telling me something?"

She swallowed visibly and stared mutely up at Rose.

"She doesn't want to wear them anymore," Avery chimed in from behind. "And she rolled over on them on purpose."

Rose gasped and blinked at Alyson, waiting for a hot denial of Avery's accusation. But none came.

"Is that true, Aly?" Rose asked gently.

She pushed back a lock of caramel-colored hair. "It's not *not* true," she said.

"You broke these glasses?" It was so out of character, Rose almost laughed. "Why?"

"Because I don't want to wear them."

Oh, this old battle? It had been fought and won, she'd thought. Being able to see had its benefits, and Aly wore her purple-rimmed glasses with pride, or at least Rose thought so.

"But you have to wear them, honey. You can't see clearly without them."

She shifted from one slippered foot to the other. "Jordie Fitzpatrick got contact lenses."

"At eight?" Rose choked.

"I'm nine now."

"Still too young for contacts, honey. One more year, just like the doctor said when we ordered these. Now, let's move it here and let Avery use the bathroom."

But Avery was actually sitting on the floor, taking it all in with that thumb back in her mouth.

"Honey." She reached over to guide it out. "You know better."

Just then, Ethan came up the steps, shaking his head and not looking at all like the funny, sweet, adorable twelve-year-old who lifted her heart.

"I don't know who died and put him in charge," Ethan grumbled, pointing his thumb in the general direction of the kitchen. "But someone better break the news to Mr. Know-It-All that he is not the boss of me or anyone else."

Without any other explanation, he brushed by her and marched up to the third floor where the boys' bedrooms were.

Something was very off this morning. Well, other than the fact that Gabe wasn't here, because when he was, harmony reigned in the D'Angelo house. And right now, nothing felt harmonious.

Right now, two years stretched out like forever.

Chapter Three

Chloe

"On Tuesdays, we see Travis."

The second Chloe uttered the words, Lady Bug leaped off the sofa, abandoned her favorite sunning spot, and darted to the beach bungalow's front door. There, she pranced on her two front paws as she pressed her wee face to the sidelight glass, her tail swishing in excitement and anticipation.

Chloe laughed, but couldn't deny...if she was a dog, she'd probably do the same thing.

"He might not come, you know. He's usually here by now."

But they both knew Travis McCall would show up at her door soon. In the month since Chloe had moved back home after The Great L.A. Debacle, as she thought of her short-lived stint as an entertainment news reporter, she and Travis had fallen into...something.

A routine? A relationship? Something they hadn't put a name to yet. Something nice. Something with potential. Something that made her heart beat with the same rhythm as Lady Bug's wee Shih Tzu paws on the tile floor.

Twice a week, after he ended a twenty-four-hour shift as a rookie firefighter, he'd just happen by the tiny beach house on her parents' property to see Chloe. Depending on what the last day had been like, he would be wired or tired.

Either way, he came in search of coffee and companionship, and then they'd spend an hour walking along the sand, recapping his last twenty-four hours at the fire station, and talking about her job search.

He always had ideas and encouragement, infused with relentless enthusiasm and reminders that the world was her oyster and all she had to do was open it. If only it were that easy.

Chloe knew why he frequently steered the conversation to that subject. After she settled into the bungalow and faced the facts of her rather unremarkable twenty-nine years, she'd made a huge decision regarding Travis.

As tempting as it was, she wouldn't go one step closer to "official" in this budding relationship until she had her career figured out. Once she had a job—even one she didn't love—she could put energy into a romance.

But so far, the job search had been a massive fail. She'd turned down the role of waitress at the family-run Riverfront Café because she'd been so incredibly bad at it in the past. She submitted her resume to the local paper, only to be told she was overqualified because she had worked for *A-List Access*, a nationally syndicated show.

She'd bombed at that job, but the line on her resume hadn't helped her.

She'd also met with a local PR firm that had offered her an entry-level job for a salary that could barely feed twelve-pound Lady Bug, so she turned it down. Raina had offered her part-time work at Wingate Properties, Rose said she could always use a hand at the flower shop, and Grace said if the bookstore weren't being rebuilt after the fire, she could work there. Even sweet Isaiah said he could use a good housekeeper at the inn.

None of those jobs interested her, but she couldn't seem to zero in on a "real" career, probably because she was paralyzed by the fear of failing again. She honestly didn't think she could take another one. And that might be the *real* reason she was holding back with Travis.

Still, he was rock-solid and quite patient.

In the past month, they'd had four movie nights, one dinner date, two trips to Yulee to get his truck fixed, and every Tuesday and Friday morning for three weeks, they had coffee and walked.

Was it wrong that she woke up this morning a little thrilled that it was Tuesday?

At least she had something to tell him—an interview with the head of marketing at a local bank tomorrow. A stretch for her journalism degree, but at least she had something to report to Travis since she'd seen him on Saturday, despite combing LinkedIn and a host of job boards.

Every possible opening she'd found would take her

away from Amelia Island, and that was another line in the sand she'd drawn.

She didn't want to leave again; she wanted to stay here, where she'd grown up and where almost all of her family lived. This was the home she wanted and the people she wanted to be near. She might *have* to take something like PR for a bank...or move. Which was the lesser of two evils?

Suddenly, Lady Bug threw her head back and barked madly, which was followed by the sound of truck wheels hitting her driveway.

"Oh, the Travis bark." Chloe abandoned the open laptop on the coffee table and stood. "Music to my ears."

She walked to the door and leaned against the jamb to peer through the sidelight for the sheer pleasure of watching long, tall, handsome Travis climb out of the truck dressed in his summer off-duty uniform of khaki shorts and blue FBFD T-shirt.

"There he is, Bugaboo," she whispered as she bent over to pick up Lady Bug so the dog wouldn't bolt toward her beloved. "Our hero."

Lady Bug squirmed in unabashed excitement.

"Hey, gorgeous," he called as she stepped outside to greet him.

The dog barked noisily.

"And you, too, Chloe," he added, making her laugh. "I wanted to come by earlier but I got stuck doing some paperwork at the station for an hour after my shift ended. The new captain is...well, can I just say that I really wish

Gabe had gotten that promotion and not run off to med school?"

"You think he'd still be here and not in med school if he'd been promoted?" she asked, relinquishing Lady Bug to his arms in lieu of throwing her own around him like she really wanted to.

"Nah. I just talked to him, and future Dr. Gabe is having no regrets," he said, inching back to scan her face with his sweet green eyes. "And mine are only that I couldn't get here sooner. Hey there, Bed Bug." He stroked the dog's little head and added a kiss, still holding her gaze. "Man, you're beautiful."

The compliment warmed Chloe even though her dog was the lucky recipient of his affection. Lady Bug looked up and gave his chin a quick lick despite the unattractive nickname he'd hung on her.

"Oof, she's got it bad for you," Chloe said, stepping back inside and beckoning him to follow. "How was the overnight shift? Any action?"

"Couple of health calls, a bad smell that turned out to be a broken A/C unit, a kitchen blaze that a very capable homeowner mostly handled on his own and...paperwork. Also, I had to clean the head and, whoa, I hate that job. I got about three hours total sleep, too."

"How about some coffee?" she asked.

"Yes, please." He followed her into the main room, which was basically living, dining, and a kitchenette all in one. The little guest house also had two tiny bedrooms and a bath, all lovingly built by a much younger Rex Wingate when Chloe was a very little girl.

Years later, her parents built the massive beach house about a hundred yards away, and this bungalow became a haven for anyone who needed privacy and sunshine.

She couldn't be more grateful to call the dollhouse her home for the time being.

"Here or to go?" she asked, opening a cabinet to pick either a ceramic cup or a tumbler for his coffee.

"Definitely a walking cup. I need air and so does this little beast." He nestled Lady Bug in his other arm, who looked tiny against his broad chest, but his attention slid to the open laptop. "How's the hunt going?"

"Pretty well. I have an interview tomorrow with the marketing guy of Lighthouse Bank. They're building an investment department and need someone to schmooze rich people on Amelia Island who might need wealth management."

"Huh. Okay. Not sure that sounds like you."

She felt her shoulders sink as she turned to him. "I don't know what sounds like me, Travis. I think I got the interview because my last name is Wingate, to be honest," she said with a wry laugh. "But to be really honest? I don't know what the heck I want to do when I grow up and that's kind of a problem, since I'll be thirty this year."

"Hey, you're talking to a guy who ditched his corporate career to become a firefighter at thirty-three and is now cleaning toilets instead of cashing fat checks. And come on, look at Gabe, going after his childhood dreams in his forties." Keeping his gaze locked on hers, he lowered Lady Bug to the floor. "You'll figure it out, Chloe."

"I guess," she said, sounding doubtful. "You and my brother-in-law had *dreams*. You use that word all the time when you talk about being a firefighter, and Gabe obviously has been nursing his dreams forever. I...don't seem to have any. Does that mean there's something wrong with me?" She held up her hand to stop the denial she expected. "I *did* have dreams of being a reporter, but after that last experience? I lost my enthusiasm for that job."

It had been a dream to land a low-level on-air job with a celebrity news show, but that had turned into a nightmare fast. The job made her feel used, dirty, and lost in L.A.

After a moment, he tipped his head toward the door. "Let's take a beach walk."

Lady Bug barked once at the word "walk," then spun in a circle and trotted toward the leash hook, making them both laugh.

"I can't believe she speaks English," Travis said.

"Certain words." Chloe poured the coffees into travel tumblers and added some cream. "Like w-a-l-k and t-r-e-a-t. And T-r-a-v-i-s."

"Really? She knows my name?"

Chloe rolled her eyes as she handed him his cup. "And your scent, your touch, and the happy sound of your truck."

"Aww, Bed Bug." He scooped her up again and nuzzled her fur. "Let's reward you with a walk."

In a few minutes the three of them were on the

beach, with Lady Bug romping on the sand and sniffing some shells. It was still hot in late September—maybe even hotter than August—but summer was officially over, so the beach wasn't nearly as crowded as it had been for the past few months.

For that reason, Chloe unclipped the leash to let Lady Bug take a few tentative steps toward the water, only to scamper away every time a wave lapped near her. Over and over again, she dared the ocean and managed to win.

They walked barefoot, quiet for a while, taking in the drama of the ocean, the rhythm of the waves, and the silliness of Lady Bug and her love-hate relationship with the water.

"So what color is your parachute, Chloe?" Travis asked after a few minutes.

"Seriously?" She grinned up at him. "The 1970s just called and they want their self-help books back."

"My mom was a big believer in whatever was in that book," he told her. "I don't know the process but I think the idea is to dig deep and find out what gives you purpose. Joy, I guess, although that sounds cliché."

"It also sounds divine," she said. "How does one find that purpose and joy?"

"I guess you have to ask yourself..." He took a sip of coffee and slowed his step, thinking hard.

"What makes you happy?" she guessed.

"I think the idea was to examine what you have experienced in your life that has been truly meaningful," he finally said. "Like what matters to you. Is it reporting the news?"

She made a face. "It used to be, but meaningful? No, the idea of being an on-air newscaster kind of tweaked my fantasies, but the work itself didn't thrill me. Or have what I would call 'meaning.'"

"What does have true meaning to you?" he pressed. "Not only work, but in life."

"Well, my family, of course," she answered without hesitation. "My sisters and parents, nieces and nephews." She lifted the leash she held and used it to point to Lady B. "That crazy little furball."

"Have you always had a dog?" he asked. The question surprised her, since she expected him to keep exploring the meaning of her life.

"No, because we had such a huge family and my mother isn't really a dog person. But I got Lady Bug the minute I could manage a pet and have been dragging her around from failed job and lost boyfriend ever since."

"Chloe!" He stopped and gave her a hard look. "You haven't failed and from what I know about your ex? He was the loser, not you."

She lifted her brows. "Look, it gives me no satisfaction to spell it out, but we both know the truth. I couldn't make it in TV news. I couldn't make it with Hunter and left him at the altar, of all massive failures. I couldn't make it when *A-List Access* came *to me* with a job offer. I couldn't make it in L.A. Heck, I couldn't even make it as a waitress at the Riverfront Café." Her voice cracked, surprising her, and getting him to put both arms around her and pull her close.

"Hey, hey," he whispered. "Don't be so hard on yourself."

The sympathy had the opposite effect, though, making her shoulders slouch with defeat. She slipped out of his touch, unwilling to surrender to what she wanted until she fixed all her pressing problems.

"How can I not be?" she asked, enough of a whine in her voice that Lady Bug hurried closer, looking up with concern in her eyes. That made her laugh and reach down for the dog. "Bug. You're so consistent, you know that?"

Chloe lifted up her little body and held her close, looking up at Travis. "She is, you know. She is the one constant thing in my life for the past six years. If anything gives me meaning, it's this dog."

"So, what does that tell you about your parachute?"

"Umm..." She put Lady Bug back on the sand, and seriously considered the question. "I could be a dog walker?"

"You could."

"Nope. Not...Wingate enough."

"What does that mean?" he asked. "You gotta have your own business with a wrought-iron gate decorated with a W? The address has to be Wingate Way or you haven't made it?"

He wasn't *completely* wrong.

"It's how my dad raised us," she said, knowing it would be hard to explain to an outsider. "Maybe that makes us overachievers, but whatever we do, we have to do it to the best of our ability, and never quit. Dad cannot tolerate a quitter."

"I respect that," he said.

"I do, too, but it's important to understand how ingrained the idea of being a Wingate is to all of us. Whether that's our job or our family life or, yeah, being the mother to a twelve-pound dog, we put our heart and soul into it. My mother is a big part of that, too. Being Susannah Wingate defines her and we picked that up over the years."

"You don't think you can find something to put your heart and soul into that is Wingate-worthy?" he asked.

"If I knew *what* I wanted to put my heart and soul into. My sisters have all figured it out. Madeline is the best seamstress for miles and has made a tidy business creating custom wedding gowns," she explained. "Tori is a phenomenal chef and when she sells her catering business, she'll turn the Riverfront Café into a destination diner, I just know it."

"And Raina is a crackerjack Realtor," he added, obviously seeing the pattern. "Rose is a very successful florist."

"Right. Sadie is killing it in Brussels, just promoted again at one of the most prestigious chocolate companies in a country famous for the stuff." She shook her head as the reality of it all hit her hard. "And Grace came back home as a pregnant widow and still managed to transform The Next Chapter into the most popular bookstore on an island where there are several. Even with the fire, you watch, she'll be back full force."

"I know she will," he agreed.

"And then there's the baby Wingate," she said glumly, tapping her chest. "It's like all the success mojo ran out. I can't hold a job, a man, an apartment, or a dream."

"You have to stop," he said, sliding his sunglasses down to burn her with a jade green gaze. "You haven't found a job you wanted to hold. You walked away from what would have been a miserable marriage. Your apartment in L.A. was roach-infested and why would you live anywhere but here? You simply haven't figured out your dream yet."

She let out a grunt, wishing this had been one of those light, happy, flirtatious walks that didn't force her to examine her many shortcomings.

"How can it be a dream if it isn't immediately obvious and at the center of my thoughts?" she asked. "How can it—"

Lady Bug's bark yanked her attention, making Chloe gasp as she saw her sniffing a dark brown dog, also untethered, but alone.

"Whoa, whoa!" She looked around for the dog's owner, but no one was nearby. "Careful there, Bug," she called, trying to gauge the safety of the other animal, who was panting like he'd just run or was maybe in need of water.

Travis moved toward them with determination, certainly willing to save Lady Bug from what looked like a seventy-pound dog. But the new arrival didn't look aggressive, only wary and uncertain.

He had a dark chocolate coat with a distinctive white marking on his snout, the face of a boxer, the tilted eyes of a pittie, and a stubby little tail that tick-tocked with emotions she couldn't quite read yet. But, oh, she wanted to.

Travis reached out both hands with his palms down, the absolute correct way to approach a strange dog.

"Hello, buddy," he said. The dog looked up with greenish-gold eyes, definitely scared and lost.

Lady Bug barked at him again, and the dog lowered himself into a submissive pose, as if he recognized the tiny white creature was the alpha.

"There you go, big guy." Travis eased to the sand to sit and Chloe came closer, her heart squeezing.

"Oh, wow. He's beautiful!" she exclaimed as she got a good look at him.

"Have you ever seen him out here?" Travis asked as he very carefully pet the dog's head.

"Never. No collar, huh?" She gave his head a stroke, too, checking his neck for a collar or tag. As she did, he turned his head and licked the inside of her arm, making her croon. "Oh, we're affectionate, are we?"

He looked into her eyes and swiped one paw over his face.

"Ahh, the universal dog gesture for 'love me more,'" she said on a laugh as she settled on the sand to rub his head.

Instantly, Lady Bug barked with jealousy and tried to crawl into Chloe's lap.

"Don't worry, Bug," Travis said, putting his hands on the tinier dog to reassure her. "Your mom still loves you. But we have to find this dog's owner."

Travis stood and looked left and right, scanning the beach. "Anyone missing a dog?" he called to a few passersby. They shook their heads and continued walking. "I'm going to ask around, Chloe. You stay with him."

"Happily. He's my friend now." When Travis left, Chloe continued to stroke the stray's head, murmuring soft words she knew would soothe him.

"What's your name, doggo?" she whispered. "Where are your people?"

He whimpered a little, rolling over for a belly rub, which she happily supplied, calming him with soothing words and sounds. Lady Bug watched with a wary eye, not thrilled with this turn of events.

"Nowhere in sight," Travis said as he jogged back.

"He must have gotten away from one of the beach houses along this section," she said. "I'll put up signs and find a local online group to see if anyone's looking for him. And my vet can check for a chip."

"I can take him to the station," he said.

She looked up at him. "Why would you?"

"Because we get strays there or abandoned dogs all the time."

"And what do you do with them?"

"Try our best to find the owner, but mostly they go to the county shelter and they can check for a chip there."

She curled a lip. "Mr. Brown is not going to a county shelter," she told him. "You know what they do to dogs there."

"They try to find the owner, or adopt them out."

"Right," she dragged the word out with distaste, because they both knew that didn't always happen. "I'll find his owner and he won't be in a cold, wet kennel. Right, you beautiful chocolate truffle?" She reached down and snuggled the dog, who was clearly starving for affection. And maybe food. "I'm going to give you some breakfast and make some flyers to find your owner. Someone loved him enough to have him fixed, so they probably really miss him."

"Wow, you do know your way around dogs," he said.

"He's missing parts." She grinned at him and stood. "Let's get you nice and fed, my darling man, and then we'll see about getting you home. We'll call you Brownie."

She started walking and glanced back at the dog, seeing apprehension in his eyes. "Or not."

He came with her then, and they walked together, her whole body and mood lifted with this new mission. "You back there, Travis?"

She turned when he didn't answer, finding him staring at her, holding Lady Bug, who wasn't quite sure about all this.

"What?" she asked.

"Nothing," he said, slowly coming closer. "But if you ask me, you look like a woman who just found...joy."

She smiled, then reached down and put a hand on

the new dog's head, which felt so much bigger than Lady Bug's.

"Is that what you gave me, boyo?" She bent over and kissed his head lightly. "I think you just gave me a bunch of things to do, because I will not rest until I find your owner or a new home for you."

"And that," Travis said so softly the words were almost lost in the sound of the surf. "Is what's commonly known as purpose."

Chapter Four

Madeline

There were few things Madeline Wingate hated as much as lost time, so a fruitless trip to Jacksonville to find the perfect lace trim for a veil that was already woefully behind schedule really messed up her day. The only thing that saved it was the distributor's parting comment that the specific lace she'd shown him—which was what this bride had demanded—was manufactured in Brussels.

So on the way back to Amelia Island, she called her sister, Sadie, her very best Brussels connection. While the phone on the other end rang, Madeline hoped that Sadie Wingate, vice-president of international marketing for Chocolat de Saint Pierre, wasn't up to her eyeballs in important meetings.

Her heart lifted when Sadie's cell clicked on the third ring, but all she heard was silence on the other end.

"Sadie? You there?" Madeline asked.

"Yeah. Hi. Madeline?" Her voice was thick, like she'd been sound asleep. Wait—was it three in the morning there or three in the afternoon?

Definitely afternoon. "Did I wake you?"

"Oh, no. No, of course not. I'm, uh, feeling under the weather. I didn't go in today."

"That must be serious for you to skip work. Have you seen a doctor?"

"Yeah, it's...I'm fine. What's up? Everything okay at home?"

"Weren't you in Copenhagen for that food festival? Did you pick something up there?"

She could have sworn Sadie groaned. "Yeah, or...no. It's a cold. Nothing serious. What's up with you?"

"I have a ridiculous favor to ask, but not if you aren't feeling well," Madeline said, already thinking how she'd break the news to the bride that the rare lace wouldn't be available.

"Please, whatever you need, Madeline," she said. "I'm not that sick and I'm not, um, planning to work for a few days."

"Why?" Madeline asked, frowning, because some-thing in Sadie's voice seemed off. Not working for a few days? That was odd. She was always working or traveling for business. "Are you sure you're okay?"

"I'm..." The pause lasted way too long. "I'm rethinking my whole life."

"Oh, is that all?" She sat up straighter behind the wheel, dropping her hand from the key she was about to turn. "Sadie! What's going on with you?"

The response was yet another long silence, giving Madeline time to picture her lively, funny, brilliant sister, who soaked up life's adventures and constantly looked for the next.

"Nothing," she finally said. "Nothing at all. Now, what favor do you need?"

"Are you thinking about leaving your company?" Madeline prodded. "Or Brussels, or what?"

"Maybe. Yes. No. I don't know, Madeline. And I really don't want to talk about it," she said, her tone unusually terse. "What did you need? Please tell me."

"I need a very specific kind of Brussels lace that you can buy at..." She squinted at the address she'd found online. "Avenue du Pont in Forest? Does that mean anything to you?"

"It's an industrial area about fifteen minutes from where I live. I could go there today."

"And get me five yards of white mesh bobbin lace?" She couldn't keep the excitement out of her voice.

"Text me exactly what you want, and I'll get it."

"I will, with a picture. Could you also overnight it to my shop? I'll send you everything and pay you hand-somely for this huge ask."

"Please. I'm happy...for something to do."

Something to do? Since when did Sadie need that? "Honey, what is going on with you?" Madeline slipped right into her most natural role, second only to being a seamstress—the "other" mother to six younger sisters.

She heard Sadie heave a heavy sigh. "I did something stupid," she said softly. "Really rash and...stupid."

"What?"

"I'm never going to tell you, so don't ask. But, whoa, I'm drowning in regret."

Madeline's heart tightened at the sound of Sadie's voice while her mind spun with possibilities. A work thing, no doubt, because work was her life.

"I'll do anything to help you, Sadie," she offered. "Name it. Anything at all."

"I might take you up on that," she said. "But for now? The way to help me is to let it drop and forget we had this conversation. And please don't tell anyone else. Can you do that?"

Keep a secret? Of course she could. Forget one of her sisters wasn't happy? Not likely. "Whatever you need," she said again.

"Thank you," Sadie said. "Send me your lace stuff and all the info and I'll handle it for you."

"I'll text you right now." Madeline tightened her grip on the phone, wishing she were holding sweet Sadie's hand. "And Sadie? Anything at all. I mean it. I love you."

"Thanks." She heard the crack in Sadie's voice. "I'll let you know."

The unsettling conversation hung over her for the whole drive back to Amelia Island, and was still top of mind when she pulled into the back lot and saw Rose talking to the driver of her delivery van.

"Hey, you!" Rose called to Madeline as the van drove off. "Am I dreaming or is my always punctual sister running behind today?"

Madeline raised both hands like the fates had conspired against her today. "I was at my fabric distributor in Jacksonville all morning selling my soul for lace to trim a veil that I absolutely have to have ASAP."

"Did you get it?"

"No, but there's a manufacturer fifteen minutes from Sadie's apartment in Brussels and that sweet angel is going to get it and ship it here." She walked closer, wishing she hadn't agreed to keep Sadie's issues private.

"Cool. I can't believe she has the time."

"Yes, in fact..." Madeline shuttered her eyes, then walked closer, crossing the few parking spots behind the ice cream parlor. "Have you talked to her lately?'"

"Sadie?" Rose shook her head and made a guilty face. "I've been so wrapped up in my own stuff. Is she okay?"

"I don't know." Madeline's steps slowed. "She was a little weird."

"Weird how? What did she say?"

I did something stupid.

Sadie's unsettling words floated around her head, along with her request to keep the conversation private.

"Not much," Madeline said, purposely vague. "But she is helping me out of a jam for a very difficult bride."

"Don't tell me it's Melissa 'I must have tulips in October' Havensworth," Rose said on a laugh. "Because she is one, uh, *particular* bride."

"That's exactly who it is." Madeline lifted a brow. "'Particular' is being kind, but then, you are."

Rose laughed. "Well, maybe while Sadie's running around Brussels solving Melissa's lace problems, she can hop over to the Netherlands and get our problem bride some tulips."

Madeline looked skyward, fully understanding the wedding issue since she and Rose frequently shared clients. "Seriously? In October? With that lace? What is that woman thinking?"

"She's spent way too much time in that 'Big Budget Bride' group on Facebook," Rose said. "Is she coming in today for a fitting?'"

"No, thank goodness. No fittings today and no appointments for the salon. I have a glorious day of utter solitude and sewing a dress I'm making on spec—all it needs is a great bride. An easier one than Melissa."

Rose gave her a funny look, as if she wanted to say something, but didn't know how.

"Everything okay?" Madeline asked, feeling a little like the family therapist.

"Yes. No. I was just wondering..." Rose took a step closer. "How come you love solitude so much?"

Madeline shrugged. "I enjoy my own company."

"Don't you ever get lonely?"

Madeline blinked at her, not even sure how to answer that.

"Oh, my gosh, Madeline, I don't mean that... It's just that you're so good at handling life on your own."

Blowing out a breath, Madeline shook off what for any other unmarried woman of forty-nine might be considered a sideways insult. Rose was incapable of delivering an insult, sideways or head-on.

"Are you struggling without Gabe, Rose?"

"A little," she admitted, then laughed. "Maybe a lot."

Madeline reached out and folded her younger sister

in a hug. "We're all here for you. Your kids and business keep you busy. He'll be back in no time."

"I know, you're right." Rose gave an uncharacteristically sad smile. "I really miss him."

"Of course you do. And if you need company? I'm here—alone—making dresses." She squeezed her again. "Come over anytime."

With one more hug, Madeline headed into her dressmaking shop. Inside, she passed the quiet salon, empty today with no bridal parties scheduled, and then walked up the narrow stairs to the comfort of her sunlit studio, and the solitude she really did love.

An hour later, Madeline fully expected her heavy heart to have lifted, which is what usually happened when she had new material and a vision. And, oh, what a vision she had.

She fluffed out yards of antique white mulberry silk for a dress that currently existed only in her imagination. She'd awakened the other night with an idea for a design that was clean and columnal, with pleating over the bust and just a touch of a spring in the hem so it glided like a dancing gown Ginger Rogers would have worn in a 1940s movie.

Something vintage and romantic and not too over-the-top.

She smoothed out the lines over her massive worktable, eyeing the direction of the threads before she raised her shears, ready to cut. But she held the heavy tool mid-air, a frown forming, still not feeling quite *right*.

Was it only her sisters' struggles that put that pressure on Madeline's heart?

It had to be. Since the day her mother had died giving birth to Raina and Rose, Madeline, the oldest, had assumed the job of worrying about three younger sisters and then three more after Dad married Suze and the years went by.

Despite not having children of her own—or maybe because of it—when one of her six sisters was troubled, Madeline felt it down to her soul.

Accepting that, she started snipping with confidence, certain she knew exactly where to make the cut as she remembered the sound of the high-pitched whine of the electric looms that she'd heard this morning in that factory in Jacksonville.

Her fingers froze.

The factory...maybe that was it. Just being in there had taken her back...back to New York, back to her days at the Fashion Institute, back to when she'd apprenticed for Elana Mau and learned the fine art of designing and making custom wedding gowns.

Back when the sound of an electric loom gave her a thrill because of who it meant she would see that day. Back when she trusted people...people like, well, Elana Mau.

Then she learned that people—all sorts of people— were capable of breaking rules...and breaking hearts.

Don't you ever get lonely?

She closed her eyes and sighed at the echo of Rose's question, putting the scissors down as if she needed her full strength to...compartmentalize. She was so good at it, so adept at sliding every single aspect of life into its proper compartment like storing bolts of fabric into her array of cubbies and bins.

Work and clients had one box, and there was another for family and friends. Design ideas, health issues, hobbies and pastimes—they all stayed in their proper mental containers. It was how Madeline structured her life, along with her calendar, phone, organized closet, structured day, and perfectly prioritized To-Do list.

But there was one compartment she would never, ever open, at least not in the bright light of day, not now, darn near twenty-five years later. She hated that dark, cold, painful place that reminded her of how utterly and completely alone she was.

Except, it was ridiculous to think she was *lonely*— especially since she so famously guarded her solitude.

She smoothed the material again and lifted the shears, determined to see this vision to completion and heard a distant sound. Was that the back door?

Setting down the shears, she walked to the top of the stairs, frowning. Did Rose take her up on the offer? Only family and her two sales staff had keys and the salon downstairs was closed, so—

"Maddie!"

Dad? She blinked in shock, unable to remember the last time her father had been here. Before his stroke last spring, of course. Back then, he'd come across the street from Wingate Properties on a regular basis, often to take her to lunch or share a coffee.

Then life changed and he collapsed at home nearly six months ago. Though greatly recovered, Dad rarely left the beach house where he and Susannah lived.

"Maddie? Are you up there?"

"Yes!" she called out, suddenly so very, very happy.

Maybe she did get lonely, because her heart soared. Or was it because her father was right there at the bottom of the stairs, beaming up at her with his ever-present cane?

"I'm coming down," she announced, because he looked like he might climb the seventeen narrow stairs that were nearly as old as he was. "What are you doing here?"

"I escaped," he said with a gleam in eyes exactly the deep, dark brown color that met her in the mirror every morning.

"Where's Suze?" she asked as she reached the bottom.

"She had to put an order in at Rose's shop, and gave me special permission to sneak over here and see you all by myself." He lifted his right arm—the one that had the most strength and didn't ever tremble—and gave her a half-hug. "Sorry to interrupt, Maddie, but I need to talk to you, and fast, before she comes to get me."

She inched back to search his face and gauge the secretive tone. And, of course, smile, because no one on Earth except Rex Wingate called her "Maddie."

Well, one other person, a little voice whispered. Once, long ago.

Back in your compartment, please!

"I need a favor and it's big," Dad said. "Huge. Massive. And so important."

Her eyes widened as she guided him into the hushed and dimly lit salon, threading a few racks of gowns to take him to the pink velvet sofa where mothers and bridesmaids waited with bated breath for the bride to exit the dressing room.

"Should I be scared?" she asked on a laugh.

As he sat, he glanced toward the back door, where he'd obviously let himself in using one of the keys everyone in her family had.

"I got all the way over here on my own, you know. No one walked me to the door, or up the steps, or anything."

"You're so much better," she cooed. "You wouldn't even know you had a stroke."

"Oh, I know. We all know. But I'm stronger than I've been for months and I want to do something...big."

"And you need my help," she said, taking his hand. "Whatever you need, Dad. You can count on me."

He gave a slow smile. A perfect Rex Wingate smile that reached inside her chest and seized her heart with love.

"Look at you," she murmured, gripping his hand tighter. "Both sides of your face match now, you know. There was a time a few months ago..."

He reached up and touched the left side of his lips. "I know. You all thought I'd be crooked forever."

"Well, you're not," she said. "Because you do relentless physical therapy and follow all the rules of your doctor and wife."

"My wife," he sighed out the words, "is the greatest living angel on this planet or any other."

Unexpectedly, Madeline's eyes filled. "No arguments from me. The day you married Susannah was one of the happiest of my life, Dad."

For a long moment, he stared at her with a glint of something in his eyes she couldn't quite read. Amusement, affection, and definitely secretive.

"That's why I'm here, Maddie. That's what I need you for."

She frowned, not following.

"In about six weeks, we will be celebrating the fortieth anniversary of that day. Did you know that?"

"Of course. November eleventh. I remember the date and the beach wedding where I proudly watched you two get happily married."

"And I want to do it all over again," he said. "I want to celebrate our anniversary in a very special way. I want to get married again, but I don't want a private ceremony on the beach like last time. I want Suze to have the wedding of her dreams and I want it to be a complete surprise."

"Oh!" She put both hands over her mouth, chills rising up and down her arms. "That's...wow. That's so sweet and romantic and not like you at all."

He snorted a laugh. "Trust me, I know. This is something she would do! She'd have the perfect party with the right people and flowers and music and..." His voice cracked as he took a breath. "I want her to have all that, Maddie. That woman has achieved sainthood in the last six months. She never lost her temper with me, she never gave up during the darkest days, and she never stopped loving me for one minute."

Madeline's eyes burned as he said the words, tears so close she knew they would fall if she blinked.

"Am I nuts?" he asked after a beat of silence.

"You're...wonderful," she said.

"I mean, a wedding for two people who got married forty years ago?"

"It's called a vow renewal ceremony and it's done all the time! I've dressed a hundred brides in their sixties, and I've seen all kinds of events. Some do a small reaffirmation of their vows, some recreate the original day, some go way over the top and—"

"That's what I want. Over the top."

She laughed, charmed by this side of a man well-known for being gruff and having no patience for fluff or pomp. "Are you sure?"

"It's what she would want," he insisted. "She was barely twenty-one when we got married, and I had four daughters and a lot of grief. Not to mention I had fourteen years on her. Back then, I moved fast to seal the deal and not let this awesome young woman get away."

She smiled at that, but the words were turning on the faucets in her eyes again. "I don't think she missed the big wedding, Dad." In fact, Madeline knew she hadn't. She and her mother—never, *ever* did she think of Suze as a stepmother—had talked about the tiny beach wedding where Madeline, then nine, and seven-year-old Tori had been the attendants.

They'd wanted Raina and Rose as flower girls, but they were three and wandered off after a butterfly without making it down the homemade aisle on the beach, with Rose humming and Raina trying to catch it.

"In fact, that beach wedding is one of our favorite memories," she added, putting pressure on his hand. "You saved all of us by marrying her."

This time, it was his dark eyes that filled with emotion. "She's been a gift from God," he said. "But I happen to know a few things about girls, since I'm father to seven of them. They want big fairy-tale weddings."

She tipped her head. "Not everyone does, Dad."

"Well, you didn't, and Chloe walked out of hers, but most girls do. I feel very strongly about this. I want the ballroom of the Ritz-Carlton with everyone we've ever known and loved in the audience. Do women wear wedding gowns to these...vow renewal events?"

"Absolutely," she said, thinking of a mermaid dress she'd made last month for a fifty-five-year-old who'd rocked it. But that was rare. "Most of the time, they wear white tea-length dresses or simple gowns."

"Well, you know her size and can make her something spectacular."

She nodded. "Of course I can do that, but are you up to planning something like this without her? Are you sure it has to be a surprise? Why don't you plan it together?"

"Because she'll talk me out of it," he said. "She'll say

it's too much for me and we should have a little catered party, family only."

"Maybe that's what you should do."

"No," he said, insistent enough that he really sounded like Old Rex. "She deserves a huge celebration and the chance to wear that long white dress she never had. She deserves giant bouquets and a catered dinner and a great big diamond ring, which I already called Worthington's Jewelry about."

"Are you sure?"

"Oh, I'm positive. Plus, I like the idea. A lot. I haven't seen very many people for six months and I know there's a whole contingent of folks who think I have one foot in the grave. I'll show them, when both feet are dancing with my bride!"

"Dad." She breathed the word, a little dizzy from the impact of it all. "Who's going to pull this together?"

"You," he said. "With the help of your sisters, but only—and I mean this with every fiber of my being—only if they swear to secrecy. I want Susannah to be surprised. Oh, and I want it to be on our actual anniversary, which is a Saturday night."

Madeline stared at him, trying to process so many thoughts, they all got jumbled. Would Susannah *want* to be surprised? Was it possible for them to pull this off in six weeks? What were the chances the Ritz would be available?

And...what would it be like to have someone love you that much?

Whoa, get back in that box!

She kicked the last thought right to where it belonged and concentrated on the problem at hand. "Dad, every venue is going to be booked for a Saturday night this coming November."

"You can find something, I'm sure. But it has to be amazing. If not the Ritz, which would be my first choice, then a museum or country club or...something special. Please, Maddie." He took both her hands. "Do this for me. And for her. She's your best friend."

She was indeed, and she'd do anything for Dad and Suze. Anything she *could* do, and he was asking for a miracle.

"But not a word to her," he said, squeezing her hands. "I want you to promise me that."

She took a breath, silent.

"Because I know you would never break a promise."

That was true. She knew what it was to be on the receiving end of a broken promise and had never broken one in her life.

"Promise me, Maddie," he pressed.

"I promise you I'll try to pull this off."

"And not a word to Suze. Not you or any of the others." He inched closer, still clutching her hands. "This is so important to me, honey. I've knocked on death's door, I lay in that hospital certain I'd never be normal, and I battled my way through every stupid exercise known to man. Through it all, I had one goal—to somehow show Susannah how much I love and appreciate her. Promise me you'll let me do that the way I want to."

She let out a soft whimper, nearly beaten. "Dad, I..."

"And all your sisters."

"I can't pull this off without them, but I will swear them to secrecy. I think..." Her voice faded as she heard the latch of the back door.

"Please, Maddie."

"Hello?" A familiar, happy voice rang out. "Rex? Madeline? Are you here?"

"In the salon, Suze," Madeline responded, still holding Rex's gaze.

"Oh, there you are." Susannah strolled into the salon through the back, a wide smile on her face.

She looked much younger than her sixty-one years, with her sassy blond hair and remarkably smooth skin. No one would ever know she was the mother of seven and had nursed her husband through six months of stroke recovery. She was a saint, and if her husband wanted to surprise her, then who was Madeline to second-guess that?

"What are you two talking about?" she asked as she came around the settee and saw their joined hands.

There was one beat of silence, then Madeline gave Dad's hands the slightest squeeze before she stood.

"Nothing at all, Suze. Just catching up on Dad's progress with PT."

"Doesn't he look amazing?" She put a hand on his shoulder. "I'm so proud of my husband." She leaned over and kissed his silver hair. "I'd marry him all over again."

A tingle shot up her spine and Madeline smiled at Dad with an infinitesimal nod.

She'd keep his secret. She'd plan his over-the-top vow renewal. And she'd make it a day her parents would both remember for the rest of their lives.

She had no idea how, but she—and her sisters—would do that for them.

Chapter Five

Rose

Rose was itching to talk to her sisters about the conversation she'd had with Suze that morning, but the flower shop was slammed all day. Not only did three separate wholesalers send deliveries that she'd have to sort and soak—a monumental physical task that Gabe always handled—but there was a steady flow of walk-ins and phone orders that prevented her from doing that.

Lizzie, her manager, usually handled the front of the shop, but she was at a dentist appointment this morning. That left Rose to split her time between the retail section of the store that opened up to Wingate Way and the back of the house, which she'd transformed into one massive workroom.

There, a long table took up the middle, mostly covered with vases and buckets of flowers, used for creating the arrangements or holding conferences with customers. Rows of cubbies along the walls stored hundreds of vases, plus candlesticks, ribbons, feathers, and an array of decorations they used for the many, many weddings Rose handled.

One whole side of the room was a walk-in cooler where all the deliveries, like the one she was about to unload, had to be stored to stay fresh.

Just as things slowed and she started to open a massive box of dahlias and mums, the bell rang, alerting her to the arrival of a new customer. She slipped through the curtained area to the store, spying a tall man with his back to her, studying the glass display full of arrangements.

"Hello. Can I help you?"

When he turned, she did a double-take, realizing exactly who he was.

"Mr. Madison." She took a few steps closer and extended her hand. "How nice to see you again."

"It's Chase," he said, shaking her hand. "And you are...?"

"Rose D'Angelo, Raina's sister. Her twin, actually."

"Oh, yes! Rose. I met you the day we closed on the house." Then he drew back, surprise in his dark eyes. "I didn't know you and Raina were twins."

"Not identical, obviously," she said, flipping her fair hair back and thinking of Raina's near-black locks.

"And she's *having* twins," he said, sounding a little enchanted. "That's so cool."

"It certainly is," Rose agreed with an easy laugh.

"So...you're the 'Rose' in Coming Up Roses?" He pointed to the sign on the window.

"I am. And I'm happy to help you with whatever you need."

"I picked this florist because of the name," he said.

"I'm looking for an unusual rose and I'm hoping you can help me find it."

"Roses are my specialty," she told him. "If I don't have it, I can find it. What kind of bouquet did you have in mind?"

"Not a bouquet, actually. One rose. But I'd like a very particular type of rose for someone special. Is that possible?"

"Of course." She nodded knowingly, but couldn't help a little twinge of disappointment. He was such a handsome man, and so sweet. Who could blame her for thinking...

Well, yeah. That was a little *too* optimistic, even for Rose. Especially when he was in here buying roses for "someone special."

"Name your rose, sir."

"It's called an Ocean Song. Have you heard of it?"

She sucked in a soft breath. "A truly extraordinary flower," she crooned. "I love that the edges are what we call 'antique' and that distinct, pale shade of violet that isn't quite lavender. That is the softest, prettiest color on Earth."

"I fully agree."

Her jaw loosened as she put two and two together. "That's where you got the name of the hotel you're building!"

He laughed. "It is. The rose has...meaning."

"How lovely. Are you looking to fill the lobby with them? Give one to every guest? They're super temperamental flowers, but you could even plant them on the property, with the right care."

"All good ideas I may incorporate, but for now, I just want to be able to get one every day for an indefinite period. Is that something I could arrange with you?"

"For delivery?" she asked, knowing how expensive that could get.

"I can come in and get it, or someone could. But sometimes I might want it delivered. Will it matter?"

"Only to your wallet. But I'm happy to arrange whatever works." She scooted behind the counter to tap the computer system to life. "First, I need to find the closest distributor for Ocean Song roses. Hang on a sec."

While she worked, she felt his gaze on her face, as if he were searching for something.

"I see it now," he said. "The twins. You and Raina."

She laughed. "We're opposite twins. I'm blond with brown eyes, she's dark with blue eyes."

"But the features, the face. Both the same."

"Very much," she agreed.

"I wonder if her twins will be like that."

The question surprised her. Raina hadn't really said a nice thing about the man when she'd come over last night, but complained that he seemed too cool and untrustworthy, taking off for a late-night rendezvous with...probably whoever would be the recipient of the Ocean Song roses.

"I don't know about her twins, but we all can't wait to find out," she told him.

Just then, Lizzie came barreling in from the back. "So

sorry, Rose! I didn't think one teeth cleaning would take that long."

"It's fine, Lizzie," she said. "One of us has to start the unload, so let's just—"

On the counter next to her, Rose's cell rang and Lizzie glanced at the screen. "It's the high school, Rose."

Her heart dropped as something told her they weren't calling with an order.

"I'd better take that," she said, gesturing Lizzie toward the computer screen. "This is Chase Madison, a new customer. Can you check the distribution base for a steady supply of Ocean Song roses?" She held up the phone to him. "Sorry."

"Of course," he said with understanding. "Thank you for your help, Rose."

She gave a wave and stepped into the workroom, holding her breath and praying Zach was okay, even though soccer practice didn't start for another half hour. "Hello?"

"Mrs. D'Angelo, this is Bill Maynard, the soccer coach at Fernandina Beach High School. Do you have a minute?"

Her heart climbed into her throat. "Is Zach okay?" she asked, skipping the niceties.

"I think so, but your question makes me wonder if you don't have the answer I'm looking for."

Frowning, she dropped onto her chair at the head of the arranging table, absently moving a stray daisy stem. "I'm not sure I follow, Coach."

"I was calling to see if you knew why Zach quit the team."

And back shot her heart into her throat as she croaked, "Excuse me?"

He gave a wry laugh. "Like I said, it sounds like you don't know the answer."

"He quit the soccer team?" She pressed her fingers to her temples, utterly bewildered by the news. Her first thought was...*Gabe. Did he know this?*

Of course not! He'd have told her. So why didn't Zach? They talked about everything. Or so she thought. "When?"

"Last week. He sent me a very brief email and I haven't had a chance to speak with him privately. I wondered if...I mean, I know your husband is out of town for an extended basis."

She tried to swallow. "He's returned to medical school in Miami," she explained. "But I don't know what that would have to do with Zach's quitting."

"In his email, Zach said there were family issues," the coach said. "I don't want to pry, but I had to ask if there's any way you and your husband could talk to him."

"Of course I—we—will. He isn't going to quit the team, Coach Maynard. It's out of the question."

"I'd love to think that's true and I know Zach's a very good kid, but in my experience? Once they quit, they're done. But Zach was such a leader on the team, even as a sophomore last year. I figured he'd be captain by his senior year, so his decision was a shock."

"To both of us," Rose said dryly. "Was he having any

problems on the team? Issues with the other guys?" She was grasping at straws, but this decision was so completely out of the blue.

"No, he's one of the best-liked kids on the team. Now, I know he plays basketball in winter," the coach continued. "So sometimes kids just want to focus on one sport, especially their junior year when they start seriously thinking about college and are really worried about their grades. Others discover that magical world of dating. I know he's been seeing Tiffany Kaplan, but I didn't think that would change his decision to play fall ball."

Yes, Zach had a lot on his plate this year, including a budding romance with a girl Rose really liked.

"I don't know if any of that would be enough for him to quit soccer, but of course I'll talk to him. I honestly have no idea why he'd make this decision."

Or did she? Gabe and Zach were connected in their love of sports, talking endlessly about every game, every player, every victory and defeat. Maybe he just didn't want to play without his father on the sidelines, calling his name.

"And I'm sure I can change his mind," she added. "Thank you so much..." Her voice faded out as the back door opened and a man walked in carrying one of the long boxes from the last delivery.

No, no. That was no man. That was her son.

"What are you doing here?" she asked, forgetting the phone in her hand.

"Uh, unloading for sort and soak. There must be a ton of flowers out there frying in the sun."

"But..."

"I got it, Mom. No problem." He dropped the box and wiped some sweat from his brow as he turned and went right back out to the delivery dock.

"Mrs. D'Angelo?" the coach asked.

"Yes, sorry. I, um, I'll talk to him and thank you very much."

She hung up and stared at the closed door, remembering breakfast and the vague response she got this morning about soccer practice and the fact that he didn't want to hold an office for the National Honor Society.

She knew exactly what was going on and she intended to put a stop to it.

"WHAT DO you think you're doing?" Rose demanded, walking out to the delivery dock behind her shop, trying to channel her inner Gabe, who would know exactly how to handle this.

Except, if he were here, it wouldn't have happened.

"I just told you—"

"You quit the soccer team?"

He froze in the act of hoisting a box over his shoulder, his eyes closing. "I'm sorry I didn't tell you but I knew what would happen."

"Uh, yeah. I'd tell you to get right back into Coach Maynard's office and tell him it was a terrible mistake and can you please get back on the roster?"

"Yeah, that," he said with a dry laugh, walking past her. "But then who would unload these boxes?"

"I would," she said.

"You can't lift this, Mom, and it's a billion degrees out here. Come on, I'm doing what Dad told me to do." He marched away toward the back door, leaving her standing on the dock in those billion degrees, sweat and tears stinging.

Gabe told him to quit the team? And didn't tell her? Well, he took the MCAT and applied to medical school and didn't tell her, so this wasn't a first.

Irritation burned hotter than the sun, but she stood there and waited for Zach to come back out, because she didn't want to have this conversation in front of Lizzie or any customers.

A minute later, the door opened again and out came Zach, earbuds in now, bopping his head to a tune that was playing. Like this was perfectly normal.

Well, it was. He'd worked here every summer since he was twelve, and often came after school to help Gabe —but not when he had sports or an extracurricular activity.

"What did Dad tell you?" she asked when he came closer.

He pulled out one of the earbuds and looked at her. "He told me I had to be the man of the family while he's gone."

She choked softly. "But he didn't tell you to get up at the crack of dawn to make breakfast, abandon an officer's role at NHS, or quit the soccer team."

"He told me to streamline my activities and suggested I consider ways to better manage my time."

"I think he meant cut back on video games, Zach, not walk off the soccer field."

He gave her a look full of that newfound maturity he'd had on display all morning. "You know you need help, Mom. We have a big family and this is a booming business."

Definitely Gabe's words, she thought. "I don't need help at the expense of your life or time."

"It's not at the expense of anything," he insisted. "I like making breakfast, the NHS office is basically a resume filler, and, let's face it—I'm not getting a soccer scholarship, because I'm not that good."

"You're very—"

He held up a hand. "Mom, bottom line is I promised Dad that I'd put the family first, so..." He tried to inch by her to get to the next pile of boxes. "That means helping out here, and if you don't let me get those boxes in the cooler, you're going to lose a few hundred bucks worth of Gerber daisies and peonies."

She stared at him, rooting for the right words to sway this kid who had his head on so straight, she rarely had to correct his course. But this time? It was on a little *too* straight.

"Honey, I think he meant things like making sure the doors are locked and helping Ethan with his chores."

"No, he didn't," he insisted. "He was very specific about helping you, helping here, and helping all of the kids, not just Ethan."

She almost smiled at him referring to his three siblings as "the kids" but then it occurred to her that it wasn't the least bit humorous. He was too young to have this on his shoulders and her anger, though it had dissipated, should really be directed at Gabe.

Because right now, Gabe was the one following his dreams and letting Zach's die on the vine, expecting his teenaged son to be "the man of the house" when he was only a junior in high school.

There had to be a better way to solve this problem.

She followed him into the back of the shop, digging for a winning argument. Then she thought of it as he stepped into the large cooler.

"What about Tiffany?" she asked.

He looked up from his crouched position in front of a box of flowers he'd just opened. "What about her?"

"Well, she told me she loves watching you play soccer, and she's in NHS, too, so—"

"We broke up."

"What? Zach! Why? And weren't you going to mention it to me?"

"Mom, I'm sixteen."

"In two weeks," she interjected.

"Fine, but I don't really have to tell you everything that happens in my personal life anymore, do I?"

"No, but I really liked her."

"So did I."

"Then why did you break up?"

"She wants a lot of my time."

"So you broke up with her to, what, replace your

father?" Her voice cracked at the thought of him making that kind of sacrifice. "I guarantee you that's not what Dad would want."

He shrugged. "Whatever. We talked, Dad and me, and we made a deal, okay? I'm doing this after school, and I'm cutting out some other stuff and I will not, I promise, let my grades suffer. I'm still going to get into UF, Mom, unless that's too expensive, then I'm certain I can get a scholarship to another college."

"And not be a Gator? That's been your dream since you could do the chomp!"

He rolled his eyes. "When I was Avery's age."

"Which makes the dream matter more."

"Would you please just relax and let me get these flowers put away?"

She stared at him, the words, the intonation, and the look so incredibly like his father, she couldn't breathe. Had Gabe asked him to do this? Maybe not this, but the "be the man of the house while I'm gone" speech would be something her husband would deliver to his beloved eldest son.

Maybe he hadn't said it in so many words, but it would be so like Zach to...overachieve.

"And guess what else?" he asked.

She wasn't sure she wanted to know anything else. "What?"

"In two weeks, when I get my license? I can pick up—"

"Stop. Don't call them 'the kids.' And I'll do the school runs, and you'll...be a kid."

She rubbed her arms against the chill of the walk-in cooler, knowing she'd lost this fight. But she would most definitely take it up with the man who caused it.

There were no customers in the front, but Rose went out to the street anyway, pulling out her phone and calling Gabe as her feet hit the cobblestones of Wingate Way.

And got his voicemail.

Almost immediately, a text popped up.

Gabe: *Hey, I can't talk now and I'm scheduled for lab tonight. Everything okay? Can we talk in the morning? Love you and miss you!*

She wasn't going to get anywhere with Gabe now, but they'd talk and they'd fix this. So she sent a simple text back:

All is well! I love you, too.

Well, half of that was true.

Chapter Six

Raina

The fact that the garage was empty the next morning shouldn't have bothered Raina at all. She shouldn't have even checked, but the door to Chase's rented room downstairs was closed and she had been curious and looked.

Why? She had no idea. She didn't want a roommate, so if hers wanted to sleep at his girlfriend's house, that was just fine.

But she did keep thinking about it, which was dumb. Still, as she walked the beach that morning, her imagination went into overdrive, ignoring the seagulls shouting at her and the splash of the waves on the cool sand.

Who was this woman he'd run off to see? What was her story? Was she a local? A tourist? What was her name? Oh, maybe a work colleague.

Of course, that was it. She was a slick sales manager at his new hotel, who wore tight pencil skirts and low-cut blouses to lure him. Someone whose marriage had gone stale and now she had a hot new boss. Someone sassy and spunky. With a name like Pippa or Micki. How about...

"How about you think about something worthwhile?" she whispered to herself as she marched back home to get ready for work, much earlier than usual.

Once out of the house, Raina forced herself to think about the day ahead. If she got a break in her schedule, she hoped to find some time to do some real shopping for the nursery. Since she'd bought the house furnished, she hadn't done much decorating. But the bedroom down the hall from hers had to be transformed into something with bunnies or bears or baby pink elephants.

Yes, she would shop later today, she decided as she stepped into the lobby of Wingate Properties and started up the stairs to her office.

"You can't do that. I made a promise!"

She stopped dead in her tracks at the sound of Madeline's voice coming from the top of the stairs.

"I'm sorry, Madeline, I could say the same thing. I made a promise, too."

And Rose? What were they doing here and why were they arguing?

"Is this about me?" she called right before she would become visible to them at the top of the staircase. "If so, fair warning: I'm coming up. Slowly, thanks to two babies on board."

"Raina!" Rose flew to the stairs, looking a little disheveled and not as happy as usual.

"It's me. Current occupant." She gave a cursory hug to her sister, looking over her shoulder to Madeline, who stood outside Raina's closed office door with her arms crossed and a look of sheer determination on her face.

"Did I miss a memo?" Raina asked.

"If we'd sent one, they would have contradicted each other," Rose said, shooting a look at Madeline.

"What are you guys doing here?" Raina asked.

"Apparently, we both came to drum up support," Madeline said. "And ran right into each other."

"Support for what?" Since neither Dani nor Blake was here yet, Raina pulled the key to her office from her bag and gestured for both of them to follow. "Come on in and duke it out in privacy. Nothing Dad hates more than family dirty laundry being aired in the office."

"No laundry is being aired," Madeline assured her as they all walked in.

"This place looks great, Rain." Rose gestured around the office that Raina and their mother had slowly taken from mid-2000s masculinity to contemporary colors and a more feminine feel.

"It does!" Madeline agreed as she took one of the cushy swivel chairs around a circular table that had replaced the private men's club sofa, as Suze referred to Rex's old leather couch. "Has Dad seen it?"

"Yes," Raina assured her. "And Suze was with me for every purchase."

"But he's not retiring officially, is he?" she asked, then snapped her fingers and pointed one at Rose. "Oh, maybe *that's* why he wants this big event. To announce his retirement. We can't take that away from him."

"So you'll just ignore what Susannah wants?" Rose asked. "I just can't justify that and I have nothing good to say about it."

Well, that would be a first, Raina thought.

Dropping into one of the chairs and waving for them to join her, Raina dug for an obvious explanation and came up with nothing. "What are you guys talking about?"

They both opened their mouths to reply, then shut them.

"You go," Rose said.

"No, it's fine. Tell Raina what you told me when we both got here."

"But you should—"

"Guys." Raina sighed with growing impatience. "Someone tell me something."

"Susannah came to see me yesterday morning," Rose said.

"At the very same time that Dad sneaked away and came to see me," Madeline added.

"Okay, and...?"

"They both want to have an anniversary celebration," Rose told her. "And they both want to renew their vows on November 11th, which is—"

"Their fortieth," Raina said, a bubble of real joy rising. "I love that idea! We should do something wonderful for them, something perfect and memorable." When her sisters exchanged mutual "I told you so" looks, Raina had to laugh. "Or not. What is this argument about?"

"It's not an argument," Rose said.

"It kind of is," Madeline countered.

Rose leaned forward and pinned her dark gaze on

Raina. "Suze was extremely clear about two things. She wants an exact replica of their original beach wedding—"

"Minus the part where you and I went butterfly chasing instead of walking down the aisle," Raina interjected with a laugh.

"Minus that legendary moment that I don't even remember," Rose agreed. "And she wants it to be a complete surprise for Dad."

"So what's the problem?" Raina asked Madeline, who shifted in her seat, waiting for her turn.

"The problem is Dad came to me privately and asked me to plan and execute a huge, elaborate, expensive 'wedding' at the Ritz-Carlton, and to make Suze a fairy-tale gown and give her the event she never got to have when she became his wife. All on the unwavering condition that it is a total surprise for her."

Raina stared at her, trying to process this. "He did?" she finally asked.

"It's out of character, isn't it?" Rose pressed.

"Not one single bit," Madeline countered. "He's never loved that woman more and is eternally grateful for all she's done. And not just in the past forty years, but these last few months since the stroke."

"She's been an angel," Raina said, marveling at Susannah's ceaseless patience and love.

"Exactly," Madeline said. "And for that, he wants to surprise her with this event. He wants everyone they know and love in attendance, at a gorgeous ballroom, with cake and a champagne tower, dancing and toasting and celebrating all night. He wants to give Suze her dream wedding."

"Which isn't what *she* wants," Rose interjected. "At least, she doesn't think it's what *he* wants."

Raina looked at them, nodding. "It's like that short story about the couple where each one sells the dearest thing they own to buy the other one a present they can't use because the dearest thing is gone." She made a face. "Do I have that right?"

"*The Gift of the Magi* by O. Henry," Madeline said, leaning back and considering what Raina had just said. "And you're not far from the truth."

"Does Suze want that big event?" Raina asked. "And wouldn't Dad would prefer a re-enactment of his happy day, something quiet with close friends and us."

"That's not what he said." Rose puffed out a breath. "And we can't ask them because it would ruin the surprise for both of them."

"But you can't surprise them both," Raina said. "They think they are in on it."

For a moment, they all just looked at each other, silent and stymied.

"How about we vote on it?" Madeline finally suggested. "Seven sisters, so it can't be a tie. We have to make one of them happy and..."

"And lie to the other one?" Raina put her hands on her belly, which had become her favorite position, and let the conundrum sink in. "I like the idea of voting, but someone's going to be disappointed or upset."

With a grunt, Rose dropped back in her chair. "Could anything else go wrong in my life?" she asked.

"What's wrong?" Raina and Madeline both asked in perfect unison.

"Well, that's a silly question," Madeline added, some of the fire in her dark eyes dissipating as she looked at Rose. "We know what's wrong, sweetie, and this isn't helping."

"Tough times in Single Parent Land?" Raina guessed. "I'm not sure I want to hear."

Rose's lashes fluttered as she shook her head. "It's fine. Gabe made the mistake of telling Zach he had to be the man of the house and, well, you know Zach."

"He's suddenly father of the year?" Raina joked.

"Pretty much," Rose said with a laugh. "Now I have to talk him off that ledge. Hopefully, I'll get a chance to talk to Gabe at length today and he can do damage control. He was in a lab late last night and we couldn't talk."

"You've got a lot going on, Rose. Maybe you don't need to take on planning such a, uh, controversial event," Raina said.

Rose tipped her head, disappointment in her eyes. "I want to do it for Suze but, no, I don't want to do it alone. And it wasn't controversial until..."

"Until I showed up with controversy," Madeline said with a wry smile. "We can work this out, Rosie. We don't have to make your life more difficult."

"Oh, all our lives can be difficult. I don't have the

market cornered on that. Life is always a challenge," Rose said, digging into her deep well of optimism.

Although if Raina looked closely, that well seemed kind of shallow these days. "I hate that this is so hard for you," she said.

Rose just held up a hand. "What's hard is even the shadow of a disagreement with anyone in this family." She reached for Madeline's hand. "I cannot stand to argue."

"We're discussing, not arguing," Madeline assured her. "But I need to make this point: Dad was near death not that long ago. This is what he wants—whether it's the party he wants or the belief that he's made Susannah happy, I don't know. But it's what he wants. He made me promise."

"And you did?" Raina asked, knowing exactly what that meant. Madeline lived by strict rules: she was never late, she was never disorganized, and she never broke a promise.

"I did," she said. "And that's why I came in here fighting. I'm sorry, Rose."

"No need to apologize," Rose said softly. "I just want something to go my way."

Raina's heart shifted at the oh-so-rare unhappiness in Rose's voice. "Let's get Grace and Chloe in here, and get Tori and Sadie on the phone. It's not too late in Brussels, and Tori is up and about for sure."

Madeline had her phone out in a flash. "I'll put it on the 7 Sis group chat. I won't go into details, just that we have a little family dilemma and we need a quick gathering of great minds."

"Perfect," Raina said. "And I need my decaf, which Dani likes to bring me, but she won't be here for at least another half hour."

"Let me get it for you, Raina," Rose said, pushing up. "The coffeemaker in the breakroom downstairs?"

"I'll come with you. Madeline, you want coffee?"

She shook her head as she texted. "I'm good."

As they walked out, Raina couldn't help putting her hand on Rose's shoulder. "I'm not used to you like this, Rosebud," she whispered. "I need my daily whiff of Eau de Rose Joy."

Rose gave her a sad smile. "I'll be fine. Gabe meant well when he asked Zach to dial back some of the many things he's doing, but Zach went overboard and quit soccer, backed out of an important Honor Society role, and broke up with Tiffany. Now I have to convince him I don't need help at the flower shop and he needs to put all those things back together."

Raina rubbed Rose's back. "You and Madeline shouldn't have this burden alone on your shoulders."

"We're all under a lot of stress," Rose said. "You, in a new home with two babies growing bigger every day."

"And one roommate." She rolled her eyes. "Who, as you know, took off like a man on a mission when some woman called and told him she was lonely."

"That lucky lady is getting one rose a day indefinitely," Rose said. "So your roommate is romantic."

Raina just looked at her, letting that sink in. "He arranged to send a rose to her every day?"

"I assume it's for the same woman. I had to take a call and Lizzie finished the order."

A rose a day? "I wonder why..."

"Usually a man sends roses because he is in love."

Raina tipped her head, acknowledging that. "But why live in my house? Why rent from me unless he can't live with her because..." She lifted her brows. "She's married," she mouthed the words, mostly because she hated saying them out loud.

"Or she's...in a small apartment, lives far away from his work, or they don't want to live together for religious reasons," Rose said. "There are a million reasons why he'd rent one place and spend the night with her when he can. Why does it matter, Raina?"

"Oh, it doesn't," she said quickly.

"'Cause you sound like, I don't know, you care who he spends time with."

"Please," she scoffed. "The only thing I care about right now is getting this anniversary issue solved. You know how I am with a problem."

Rose put her hand on Raina's back. "The fixer. Just fix it my way, 'kay? Twin bond and all."

THE IMPROMPTU MEETING took a while to get underway, since Tori was at a farmers market, Sadie never replied to the text, and Chloe had to dress for a job interview in town.

While they waited and Dani ran to get more coffee and pastries, Grace came over from the inn and filled them in on the rebuilding project, just getting started after a fire had shut down her bookstore.

"It's actually going to be an amazing renovation," Grace told them, her hazel eyes lit with a joy that none of them had seen in years. "You know, Isaiah says God has a plan and when you're in the middle of the storm—or fire, in this case—it's hard to see. But I'm going to end up with a showplace for a bookstore."

It was impossible not to notice the change in Grace since the fire—well, maybe since Isaiah Kincaid came to town and into her life. Even her daughter's autism diagnosis seemed to be a challenge Grace could take in stride.

"Isaiah suggested we add even more reading nooks," she said as she animatedly clicked and shared pictures from Pinterest on her phone. "We're going to expand the kids' area so we can have more events and maybe even host small birthday parties. God willing, we'll be done by the time Nikki turns four."

"Because she might not like the other kids getting parties first?" Madeline asked.

"No." Grace angled her head and smiled. "She might not love it, but, you know, she's really learning the concept of sharing and caring. It's not easy for her, but Dr. Alberino has been a miracle worker and, of course, Isaiah is like a balm to her heart."

"And yours," Rose teased. "You're welcome," she added with a wink.

Grace laughed, no longer insisting that she and the man who was now managing their family inn were only friends. It was obvious they were much more, and fast becoming a small family unit, especially with Grace living in the third-floor apartment at Wingate House while her bookstore and home were being rebuilt after the fire.

"And we've officially signed her up for piano lessons," Grace added happily. "She's truly found her little island of genius!"

"We?" Rose launched a brow north.

"Yes, Rose. Isaiah and I—and Nikki—are a 'we' and..." She blew her sister a kiss. "*We* couldn't be more thankful for the push."

"I'm here but don't have a lot of time!" Chloe called before she sailed into Raina's office, looking quite snazzy in a soft pink jacket and black pants.

As they all raved over her outfit, she flicked her hands and dropped onto the closest chair, brushing those pants and plucking at them. "Yes, thank you, lovely except for the dog hairs from both my creatures."

"Both?" a few voices raised in surprise.

"Don't ask, I don't have enough time." She smoothed her long blond hair, currently clipped back to add to the air of professionalism. "Also don't ask about the interview, because I don't even want the job but unemployment is starting to wear me down."

"You can work here," Raina said.

"Or at the flower shop," Rose added.

"Or at any business on Wingate Way," Grace chimed in.

"Including mine!" Tori's voice came out of the laptop Raina had set up in the middle of the table.

"Oh! I didn't see you there, Tori," Chloe exclaimed on a laugh. "And I think you know that the Riverfront Café is better off without me, the World's Worst Waitress. How's the temporary management working out, by the way?"

"The café is running, maybe not at a clip like it was this summer," Tori told them through the screen. "But the good news is we're making progress on the legal front and Trey is starting to make concessions on the custody issue. My sous chefs are salivating to buy my business and my kids can't wait to get back to Amelia Island. I'm sure that by Christmas, we'll have this whole thing figured out and Kenzie, Finn, and I will be moving down there permanently."

A noisy cheer went up in the group, with Rose and Raina high-fiving and Chloe throwing a victorious fist in the air.

"You'll come back before that, though, right?" Madeline asked.

"Well, it sounds like we're coming down for a vow renewal ceremony, whatever that is."

"I filled her in," Madeline said. "But Chloe and Grace don't know everything yet."

"And where's Sadie?" Rose asked, exasperated. "Does she ever answer a text or call anymore?"

"I've tried her twice in the last two days," Grace said. "I don't even know what country she's in."

"I just called her office and talked to her assistant," Madeline told them. "She's not in today. I talked to her yesterday, but Chloe has to leave soon, so let's get down to business and try to figure this out without Sadie."

Rose and Madeline explained the predicament in great detail, each not so subtly pushing for what they thought was the right answer.

While they did, Raina realized they were missing a big piece of information. Was the Ritz-Carlton even available that day? Without interrupting the discussion, she shot a text to Dani, who was at her desk outside the office.

While waiting for her efficient assistant to find out, Raina listened and looked around at each of her sisters, trying to guess where they'd stand. Grace and Chloe would be on Team Suze, no question. Yes, they were Susannah's biological daughters, as was Sadie, but that wasn't the reason for Raina's opinion.

Chloe had recently walked out on a massive wedding and knew what was involved in planning one. Grace would always choose low-key over big splash. That's just who she was.

Tori might like the fancy all-out event, which probably seemed simple to her, a professional caterer. Like Rose, much of her business involved weddings, so they weren't daunting.

Madeline and Rose's positions were clear, of course.

"What do you think, Raina?" Chloe asked her. "You've been quiet."

Raina took a second to consider her response, but her whole problem-solving brain was aching to fix this quandary.

"I think it doesn't matter what we want," Raina finally said. "Because what we want is to make both our parents happy. What about a compromise? You know, something that combines both their visions? I just don't know if that would make them both happy, or disappoint them both."

"What would a compromise look like?" Grace asked. "A beach wedding, then a big reception?"

"That's not a bad idea," Madeline said.

"Oh, maybe we could work with that," Rose said.

"But he wants it in the church, right?" Chloe grimaced. "I don't actually want to walk into St. Peter's ever again."

A tap on the door quieted them as they turned to see Dani open it up and look at Raina. All she did was shake her head and whisper, "They actually laughed. I checked the Omni, too, and a few country clubs. *Nada.*"

Raina blew out a breath and looked around as Dani left, closing the door behind her. "Guys, there's no venue available that day."

Dead silence descended as they looked at each other.

"Well, I guess our decision is made." Rose bounced a bit in her chair. "We'll reproduce their wedding on the beach, and have a small but fabulous party at their house. Exactly what Suze wanted."

All the color drained from Madeline's face as she slowly shook her head.

"You're not breaking your promise," Rose said quickly. "There's nothing available."

Madeline closed her eyes, her disappointment palpable. "It's so important to him," she said, the ragged edge in her voice tearing Raina's heart in two. "I wanted to give this to him. Not that he wants that event, but he wants to give it to her. I know I keep saying that, but..."

A teardrop meandered down her cheek and they all let out soft whimpers in sympathy.

"Maybe instead of their house, we can go to the exact beach where they got married," Rose said, clearly wanting to do anything to ease Madeline's pain.

"South of the Ritz? Last time I was there, it was a construction site," Madeline replied.

Raina sat up a little straighter and snapped her fingers. "Wait a second. It's not a construction site, it's a boutique hotel and I happen to be living with the owner. Not that he ever sleeps there, but he pays rent."

Suddenly, all eyes in the room—and the pair on the laptop—were on her.

"I could ask Chase about Ocean Song," she said. "It probably isn't booked, because it's not officially open yet. I know it's not quite the Ritz, but I've heard it's gorgeous and there is event space."

"And it's on the beach where they got married forty years ago," Madeline said, looking intrigued.

They all reacted, leaning forward, chattering at the

same time, the noise in the room rising as the idea took shape.

"Awesome!" Chloe exclaimed, standing up. "Problem solved? Or almost solved? I have to run, you guys."

"When can you talk to Chase, Raina?" Madeline asked.

"I should see him tonight, if he comes home." She rolled her eyes. "I have a tenant coming in for a meeting now, but why don't I just take a drive to Ocean Song today and check out the space and talk to him?"

Everyone loved that idea, which brought the gathering to a close. They hugged each other goodbye, and Raina promised to do her best to solve the problem.

"It's what you do, Rain," Tori called out from the laptop screen.

She blew her sister a kiss and hoped this would be an easy problem to solve. Although she was starting to discover that nothing with Chase Madison was ever easy.

Chapter Seven

Chloe

Gil Huxley, senior VP of marketing for Lighthouse Bank, leaned back as their interview came to an end, beaming at Chloe with a wide smile and warm blue eyes.

"What can I say, Ms. Wingate? I'm thoroughly impressed."

"Thank you," she said, keeping that light, bright voice she'd used since she'd walked in to meet with the fifty-something man who lived, breathed, and clearly loved the banking business.

"You'd have to meet with my boss, of course, and our head of HR, but I can see us making an offer. Once you accept, we'll get you into an intensive training program to learn how to embody the Lighthouse mission statement and customer focus. How do you feel about that?"

Like throwing up, she thought without taking the smile from her face. "Honored," she replied. "Flattered and...interested."

God strike her down for lying. She was so not interested. Her interest level was sub-zero and falling.

But she *needed a job*. And the salary he'd mentioned was actually more than *A-List Access* had paid her, so she'd be a fool to turn it down.

He stood and reached out his hand. "Thank you for coming in. My assistant will give you the packet we discussed and we'll call you to schedule the next round. I'm very optimistic."

She shook his hand, still smiling like she was optimistic, too. "That's great, thank you, Mr. Huxley."

"It's Gil. And may I call you Chloe?"

"Absolutely."

"And I will be calling," he said with a definitive nod. "You can count on it."

She wasn't sure what he saw on her resume or heard in her responses to his questions—especially that doozy about who her favorite fictional character was and why. Had she really said Dr. Doolittle? Yes, because her brain was on her dogs. But *Doolittle*? Was that a subliminal message or what?

At least she wouldn't have to leave Amelia Island if she took this job. She'd be miserable, but she'd be home.

After walking out of the office back into the warm air, Chloe's mind immediately went back to the one thing that seemed to matter: the stray dog. She swung by the office supply store that had printed the flyers she'd created yesterday, and checked Facebook on her phone. So far, no one had claimed...the dog.

She had purposely not given him a name so she wouldn't get attached. Although when he'd jumped on the bed in the middle of the night and tried to sleep there, Chloe was feeling mighty attached.

Lady Bug was having none of that, however, and she barked him right back down to the bed on the floor. Chloe had bought him a bed, and food with new bowls, and a collar and leash and a few toys. He had to be sad and scared, she'd explained to Lady Bug, who had spent the last twenty-four hours giving judgey and unhappy looks to Chloe and the new arrival.

She'd thought about him more than the possible job, she realized, rushing home to bring both dogs treats and love for being so good while she'd been gone.

She started to call a greeting as she reached the front door but frowned and inched back at the sound from inside the bungalow. Lady Bug's bark was loud and non-stop, a little frantic, too.

"Is everything okay in there?" She poked at the keypad with a low-key concern building and opened the door. "Bugaboo? Are you all..."

Her voice faded and turned into a slow, noisy gasp for air as she stood speechless and tried to take in the...snow. Or feathers? Stuffing. Something white all over everything.

"What happened?"

Lady Bug charged forward with the non-stop bark, like a staccato rifle of disgust, fury, and blame. Chloe still couldn't speak, dropping a few of her bags as she looked around and...found what was left of three sofa pillows, chewed beyond recognition.

No Name the New Dog bounded over, looked up at

her, his greenish-gold eyes hungry for approval, his tail tick-tocking with joy.

"No, no," she managed to say. "You are not a good boy. You are a..."

Lady Bug twirled once, finally silent, totally vindicated. It would have been funny except...it was so not.

"You want to get us booted out, Brownie Mix?" she asked. "'Cause your landlord is not going to be happy. If I know my mother, those pillows cost a fortune."

The dog stared at her and Lady Bug barked once to underscore just how much trouble he was in, then took a stroll around the mess like she was judge, jury, and prosecuting attorney examining the crime scene.

"You"—Chloe pointed to her newest problem, trying to think of what could discipline him—"cannot get a 'Mommy came home' treat."

He responded by bounding around the small room, circling her, jumping on the sofa, and leaping back off at her feet, his large pink tongue out as he panted.

Chloe bit her lip to keep from laughing.

"But I'll take you out, because clearly this bungalow ain't big enough for the two of you."

Lady Bug sniffed, barked, and walked away toward the bedroom, no doubt to go under the bed and pout.

"I'll take you, too, Bugger!"

There was nothing but silence from her baby, which broke Chloe's heart.

She followed the dog and got on her knees, lifting the bed skirt to see Lady Bug, who looked back with a mix of sadness and anger in her eyes.

"I know, I know. You hate this. Did you think I was going to blame you for this mess? C'mere, angel." She reached in and snagged her, gently easing her out to sit on the bed.

Cradling and rocking the way-too-emotional dog, she whispered, "I'm not going to keep him, I promise. But I can't take him to a shelter because bad, bad things could happen to him. You don't want that, do you? Well, maybe you do right now, but we'll find who owns this guy, I promise."

Lady Bug looked her right in the eye and growled, and then Chloe did laugh.

"You're mad at me? I'm the one who should be mad. You're the alpha here. You're the big sister. You think any of my sisters would have let me get away with this?" As she talked, Chloe smoothed her silky fur, stroking her head just the way Lady Bug liked it. "You have to teach him what's what, Bug. You have to set the example. I know, I know," she cooed, the words finally soothing the dog. "You want a treat?"

She wiggled out of Chloe's hands, hopped on the floor, and shot under the bed again.

Not soothing her that much. "Okay, okay. I get it. You're having a moment. No problem."

Pushing up, Chloe caught sight of the other dog in the doorway, watching the whole thing with nothing but longing in his eyes.

"Now you want cuddles?" Chloe surmised. "What kind of message would that send, huh?"

He dropped down to the floor, paws out, head cocked, full adorableness on display.

"Dude, you can't charm your way out of this one." She stood and bent over, unable to not pet him. "Why did you do that, buddy?"

He rolled over and offered his belly, and, Chloe guessed, an apology.

"Come on," she said after giving him a rub. "But you have to chill, doggo."

In the living room, she sighed noisily at the mess, no clue how to handle a dog that misbehaved. Lady Bug would no sooner chew up a pillow than she would take a long swim in the ocean. But this guy?

He *needed* a long swim in the ocean.

"Let's get this cleaned up and take a walk. Maybe someone will recognize you while we hang some flyers on a few of the steps and pilings, okay?"

He barked, then turned toward what was left of one of the pillows, lifting it in his teeth and bringing it to her like a prize to thank her for whatever she said, did, or bought. It didn't matter—that was love in his eyes.

After she changed from interview clothes into shorts and a tank top, she did her best to clean up the mess, making a mental note to stop into Mom's favorite décor store on Centre Street and buy replacements.

"Come on, pillow chewer. Let's see if we can find your owner." She brought the new collar out and sized it to fit him, then found the leash and the flyers. "Lady Bug! We're leaving! Let's go, girlie."

Nothing. Not even a bark.

"She's on strike," Chloe whispered to the other dog, who was already tugging her toward the door. "I hate to break it to you, big boy, but I don't think she's a fan."

Unconcerned, he pressed toward the door, ready to roll.

"Bye, Lady Bug! We're leaving without you!" she called with a deliberate warning in her voice as she opened the door. "Unless you want to come—"

Very slowly, with more attitude than a twelve-pound dog should have, Lady Bug emerged from the hall, probably having to go to the bathroom even more than she wanted to sulk under the bed.

"There's my lamb chop!" Chloe grabbed her leash and clipped it on, adding a kiss. "Way to be a big girl."

The second she opened the door, the new dog shot out and the leash yanked so hard, it nearly pulled Chloe over. "Whoa! Careful there!"

Instantly, Lady Bug trotted up to him and barked once right in his face.

He dropped down to his submissive pose, the whole thing making Chloe crack up.

"You tell him, Bug. We got manners around here."

Closing the door, she let the bigger dog lead her down toward the sand. "Now, let's go see if someone's looking for you—whoa!"

He launched forward, pulling her along, and thus making poor Lady Bug's tiny legs flip wildly in the sand. Chloe stepped it up, jogging with him, just as she heard her name called.

Looking up, she saw her mother on the deck of the beach house, waving at her.

"Who's that?" her mother called.

"And there's the lady who no doubt had those pillows custom made, boyo. Yeah, I know it's a beach bungalow, but you haven't met Susannah Wingate." Then, she waved back. "Temporary guest. Can I bring him up?"

"Of course."

She led the dogs in the direction of the house, right to the beach steps. No surprise, the big dog loped up, taking them two at time, then froze at the sight of her mother, once again wary of a stranger.

"Did you get another dog?" Susannah asked, coming closer but looking just as uncertain as the new arrival.

"I found him lost on the beach yesterday morning. Mom, meet...Brownie Mix."

"Well, hello...." She bent down but looked up at Chloe. "*Brownie Mix?*"

Chloe bit back a laugh. "I know, it's on the money but if I give him a cute name I'll get attached. And surely this angel has an owner."

"He's pretty," Susannah said, slowly reaching her hand out. "Safe?"

"So far. Unless you're a sofa pillow."

Her mother gave a questioning look.

"Please tell me they weren't custom and that I can replace them with a trip to Home Goods."

That made her mother laugh. "It's fine, Chloe."

"You say that now, but God only knows what he could do to that bungalow." She held up the paper bag full of flyers. "I tried social media and now I'm going to post these along the beach, because someone has to be missing this guy." Chloe gave his head a scratch. "But he wasn't wearing a collar, isn't chipped, and no one is claiming him."

"Did you take him to your vet?" Mom asked.

"Yep. He's healthy, with no critters or problems, which only makes me certain someone who loves him has lost him." She gestured to the oversized wooden deck with several seating areas, a summer kitchen, and a bank of French doors leading into the house. "Can I let him take a walk around?"

"Of course. And stay for a minute. I feel like I haven't talked to you for a few days."

Chloe unhooked both dogs and Lady Bug, a regular, ran straight to her favorite ottoman, which gave her a view of the entire deck and the steps from the beach.

But old Mixie loped around like a horse just let out to pasture, nearly knocking over a plant and heading straight for the back stairs to escape.

"Oh, no," Chloe called to him, but Lady Bug leaped off the ottoman and flew across the deck, catching up with him. She barked in his face, jumped and nipped his shoulder, then barked again.

It worked, bringing the bigger dog to a stop.

"Good girl, Bug!" Chloe reached into the little container hanging from the leash and shook it, the sound of treats getting Lady Bug to come closer, and Brownie Mix followed, so she gave him one, too.

"Come and sit," her mother said, guiding Chloe to a

favorite grouping of rattan chairs, both dogs following to sit quietly on the deck.

"You're going to keep him, aren't you?" Susannah asked on a laugh when Chloe rewarded that behavior with another treat.

"Not while I'm living in that bungalow," she said. "It's too small for a dog his size. So's my income."

Susannah tipped her head in concession. "How was the interview?"

"Eh...banking. Not my cup, but then neither is unemployment. So, I might consider the offer I expect to get."

"Just wait until the right thing comes along, honey."

"Mom, I can't mooch off you and Dad in the bungalow forever. I'm staring down the barrel of thirty and I..." She shifted in the seat. "God, I hate this subject."

"Then change it," her mother said with a loving smile. "Have you talked to Rose today?"

Instantly, she remembered the anniversary party and wanted to tread very carefully and not reveal any secrets —like Dad's idea or the fact that all of the Wingate women, minus Sadie, were currently planning the Great Anniversary Compromise.

"Um, yeah, we've talked. Had some texts. She said she has something to talk to me about," she said, purposefully vague. "Any clue?"

"Every clue." She gave a sly smile, leaning forward and glancing toward the closed French doors. "I asked her to plan a vow renewal ceremony for our fortieth anniversary, but it has to be a surprise for your father."

Was there anything worse than knowing a secret

when you weren't supposed to? She chose her words carefully. "Awesome idea, Mom. What do you have in mind?"

"Oh, who do I hear out there?" One of the French doors opened and her father stepped out into the late afternoon sunshine, looking so good and healthy that Chloe nearly leaped from her chair.

"Not a word, Chloe," Susannah whispered quickly. "It's a surprise."

She gave her mother a confirming look and drew a sneaky X over her heart. "Hey, Daddio," she called. "You're looking good. Meet my temporary houseguest."

"She's calling him Brownie Mix," her mother added with a laugh of disbelief.

The dog headed over to Dad, moving slower than usual, which touched Chloe. Did he understand Dad wasn't as steady on his feet as others? In case he didn't, Chloe snagged the collar to be sure he didn't jump.

"He is certainly handsome," Dad said, leaning down a bit like he was greeting a child. "Are you a good boy?"

"Not even close, but Lady Bug's getting him in line." She came closer and gave her father a hug and a kiss. "He's a short-term guest, I promise."

Dad ambled over to join them, still using a cane. But he was moving so well, Chloe suspected that extension of his right hand had become a bit of a prop that he enjoyed using.

As Dad settled into the seating area to join them, Chloe let go of the dog, who instantly moved closer to Rex, giving him a sniff, then sat next to his chair.

"You made a friend, Dad."

"Good boy." Rex tried to reach down and pet him, but it was awkward and he couldn't reach. The dog moved a little closer, touching Chloe's heart even more.

Chloe explained how she and Travis found him, and her plan to find his owner.

"What happens if no one comes to get him?" her mother asked.

"I don't know, but I won't keep him, Mom, I swear."

"Why not?" Dad asked. "He's a fine creature."

"Tell that to Mom's former pillows."

Dad snorted and studied the dog intently. "Well, I say if you want to keep him, you should."

She let out a sigh and looked from one to the other, sad she had to have this conversation again. "Until I get my own life in order, I can't take on more responsibilities. I love the idea, but I don't think it's the right time in my life."

"No luck, huh?" Dad asked, and she could swear she saw the disappointment in his eyes.

"I had an interview at Lighthouse Bank today," she said, forcing light into her voice. "They're looking for someone to handle PR for a new division."

"Who did you meet with?"

"The senior v-p of marketing."

"Gil?" Dad's brows shot up. "Good man. Very smart. What did you think?"

She mentally debated how honest she should be, especially since she'd forgotten Dad knew everyone on

Amelia Island. He'd even offered to make some calls for her, but she didn't want to go there. Yet.

"What do you think she thought?" Susannah asked with a wry smile. "PR for a bank? Does that feel like Chloe to you?"

"I don't know," Dad said. "Does it feel like Chloe to Chloe? Because that's who matters."

"It feels like...a stretch from my degree and what I thought I wanted to do with my life." *Also my personal idea of hell*, she added mentally, but had a feeling Dad would challenge her on that.

"Forget your degree, Chloe. What does your heart want to do?" he asked, the question surprising her a little.

"I don't know," she admitted. "I honestly don't know what color my parachute is." As she dropped her head back with a groan, the new dog immediately jumped up and tried to get on her lap. "Oh, you're an empathetic thing, aren't you, Mixie? Moxie? How about...Chocolate?"

She made room in the big chair and let his full weight press on her lap when he climbed up, which got Lady Bug's attention in a big way.

"Just pick one," her father said.

"What? A name or a color for my parachute or a job for my lost and floundering self or which of these needy dogs should get my love? 'Cause that last one is the only option that appeals to me."

Her father gave a knowing smile. "You'll figure it out, Chloe. Just don't quit until you do."

Of course he'd say that. Dad was a driver, the great

motivator, a man who loathed a quitter more than anything. He was the reason all of her sisters followed their hearts' desire and thrived. All but Chloe.

She wrapped her arms around the dog, getting a surprising amount of comfort from him. "Trust me, Dad. I'm trying."

"Chloe." Her mother leaned forward and put a hand on her leg. "You can stay in the bungalow as long as you need to. You can keep however many dogs you want. You can take your time and figure it all out. You know we love you."

Her heart just about folded in half.

"Thanks, Mom. I really appreciate that." With that, she patted the dog and eased him to the deck. "Now, I have to walk him and see if we can find his owner, and post a few of these flyers. Can I put one down on your steps?"

"Of course," Mom said, standing to wrap her arms around Chloe. "I love you, honey."

"Love you more, Mom. And you, Daddio." She leaned over to kiss her father, who looked up at her, an intensity in his dark eyes that she knew all too well. She braced herself for the "Wingates don't quit" lecture or maybe a variation of "the first three letters in Wingate are w-i-n" and a "go get 'em" speech she'd heard a lot.

To be fair, since his stroke, she hadn't heard anything like that. But then, she was busy being a runaway bride and failing in her TV career.

"Why don't you build a temporary fence next to the bungalow?"

She inched back, so not expecting that. "Excuse me?"

"For the dogs to run and romp. You can't take this big boy on twenty walks a day, so have that handsome firefighter of yours build a pen and maybe put up an awning for sunny days."

"Right here on the beach?"

"Why not? It's my property and I say make the dogs comfortable."

She let out a sigh, and relaxed. "That's sweet of you to offer, Dad. But I don't think I'll have him that long or, God willing, be living in your bungalow."

He narrowed his eyes. "You heard your mother, and I agree. However long you like. You are our daughter and we love you and you can stay forever, and do it with a passel of pooches, if that makes you happy."

Suddenly overwhelmed, she reached down and gave him a hug. "Thank you." And another kiss to her mother. "Thank you both."

Feeling lighter and so loved, she leashed up the dogs and headed off. "Come on...Pepper. Hershey. Oh, I know! Snickers!"

She heard her parents laughing as she made her way down the steps to the sand and turned to head north on the beach.

"It's hard not having a name, huh?" She gave his head a gentle stroke. "Kind of like not having a job. Everyone wants to give you one, but you only want the one that feels right."

And that, in a nutshell, was her problem in life.

Chapter Eight

Madeline

The Ginger Rogers gown, as Madeline thought of her latest creation, was coming along nicely. She used any spare time—like today's allotted forty-five minutes for lunch—to work on it. But only because the lace for Melissa Havensworth's veil still hadn't arrived when the eleven-thirty FedEx delivery came and went.

And that was a problem, because Melissa would be here tomorrow afternoon at three for a fitting. Yes, she could buy another week, but the bride wouldn't be happy and a veil delay really wasn't Madeline's style.

She texted Sadie again, knowing her sister was crazy busy, but she'd *promised* to get the lace and overnight it to Madeline. International mail could take a few days, but Sadie had sent a text that promised it would arrive today.

"Did you get a tracking number? Still waiting for my lace," she said out loud as she thumbed the words, trying not to sound impatient.

But didn't a promise mean anything to anyone? What good was making one if you weren't going to keep it?

She stepped back and looked at the dress laying

inside-out on her worktable, trying to decide if it should have cap sleeves or something softer. Something more mature. Something for...Susannah.

Was this the dress for her mother to wear at the vow renewal? Dad had wanted a fairy princess ballgown. Susannah told Rose she imagined herself in something short and simple.

But this was a *perfect* compromise.

Buoyed by the thought, she headed off to find matching chiffon she might use to make a draping portrait sleeve that would look beautiful on her mother. Something like—

She heard her phone buzz and pivoted, praying it was Sadie with an answer. One glance at the screen and her heart lifted.

Sadie: *At your house.*

What? The package had been delivered there instead of here? She'd been so clear where Sadie should ship it!

She started to stab back a response, but stopped herself. Sadie had done Madeline a huge favor by getting the lace, and if she walked home now and got the package, she could have that veil finished by tomorrow morning, right on time for Melissa's final fitting.

"So much for you, Ginger Rogers," she said to the dress that, like all of her creations, had a secret personality that only Madeline knew. This one was graceful, gorgeous, well-balanced with just a bit of a surprise flair and, of course, utterly lovely.

What better dress for Susannah, who fit that description to a T?

Thinking about that, she slipped out the back, hearing the laughter of a small group of ladies who were in the salon today with a bride-to-be having her special moment. As she passed the salon, she slowed and peeked in, catching the very moment the young woman stepped out of the dressing room in the gown Madeline had called "Sunlight on the Water," since it sparkled with a shimmer of sequins under the top layer of sheer tulle.

Madeline sucked in a breath at how beautiful the young woman looked, even with the dress clipped to fit her narrow frame. She took another few seconds to observe the reactions from the bridal party and the tears from the bride-to-be's mother.

This moment in the fittings always got her, Madeline mused as the ladies fussed and the bride twirled. As her salon manager chatted and took pictures, the mother of the bride was typically emotional, making Madeline wish she could have given that memory to her own mother.

Well, too bad, she thought, stuffing the very idea into the compartment where it belonged. That ship had sailed and Madeline wasn't on it.

Instead, Susannah would give that moment to all seven of her daughters when she donned the Ginger Rogers dress for her vow renewal.

Madeline stepped outside into the parking lot, but it was too nice a day to drive the short distance to the brick walk-up townhouse where she lived across Centre Street and off Ash. Feeling wildly spontaneous and not at all following her strict schedule, she slipped around to the front of her store, walking over the stone path between her salon and the ice cream parlor that separated Madeline Wingate Designs from Coming Up Roses.

Just as she reached Wingate Way, she caught sight of Silas Struthers, the man who owned Amelia Creamery, on his knees putting a sign in the window.

"For lease?" she read out loud. "Silas, are you leaving us?" It was impossible. He'd leased the store forever!

The older man stood, brushing back some thin gray hair. "Oh, hello, Miz Wingate." He nodded, always such a gentleman and a staple in Fernandina Beach. Silas and his wife, Milly, had been making homemade ice cream for tourists for at least twenty years. "Yes, I got permission from your sister, Raina, to post this. I'm afraid I had to give my notice, but we're staying through the holidays, I promise."

"You're retiring?" she guessed.

"Milly's mom isn't doing so great, so we're going to relocate up to Virginia to help her. Not exactly what I want, but family is what matters and who comes through when you're in a bind, right?"

"Oh, yes," she agreed, suddenly happy she hadn't given Sadie grief over text for sending the package to the wrong address. "I hope your mother-in-law is okay, but I'm sad you and Milly are leaving us high and dry without the best ice cream in the state of Florida."

"Thanks so much. But you think you're upset? When I told Raina, she darn near started to cry, but I think it was because those babies love my Rocky Road."

She laughed, knowing Raina's craving for Silas's ice cream. "We're all going to miss you," she said.

"Thanks, hon. I hope you get good neighbors."

"Whoever they are, they won't make ice cream like you." She gave him a warm smile and waved, crossing the street to make her way home at a speedy clip. The sooner she got the lace, the sooner she could be back on schedule for Melissa's fitting.

She walked down the side street to the row of brick townhouses, all new but built to look like they'd been there for a hundred years. Madeline had bought the first one that hit the market, crazy about the idea of having a maintenance-free yard right in the heart of town.

As she reached the front door of her unit, she scanned the steps for a package that...wasn't there. But this was where FedEx always left boxes.

Pulling out her phone, she texted Sadie with a picture. "Not here."

A second later, her phone flashed with a reply.

Sadie: *In the back.*

The back of the building? Why? Frustration zinged as she headed to one of the narrow alleys between two of the townhouses that led to a small back area for resident parking and back doors to the units.

How did Sadie know it was here? She texted the question as she walked, coming around the corner as she waited for the response. No doubt FedEx had sent her a picture, since they did that sometimes, but why would they—

"I know because I'm holding it in my hands."

Madeline gasped at the familiar voice, almost immediately followed by her sister, who appeared in the recessed door of Madeline's townhouse.

"Sadie!" she screamed, nearly dropping her phone in shock.

"Shhh! I'm hiding." She held out a box. "Special delivery, sis."

"What?" Madeline pressed both hands to her chest, still not processing the unexpected arrival. And the words. "Who are you hiding from?"

Sadie put the box on the ground, then stretched out her arms. "Everyone but the person who said they'd do anything for me. Well, this is anything."

Madeline took her hug, a little tentative because of how confused she was, then gave her sister a squeeze. "You better have an explanation."

"You better have a few hours in that airtight schedule of yours."

Drawing back, she searched Sadie's face, taking in the features of a woman she truly loved and missed. Everything was there—the sweet eyes that could be light brown or green depending on the light, the easy, wide smile, the delicate features, the halo of wild golden-brown waves that fell just past her shoulders.

But something wasn't right. Her eyes looked sad, her smile was missing, and had she even combed that mass of hair today?

"What are you doing here?" Madeline asked, holding her tightly. "And what the heck do you mean you're hiding?"

"No one can know I'm here, Madeline. No one in the family, no one who is looking for me. No one."

"What?"

"Can I go inside?"

Madeline picked up the box. "Just come with me to the studio and we'll talk."

"No. If you insist, I'll leave and you won't see me again until...for a while."

"Sadie!" She gripped the box in frustration. "Why?"

"Let me in and don't tell anyone I'm here and I'll... well, I won't tell you. But I won't leave."

It wasn't much of a deal, but Madeline accepted it, letting her schedule get shot to hell. She brought her little sister into the house, deeply troubled by all she was asking.

BY THE TIME Sadie had settled in—bearing all of one carry-on sized suitcase and a handbag—and had something to eat, Madeline's frustration had abated a little bit. Mostly, she was overjoyed to see her sister, especially once it was clear she wasn't in danger or hurt. Whatever had brought her here was personal.

Now it was just a matter of getting it out of her.

But Sadie was tightlipped. She asked more questions than she answered, steering Madeline to tell her all about the anniversary party dilemma and what they'd decided, update her on Dad's health, and get the latest on all the sisters.

Madeline obliged and by the time she'd finally finished, Sadie was stretched out on the sofa, satisfied and sleepy.

"You are not going to stay here without an explanation," Madeline said.

"Are you going to kick me out?" she asked with a sly smile.

"Sadie, come on. You trusted me enough to come here and nowhere else. Now trust me enough to tell me what's going on."

"I brought you lace, as promised. I know you never break a promise and neither do...well, sometimes I do." She made a face. "I guess it depends on the promise."

Madeline grunted. "What does that mean, Sadie?"

"It means that..." She sat up a little, using her fingers to comb back some of her unruly hair. "I told you enough already. I did something, Madeline. It was reckless and dumb and came at a cost."

Madeline stared at her, not completely shocked by Sadie doing something reckless. She was a natural-born adventurer, and a little too fearless for her own good. Living in Brussels, traveling the world, building the Saint Pierre chocolate brand one truffle at a time was the most settled this little tumbleweed had ever been.

"And..." Madeline urged when Sadie stayed quiet.

"And the cost was my job. I quit."

"Oh. Wow. Well, that's big news. I'm not sure why it has to be a secret—"

"No one can know I'm here, Madeline," she insisted. "I don't want to be found. I don't want to explain. I don't want to see anyone. I just want to hide in this townhouse. No one ever comes here, right?"

Madeline winced at that.

"I just mean you don't entertain a lot," she added quickly. "Has a pillow ever been at an angle? A dish left in the sink? A towel on the floor?"

"Over my dead body," Madeline joked. Kind of joked. "But you're right. This isn't a frequent hangout for Wingates or my vast network of friends and associates."

Sadie smiled at the sarcasm. "Plus, you are the most trustworthy Wingate."

"You can trust any and all of us," Madeline said, automatically rising to their sisters' defense. "We're all in the midst of a big secret planning session and it never for one second occurred to me that anyone would break a confidence."

Sadie nodded. "I trust all of them, yes. But keeping the fact that I'm here, on Amelia Island, and laying low a secret? Rose would have to tell Gabe or Raina. Chloe couldn't keep it from Grace and she might casually mention it to her new boyfriend. Mom and Dad don't go to the bathroom without telling each other, and Tori's not here, so you..."

"I can be trusted," Madeline said, bristling a little. "But only if you tell me the whole story."

"It's not important."

"Not important?" Madeline scoffed. "You quit your job, flew four thousand miles, and are skulking around my parking alley. I'd say something's important."

She dropped back to a reclining pose and draped her

arm over her face. "I told you I did something stupid, and it came back to bite me. I cannot show my face in that company—possibly in all of Brussels; actually, the entire continent—and I'm going to lay low here until..." She let her voice fade to nothing.

"Until what?"

"Until it blows over."

"How is that going to happen?" Madeline asked, hoping she could come at this through the back door.

"Once, you know, legal stuff is handled."

"Legal stuff? Sadie, are you in trouble with *the law*?" It seemed preposterous, but so was this request she was making.

She dropped her arm and stared at Madeline. "Please, please, *please*. I cannot and will not elaborate. It's shameful and, frankly, personally agonizing for me."

Madeline started to argue, then closed her mouth. She had no desire to cause anyone agony, especially her beloved sister. But had she stolen something? Done something illegal or deceitful? The very idea was so out of character.

"How long?" Madeline asked.

"How long will I be here in hiding? I don't know. Not too long, I hope."

"Could you disappear again?"

She shook her head. "No, I'm not going anywhere."

"What if someone does come over here to my little empty house? Every Wingate knows the key code. Suze could walk in anytime."

She looked horrified. "How often does she do that?"

"Never, but..." Madeline shrugged. "I guess I could change the code and then anyone coming would have to give me a heads-up."

Sadie sat up, tears filling her eyes. "Thank you," she whispered.

For a long time, Madeline didn't say anything, watching her sister, wondering what—or who—could have driven her to this.

"Once you clear things up," she finally said, "will you stay on Amelia Island?"

"Stay?" she choked softly. "Have you met me?"

"So, whatever happened to you or whatever you did, it hasn't changed you."

She swallowed and her face grew extremely serious. "It changed me plenty. I need you to promise that you won't let anyone know I'm here. I'll tell you this much—someone might be looking for me and I do not want to be found by...anyone."

"Okay," Madeline agreed on a slow sigh.

"Is that a promise?" Sadie pressed. "Is that an absolutely cannot-be-broken, swear-on-your-life, Madeline Wingate promise?"

Madeline didn't respond. That was a big, big promise and she wasn't sure.

"Madeline?" Sadie slipped off the sofa and came closer on her knees. "I'm begging you."

"Will you tell me, someday?"

She angled her head and looked hard at Madeline. "Don't you have any secrets?"

Hissing in a soft breath at the question, Madeline stayed very still.

"I mean, isn't there one thing in your life, in your past, that no one knows? Maybe just one other person and that's the way you keep it? Hidden from the world and from the family? Don't you have anything like that, Madeline?"

Chills rose on her arms and suddenly Madeline felt... naked. Exposed and cornered and aching to run rather than answer that question with the truth. Of course she had that secret. She had one she'd carried around for twenty-five years, a secret that held her down, kept her alone, and made her the promise-keeper she was today.

Because when someone breaks a sacred promise, it hurts. It changes a person, like whatever changed Sadie.

"I promise," she whispered, putting her hand on Sadie's creamy cheek. "Your secret, even if I don't know it, is safe with me."

She closed her eyes and nestled her cheek into Madeline's palm. "Thank you, sweet sister. And I promise..."

"To tell me someday."

Sadie opened her eyes. "Not to make too much of a mess while I'm living here." She laughed, suddenly alive and beautiful and Sadie again. And really, that was all Madeline wanted.

Well, that and the truth. She'd bide her time and get it eventually.

But she wouldn't break her promise to Sadie.

Chapter Nine

Raina

When it opened, Ocean Song would be a hotel unlike any other on Amelia Island. Raina had suspected that when she'd first driven by the construction site a few months ago. But now, closer to completion, she could see the exclusive waterfront property was truly one of a kind.

Before driving out this afternoon, Raina had done a little digging through her personal resources to learn that the new property would have twenty-two individual suites, each with small private pools and ocean views. Most important, there was a beachfront structure called Magnolia Hall for private events, a banquet room enclosed by glass bifold doors to offer "indoor/outdoor" entertaining for large parties.

Large parties like the hundred and fifty people Madeline thought would be on the guest list for Susannah and Rex's vow renewal.

And if that hall was anything like the sleek, bright and blinding white main building with a palm-lined portico that greeted her when she pulled up, it would suit both her parents and thrill her sisters. All she had to do was get it.

She parked in a lot mostly filled by trucks and one white Mercedes coupe—guaranteeing Chase was onsite —and then walked under the portico to the glass entrance. Inside, the spacious lobby was warmed by sand-toned hardwood floors that gleamed in the sunshine.

The view beyond the wall of glass at the far end of the lobby proved Mother Nature knew no limits for the possible shades of blue. The vista—the whole ambiance, Raina had to admit—was nothing short of glorious.

Raina looked around for an employee or someone who could send her in the right direction, and spied a carpenter putting finishing touches on a built-in wall unit behind a long reception desk.

"Excuse me?" she asked him. "I'm looking for the management and sales offices."

The man in his mid-forties stood up and pulled out an earbud, glancing at her, unable to keep his gaze from dropping for a millisecond to her protruding belly. "Who are you looking for, ma'am?"

"Chase Madison," she said.

He gave her a dubious squint. "Well, he went out to the courtyard because something's up with the pool tiling but you can't go there without a hardhat. He's adamant about that, which you'd know if you met him before."

"Oh, I've met him," she said, looking around for the courtyard. "I actually live with him," she added with a wry laugh that faded when she caught sight of Chase, phone at his ear, yellow hardhat in the other hand, walking toward the glass doors from outside. "And there he is. Thanks!"

Clearly preoccupied, Chase yanked the door open and came to a stop just as she reached him, his face registering surprise.

"Raina! What are you doing here?"

"Hey, hi." She looked up at him—did work boots make him even taller?—and gave her warmest smile. "I come looking for a favor. Are you very busy right now?"

"I am, but..." He gave a soft laugh of disbelief, then held up a finger as he listened. "One sec. Hey, Dave? Let me get back to you."

As he finished his call, she couldn't help noticing he wore faded jeans, boots, and a soft white T-shirt with just enough dirt for her to wonder if he was out there doing the tiling with his crew.

Somehow, she'd imagined him working in a linen shirt and dress slacks. She'd have been wrong. Turning away, she fought a smile, knowing her sister Tori would hang a nickname on this great-looking man like...Hotty-pants 2.0.

"So, this is a pleasant surprise," Chase said to her, sliding the phone into his pocket. "What kind of favor do you need?"

Based on the unfinished feel of the place, a rather big one, but Raina didn't want to plant that seed quite yet. "Well, I was wondering—"

"Chase! There you are." A woman came rushing down the hall, moving swiftly, considering she looked to be in her mid-sixties, carrying a long, thin cylinder of wrapped tissue that she held out to him as she got close to them. "I picked up your order."

"Thanks, Jules. Oh, this is Raina Wingate," he said, taking the wrapped object from her hand. "Raina, my assistant, Julia Laramy."

"Oh, Raina!" She extended a hand with a warm smile, shaking Raina's. "How nice to meet you. You bought the beach house! Congratulations!" Then she turned to Chase. "You wanted to get that rose over there before Paul showed up, right? You have less than an hour. Or I can drop it off."

Raina's heart shifted in her chest, realizing what was in the tissue. So, was Paul the husband? Surely Chase wouldn't be that open about his...affair?

"I'll get it to her," he said. "After I talk to Raina. Thanks, Jules."

His assistant nodded and took off down the hall with a quick goodbye, and Raina peeked into the tissue, getting a glimpse of lavender-tinted petals.

"Ah. The famous Ocean Song rose?" she asked, getting a quick look of surprise from him.

"It's famous?"

She shrugged. "My sister is the florist."

His eyes glinted with a smile. "And you two discussed my order?"

"Full disclosure? We discuss everything. And we both thought it was...romantic."

"You did?" He seemed amused by that, looking into the tissue himself. "Well, I suppose it depends on how you define romantic, but, yes, that's the idea."

"Then I don't want to keep you from delivering it," she said. "Maybe we could—"

"How much time do you have?" he said, cutting her off. "Right now, I mean."

"I'm free this afternoon. Unless you want to schedule a time that's better..."

He put a hand on her arm. "I'd like you to meet someone. Would you come with me to deliver this rose? On the way, you can tell me what you need."

Go...to meet his girlfriend? The invitation was far too intriguing to turn down, so she nodded in the direction of the door. "Let's go."

As they walked to the front, he slowed his steps at the reception desk where the carpenter was still at work, bent over a shelf.

"That you, Jeremiah?" Chase asked.

The man straightened and smiled. "Oh, hello, Mr. Madison. I see you two found each other."

"How's our patient?" Chase asked.

Jeremiah beamed at him, nodding. "Josh? Oh, he's much better, thank you. Kind of tough to slow down my nine-year-old, but that fall sure did. He's doing okay, though, and swears he'll play Little League come spring."

"I bet he will," Chase said, turning to include Raina in the conversation. "Jeremiah's little boy fell off the monkey bars at school and —"

"Broke his arm," she finished, instantly knowing there was likely only one third grader with a broken arm in the small Amelia Island population. "My niece is in the class where it happened at Coastal Oaks Elementary. She was on the playground and told me all about it. I'm glad he's doing well."

"Really?" Jeremiah asked. "She was there? What's her name?"

"Alyson D'Angelo. Does your son know her?"

"I don't know," he said with a slow shake of his head, regarding her with even more interest. "Did she get a good look at what happened? Because there seems to be a little controversy over what caused the fall."

"I don't know, but I'll ask her," she said.

"Thank you and..." He glanced down at her belly. "Congratulations to both of you."

"Oh, no!" they both exclaimed in unison, shaking their heads and laughing awkwardly at the mistake.

"Can't take the credit," Chase said. "We're just..."

"Oh, sorry." Jeremiah turned beet red. "When she said you lived together, I just assumed..."

"Fair enough," Raina said, knowing she hadn't explained that to him. "I promise if Alyson can shed any light on your son's accident, I'll let you know."

"Thank you," he said, nodding and turning back to his work.

Chase blew out a soft breath as they walked away. "Sorry about that."

"It's fine," she assured him. "And I'm happy to hear little Josh is doing okay. Alyson said his bone was sticking out of his arm. I got a description in *way* too much detail."

"It was bad," Chase said. "I actually took Jeremiah to the hospital because he was too upset to drive, and the poor kid was really shaken up." Chase led her to that white Mercedes and opened the passenger door for her.

When he climbed in behind the steering wheel, he still held the rose.

"Here," she offered, taking it from him. "And can I just compliment you on nailing some incredible real estate for this place? I grew up on this island and I know this is one of the nicest beaches around."

"Thank you. It's been quite a journey and..." He threw a look at the building when they drove past. "We are so not done yet."

Oh, boy. Better get this out there and see what his response would be. "Well, I sure hope it's done by mid-November for a reception we're dying to hold here."

He tapped the brakes, turning his head to her. "You're getting married."

"Me?" She gave a quick laugh, mostly to cover the fact that he sounded surprisingly...disappointed. "I'm not even divorced yet, remember?"

"Oh, that's right. So which of the many lovely Wingates is tying the knot?"

"*Re*-tying," she corrected. "Rex and Susannah are celebrating their fortieth anniversary on November eleventh and my sisters and I want to throw them a vow renewal ceremony on the beach, with a big party. Here, if possible."

His attention on the road, she saw him calculate the dates. "That's in six weeks."

"Yep. And you don't open until..." All she'd been able

to find was a vague date for next year. "When do you open, exactly?"

"Officially? After the holidays, in early January. I've got some marketing people thinking about a soft opening in December, minus the traditional Christmas décor, but only to work out kinks with a gentle and friendly audience."

"Move it up a few weeks and we could be so gentle and friendly." She grinned at him. "Wingates are famous for both."

He laughed softly, blowing out a slow breath as he considered the request. "Rex and Susannah, huh? Very sweet."

"It's even sweeter when you find out that Rex wants to surprise Susannah with an over-the-top fairy-tale wedding and reception for a few hundred at the Ritz, while Suze has told us she wants to surprise *him* with a re-enactment of their tiny beach wedding."

He looked astonished. "And neither knows that?"

"Nope. They came to us separately and certain. We nixed the Ritz—"

"I'm sure it's booked."

"Everything is," she told him.

"And that's why you came to Ocean Song."

"I'm here because my sisters and I are looking for the perfect compromise in size and glitz, plus there is the weird but true fact that the Ocean Song beach is the *very* beach where they got married forty years ago."

"No."

"Yes, and apparently I was there, but Rose and I were

three and more interested in chasing butterflies than being flower girls. But it is 'their' beach and, hey..." She fluttered the tissue-wrapped rose. "Surely a romantic guy like you can appreciate the significance of that."

He chuckled and glanced at the flower, then back at her. "Romance is in my blood," he said softly.

"Ah, yes. The Sicilian. Any chance the place called Magnolia Hall will be done?" she pressed.

"Only if you want to see a grown man cry—that would be my construction manager, Dave."

"He can cry at the ceremony," she said, sliding into negotiation mode as easily as he downshifted and turned off the main road. "And get free champagne."

That made him laugh again as he turned onto a cozy residential street. "He'll need it if he has to pull off that miracle at Ocean Song."

She eyed the flower again. "So is the resort named after this type of rose?"

"Yes, but it was only my working name for the project," he said. "Turns out the investors loved the name, so we kept it."

"You have partners on the project?" she asked.

"Financial only. And a few consultants for design, marketing, and hotel management, since it's the first hotel I've ever done."

"Really?" That was a surprise. "Pretty big under-taking for your first commercial property, isn't it?"

He shrugged. "I'm a go-big-or-go-home kind of guy. Plus, the concept is exactly what this market needs."

She couldn't argue that, but his entrance into the

competitive hotel business fascinated her. "I thought your business was vacation rentals."

"It is, but hotels are coming back," he said. "Believe it or not, the vacation home rental concept isn't for everyone or for every type of vacation, and people are flocking back to hotels."

"I've heard rentals are slowing because interest rates are high and the boom buyers' loans are all coming due."

He gave her a quick smile, as though he appreciated her equal knowledge of the market. For a flash, she was transported back to the early days with Jack, when they'd talk real estate into the wee hours of the night.

"But people will always go on vacation," he continued, apparently not haunted by bittersweet memories like she was. "And they want the amenities like room service and pool bars, daily maids, a concierge, a gym, and...pampering. Ocean Song has all that, and more."

"Sounds lovely. What made you choose Amelia Island?" she asked, knowing his vacation properties were all over the country.

He slowed the car and pulled into the driveway of a small ranch home, shaded by oaks and tucked far off the street. "Because someone I care about very deeply lives here and I wanted to build her...a legacy."

She looked from the house to him, as curious about the person who lived there as the soft and tender note in his voice.

Without elaborating, he turned off the ignition and slid the rose from her hands. "Come and meet the woman I love."

INSIDE, it was dim but not gloomy. Shades were closed in a tiny, sparsely furnished living room and the small house smelled...warm. Cozy, even. Like someone had baked cookies earlier and the comforting scent lingered.

"This way." He guided her into a narrow hall, stopping at a door left ajar. He eased it open to reveal a double four-poster bed with a tiny white-haired woman sound asleep.

Raina looked up at him, taken aback. "Who is this?"

He gave a slow smile, a light in his eyes she'd never seen before. "Analucia Cardinale," he said, his words barely a whisper. "Don't fall in love too hard, she isn't long for this world. She's ninety-seven, can't see a thing, and slips into incomprehensible Italian much of the time." He leaned close to her ear and added, "My nonna."

Chills fluttered up her neck. His...grandmother?

"Nonna?" he called gently, stepping into the dimly lit room to go to the side of the bed. "It's me."

Her lids fluttered and she turned, showing a face that had lived every one of those ninety-seven years, with a large nose that looked like it was the only thing about her that didn't get smaller with age.

"Carlo." She reached a weathered, spotted hand to his face and muttered something else, probably in Italian, because Raina didn't understand a word.

He took her hand and eased himself onto the side of

the bed. "I brought you something." He placed the rose, still in the tissue, in her other hand. "Ocean Song."

"Ahh." She lifted it to her nose and inhaled. "*Mi amore*, Carlo." She drew the name out this time, almost singing it. "He still sends me my favorite rose from heaven."

"And I brought a friend, Nonna. Would you like to meet her? Do you feel up to company?"

"*Si, si.*" She tried to push up, but didn't get very far. Her dark eyes moved, though, as if she scanned the room, then she closed them. "Bring her to me."

He gestured to Raina and she joined him at the side of the bed.

"Nonna, this is Raina."

"Rain...like the rain from the sky?" she asked, turning and looking toward Raina but not at her. This close, Raina could see her eyes were cloudy and distant and her face bore deep, deep creases that looked like she'd lived her life laughing in the sun.

"Yes, lots of people call me Rain," she said as Chase guided her to replace him next to his grandmother. "Can I call you Nonna, too?"

The old woman gave a gummy smile and reached out her hand, which Raina took immediately, feeling the smooth parchment of her skin and the raised knuckles from arthritis and age.

"*Si, si...*" She let go and lifted a hand toward Raina's face, touching her cheek with a featherlight finger. "*Bella, bella. Piogge.*"

"She says you're beautiful," Chase said. "*Piogge* is the Italian word for rain."

Raina smiled against the palm. "Thank you, Nonna. So are you."

"I was," she said. "My Carlo told me I was the prettiest girl in Palermo."

"I bet you were," Raina said, unable to keep from smiling at the pure sweetness of this angel.

Sometime, when she could think, she'd have a good laugh over how wildly she'd misunderstood Chase's late-night departure and the roses. A married woman in pencil skirts? But now, she just wanted to soak up the simplicity of this dear old woman.

"Carlo was your husband?" Raina guessed.

The cloudy eyes shuttered with a moan. "*Mi amore,*" she whispered. "He is gone now, and so is my daughter, Marguerita."

At the sad note when she spoke the name, Raina looked up at Chase. "Your mother?" she asked softly.

His eyes barely closed in confirmation as his grandmother lifted the rose toward him. "*Per favore.* Paul said there's a clean vase."

"Of course. You talk to Raina." He left the room with the flower, giving Raina a moment to catch her breath from the unexpected emotion swirling in her.

"Paul is my nurse," Nonna said. "He's so sweet but sometimes he can't come at night. Then Chase stays with me. Just overnight. I don't need someone all day, too. But sometimes, at night, it's lonely."

Whoa, Raina had been off-base in her assumptions.

"He's a good boy, my Carlo, *si*? I know, his name is Charles. Or...Chase." She made a face that showed exactly what she thought of the nickname. "But so handsome, *si*?"

Raina smiled. "Very."

"And he can cook like his grandfather."

"I've seen him at work in our kitchen," she said, and Nonna's eyes seemed to focus for a second.

"Ahh, so you're..."

"Living in the same house," she said, instantly realizing how that might sound, but surely his grandmother knew the arrangement. "I bought the beach house from him and he's...renting there."

Once again, her eyes shuttered. "Ah, that lovely house. I love it."

"I do, too," Raina said.

"But I couldn't manage the steps or the beach." She patted Raina's arm. "But so nice for you two."

"It's...nice." And there wasn't a "you two" but she didn't know how to say that.

"What name is Raina?" she asked. "Not Italian."

Raina laughed. "No, it's short for Regina, which is a feminine version of my father, grandfather, and great-grandfather's names."

"Ooh!" She squeezed Raina's hands. "That's nice. I like a big family."

"Then you'd like mine. There are seven of us, all girls."

Her eyes grew wide. "Seven daughters! *Mio Dio*!"

"Did you have...more children?" Raina asked, so curious about this woman's nine decades of life.

"*Non, non.* Just my Marguerita. And she met that American boy, the soldier, Lieutenant Madison. He took her away but then, we come here, me and Carlo, when the baby was born. To help Marguerita and then...the accident."

An accident with Chase's parents? Raina frowned, leaning closer and not sure she understood. As she did, Nonna's hand dropped a little lower and bumped Raina's stomach.

"Oh!" The old eyes flashed as she pressed, splaying her hands over the baby bump. "This is not...the pasta."

"Not all of it," she said on a laugh. "I'm pregnant."

"You are?" That put a light in her foggy eyes. "How...wonderful!"

"It is," she agreed. "I really couldn't be happier."

She murmured Italian and brazenly splayed her hand over Raina's belly, her large nostrils quivering as she took a breath. "Is it...are you...Carlo!"

Chase walked into the room, holding a vase with the rose on display. "Yes, Nonna?"

"She is...a baby!" She did everything to push herself up, but it was clearly too much for her.

"Two babies," Chase said, chuckling. "Did Raina tell you she's having twins?"

"Oh! *Dolce madre di Dio!*" she exclaimed. "When would you tell me?"

"Oh, Nonna," he said. "It's not—"

"The line! It continues!"

Raina felt her eyes widen as she turned to Chase, sharing the same expression they had when Jeremiah had made that mistake.

"Carlo! Carlo!" Nonna reached trembling hands all over like she was searching for something. "*Mi rosario!* I must pray!" She finally landed on something, lifting a string of black beads. "Holy Mother, *grazie! Grazie mille!*"

Raina stood slowly, realizing how very wrong Nonna's impression was, turning to Chase, who came to the bed and opened his mouth to tell her.

But that weathered old hand grabbed his as tears sprung. "You make me so happy, Carlo! I am so... Oh! I don't know the word! *Felicita!*"

She didn't need to know the words; Raina could feel the woman's tiny body vibrate with excitement. "Two babies to carry on the Cardinale family tree! *Molto grazie*, Carlo and Rain!"

Tears started to meander down the network of creases on her face, a sob shaking her shoulders.

"Nonna, Nonna." Chase bent over to wrap his arms around her and settle her. "Calm. Calm down. You're too excited. Your heart can't take it."

"*Non! Felicita! Felicita!*"

He straightened a bit, looking at Raina, who imagined her own expression was as stricken as his. "She's happy," he said.

No kidding. But she was wrong!

"Stay calm, Nonna. This isn't what—"

"Rain! Rain! To me, *bella*." The old woman nudged

Chase away and reached for Raina. "*Per favore*. Please, please."

Raina let Nonna take her hand and pull her closer. "When the babies come? When?"

She swallowed. "The end of January."

With a string of Italian under her breath, she gazed up at Raina, those ancient eyes looking the clearest they had in the twenty minutes they'd been together.

"You name one Charles," Nonna said.

Excuse me? Did she say...Charles?

"I...don't...know...the genders..." Raina could barely speak.

"Not Carlo, I know, so Italian!" She waved a gnarled hand. "Charles Cardinale Madison. One of them."

"They might both be girls," Raina whispered, utterly unable to break her heart with the truth.

"*Non, non.* A boy. One must be a boy! I will pray." Her eyes closed again as she brought the rosary to her lips and kissed it. "*Ave o Maria, piena di grazia...*"

Raina just stared at her, vaguely aware of Chase taking her arm and guiding her away from the bed.

"Nonna, we have to go, but first you have to know..."

She continued to pray in Italian and Raina braced herself for her response when Chase said the babies were not his. But the words didn't come. And old Analucia was drifting off to sleep, to dream of great-grandbabies that were not hers.

He sighed. "Let's go now," he whispered.

"Chase!" she hissed, blinking at him. "You can't let her—"

"Shhh. Let's go. Paul will be here in ten minutes, so she won't be alone. Come on, let her sleep."

"But she..."

"Let's just go to the car."

With a quick goodbye to his sleeping nonna, Chase ushered Raina back to the hall and the living room, then right out the door.

She froze in the driveway and stared at him. "You can*not* let her believe these babies are yours."

For at least four or five heartbeats, he stared at her, emotions darkening his eyes to the color of espresso and just as strong.

"Raina, she's very sick. She has months left at the most. That's why I sold my house, why I went to Palermo to manage her final affairs. She's dying and..."

"And you want her to die believing that lie?"

"It's not a lie, it's...a wrong impression. And one that's made her very, very happy."

"That was obvious."

"It's all she's ever wanted. She and Carlo, my grandfather who grew Ocean Song roses in the garden in Palermo. A child, a legacy, the continuation of the family —it was all she wanted. And when my parents died, I..." His voice grew thick. "Who does it hurt if she dies happy?"

She just stared at him, unable to answer that question as another one formed in her head. "Did you bring me here so she would make that mistake?"

"No!" He seemed genuinely stunned at that. "She's all but blind. I never thought she'd even see what you looked like, let alone know you were pregnant. I just wanted you to meet her."

"Why?"

He gave a mirthless smile. "Because I could tell you thought I had some kind of side chick who only wanted me for late-night chicken parm calls."

She almost laughed. "I did, um, assume... Never mind. Chase, you can't let her think that. It's not true."

After a beat, he reached for her hand, clasping it in his. "How about a deal, Raina?"

"I don't..." She let out a sigh. "What?"

"Do this for me. Just let her believe that until her time is up. And, in return, I will move heaven and Earth to give you that space you need for your parents' party. The banquet top to bottom at cost. Would that be an arrangement the great fixer and dealmaker Raina Wingate would agree to?"

Something in his voice, in the question, actually made her dizzy. She closed her eyes and clung to his hand, knowing the whole deception was wrong...but very right, too.

"You don't have to make it a deal, Chase. I'll...do it." Holding his gaze, she narrowed her own. "But I'm not naming a baby Charles. No offense."

He laughed. "None taken." Still holding her hand, he tugged her closer. "Do we have a deal?"

She finally exhaled and nodded. "Yes."

Closing the space between them, he dropped a light kiss on her head. "*Grazie,* Raina," he whispered. "*Grazie mille.*"

Chapter Ten

Rose

"Am I hitting you in the middle of dinner?" Gabe's voice on the other end of the phone, no matter how mad Rose thought she was at her husband, always gave her a small thrill. These days it kind of made her ache, too. "It's the first chance I had to call all day."

"Hey." She walked away from the counter, squeezing her eyes to wipe her brain of everything else and focus on him. "I'm cooking, all the kids are doing homework. You know, the usual."

"My favorite moment of the day," he said. "Well, second favorite. Waking up next to you is number one. Also going to sleep. Man, I miss you, Rosie."

"I know. I miss you, too." Glancing around and not having any idea when one of the kids might walk into the kitchen, she headed toward the back door, stepping out to the patio and the yard beyond. "How did the lab go last night?"

"Long, hard, a ton of work. Basically, medical school. How's it going up there, babe?"

She sighed, not wanting to attack on the Zach issue,

longing for just a chance to catch up. She walked by the greenhouse, the scene of so many happy hours with Gabe, and settled on a bench he'd built for her, looking across the yard and into the trees with a noisy sigh.

"That doesn't sound good," he said.

"It's lonely," she admitted. "Life isn't really a ton of fun without you." And that, she realized, was the bottom line.

"Yeah, fun is a distant memory. How are the kids?"

"Well, let's see. Alyson broke her glasses because she wants contacts, Ethan is really struggling in math, and Avery is sucking her thumb again."

He groaned lightly. "Okay, well, I still say no on the contacts until she's ten, maybe we can get a tutor for Ethan, and should we try the thumb guard thing again?"

"I can't put her through that again," she said. "She'll stop, but...the real problem is with Zach."

"Really? I talked to him the other night and he seemed great. He told me you were struggling, but we ironed things out."

Oh, he ironed them out all right. She closed her eyes and leaned back. "And then he made breakfast at dawn, quit soccer, bagged the officer's role in NHS, broke up with his girlfriend, and showed up at the shop today to... be you."

Gabe was dead silent for a few heartbeats, then she heard him swear under his breath.

"He was born an overachiever," Rose said softly. "So what did you expect him to do when you told him to basically take over as the father of the family?"

"Oh, Rose, that's... He quit soccer?" He choked out the question. "What the heck was he thinking?"

"That you gave him a more important job."

"This is not..." His voice trailed off. "Yes, it is. Totally my fault. I asked him to step it up and to be sure to be there for you. I'm not that upset about Tiffany, to be honest, but soccer and NHS?"

"There was no reason to break up with Tiffany," she countered. "He really liked her and she's a nice girl."

"But things were getting a little too serious. He told me that."

"Serious, like...he's falling in love?"

Gabe laughed softly. "I think the word you're looking for is 'lust.'"

"Zach?" she barked. "He's not even sixteen!"

"Wake up and smell the new world, sweet Rosie. Don't worry, I talked to him. Honestly, we talked more about that than him helping out at home."

She cringed. "How serious? Are they..." Shuddering, she shook her head. "I really don't want to think about it."

"Nothing's happened," he assured her. "But he's a boy and she's a girl and hormones are crazy."

"He told you that?" Rose asked, a little jealous that her firstborn hadn't confided in her. Then again, her reaction probably wouldn't have been as cool as Gabe's.

"He danced around the subject, but if he broke up with her, I guess the dance is over."

"But what about all the extracurricular stuff and quitting the team? What are we going to do?"

Gabe was silent for a long, long time. Then, she heard

him grunt softly. "Rose, I hope I didn't make a huge mistake."

"By talking to him?" she asked, but only because she wanted to be gentle. She knew what he meant.

"Med school."

Her very first instinct was the most human one—to fire back with, *"Ya think?"* But Rose would no sooner make Gabe feel any worse than she would stick that awful thumb guard on Avery.

"No, honey," she said softly. "This is a bump in the road."

She heard him huff out a breath.

"Gabe, listen to me. This is what you wanted more than anything, and you got it. You can't let one overreaction from Zach bring this dream to a halt."

"Well, I got bad news about some of my credits I thought they were going to accept. I have to repeat a few classes. I can do them at night and give up EMT hours, but that will mean less money."

As his voice grew thick, she could imagine him dropping his head, combing his fingers through his dark hair to pull it back, trying to make things right for his family.

Her heart swelled with love for him.

For their entire marriage, Gabe had given selflessly to her and their kids, and, in the process, lost himself. Maybe that happened to a lot of men, and maybe that was why there was such a thing as a mid-life crisis, and the reason two of Rose's sisters' marriages had ended.

If all she needed to do to make her husband feel

happy and content was be a somewhat single parent for a few years, she could do that.

She loved him that much.

"Listen to me, Gabriel D'Angelo."

He chuckled, probably because when she used his full name, he knew she meant business.

"All right, Rose-Colored Glasses," he countered with a soft laugh. "Gimme a dose of pure positivity to keep me going."

"Darn right I will," she said. "Honey, you are going to be Amelia Island's most amazing doctor. You are going to wake up next to me and go to sleep next to me and enjoy more dinners with this family for the next forty years. We can get through this, both of us. And so can our kids, who are incredible."

He sighed again, but she hoped her words were getting through to him.

"I'll talk to Zach," he promised her. "I'll set him straight. And maybe I can Zoom with Ethan later and work on that math. After that, let me FaceTime the girls and do their prayers with them."

She whimpered a little. She hadn't even told him about the missed prayers, but he knew. He knew because he was Gabe.

Her eyes filled as she pressed the phone to her ear. "I love you so much," she whispered.

"Not as much as I love you," he countered. "And promise me, after I pray with the girls tonight, you and I can just talk until we're both asleep."

"I promise."

With a few more I love you's and promises, they said goodbye, and Rose felt better than she had in days.

ROSE KEPT ALL her promises except the last one. She wanted to call Gabe later and talk until they were asleep, but Raina showed up and announced they had to talk. So, once the kids were settled, Rose and Raina went out to the greenhouse together. There, Raina told her about the deal she'd made and how much she was struggling with it.

"I don't know," Rose said, closing her eyes to imagine an old dying woman given a gift of joy. "Remember a few months back when I met Annabelle Green, the woman who was our mother's friend? She died before I could talk to her a second time. Oh, that hurt. Not only did I want to know more about Charlotte, I wanted to tell her that our mother lived a short, but very good, life. I wanted to give her that peace before she died and I couldn't."

Raina stared out into the night through the glass, deep in thought.

"It's a lie," she finally said softly. "What if there's an afterlife and she gets up there and finds out we lied to her?"

Rose laughed softly. "She'll understand why."

"I get his motivation—"

"Love for his grandmother."

"Who raised him after his parents died." Raina turned, tucking her feet up. "They had quite a story, too.

His mother was born and raised in Palermo, in Sicily, and after the Vietnam War ended, lots of American soldiers vacationed there. Marguerita met a young lieutenant, William Madison, fell madly in love, married him, and moved to the States."

"See, romance *is* in his blood. That's why the flowers."

"His grandfather grew Ocean Roses in their garden," Raina told her. "He takes her one every day to remind her of him."

"Oh." Rose put her hand on her heart. "I can't bear the sweetness."

"When Chase—who is actually Charles, after his grandfather, Carlo—was born, his mother got very sick with appendicitis. She nearly died and Nonna decided to move here to help her. It was a big battle, but Carlo finally agreed, leaving his family. Thirteen years later, William and Marguerita—who went by Maggie—were killed in a boating accident. Nonna and Poppy raised Chase from there."

Rose closed her eyes, swamped by how people survived such grief. "So he adores his grandmother."

"Beyond words. And her last, only, and dying wish is that he have children and carry on the Cardinale line," Raina said. "He's been in Sicily the past few weeks because she's written letters to her family there—nieces and nephews, I guess, and friends—to say goodbye and give them gifts. What if one of them gets wind of this?"

"Then he'll tell them she made a mistake and it felt

right to let her think the babies are his. He'll be a hero for loving their aunt and friend so much."

"I guess, but..." She cringed. "If anyone gets the wrong impression, especially since we're living together, well, it would be very embarrassing. Wingate is a well-known name and I am technically still married. I don't want a scandal. It would break Suze and make me feel awful."

Rose nodded, thinking on that. "I don't think it will get out, but I understand your concerns, especially sharing that house. Why did he sell his beach house anyway? Why not move his grandmother there, or why doesn't he stay with her since he did? Why live with you?"

"I asked him that," Raina said. "She lived at the beach house and got very, very sick and close to death. He moved her into assisted living with round-the-clock nurses and she hated it, but liked one of the nurses, who is a really nice guy named Paul."

"So, not her *husband*," Rose said dryly, rolling her eyes.

"No, I totally misconstrued that. But after she got out of the assisted-living situation, she didn't want to ramble around that big beach house, so he rented this tiny house and hired that nurse to be her night nurse. It's only two bedrooms, so Paul needs the other one. I do suspect Chase has spent more than a few nights on the couch, just to be close. He put his own house on the market because he knows she won't be around long and the timing was right. She surprised him and rallied, but she's still very old and fragile, but dreaming of a great-grand-child. And wham, in walks pregnant Raina."

Rose gasped. "Did he plan this?"

"I asked him that, too, and he swears he did not. She's blind and only felt my stomach by accident. Maybe he did, I don't know. I know you think he walks on water, Rose—"

She laughed. "I didn't say that. But the daily rose is sweet, you have to admit."

Raina lifted a brow. "He's divorced twice, so..."

"So, he made mistakes." Rose leaned in. "It can happen to anyone and doesn't mean it's his fault."

Raina laughed at that. "Yeah, yeah. Hey, pot, have you met the divorced kettle?"

"And your divorce is certainly not your fault," Rose reminded her. "Has he told you about them?"

"No." She shook her head. "I'm not sure I want to know."

"Why not?"

Raina just shifted on the loveseat, clearly uncomfort-able. "I don't know. All I do know is that I agreed to dupe this old lady—"

"Don't think of it like that." Rose reached out and put a hand on Raina's shoulder. "I think you are giving her an extraordinary gift. Plus, we get the space for the party."

Raina snorted. "Come on. You and I both know I would have said yes even if there were no hotel space involved. Why?"

"The question to me is why not, Raina. It's a kind thing and it doesn't hurt a soul."

"I guess." Raina sipped some tea, gnawing on her lower lip. "It's like I can't say no to this guy. Buy his house, sure. Let him rent a room, of course. Pretend to be the mother of his children? No problem!"

"You fell madly in love with the house, his rent covered your mortgage payments, and you agreed to the baby thing because anyone with a heart would have done the same thing."

"I guess." Raina blew out a breath. "But it's scary. What else will I say yes to?"

Rose bit back a laugh and Raina looked sharply at her.

"What's funny?" she asked.

"Nothing. It's just..." Rose eased closer to whisper, "Maybe you're...attracted to him."

"Shut it, Rosebud! I'm pregnant and not even divorced, for heaven's sake."

"So what?" Rose countered. "Neither of those things has made you less human. He's very good-looking, obviously has a kind heart, and he's a success in life. He's, what, fifty at the most? So seven years older and well, if you ask me, quite a catch."

"A catch if you're fishing for another man, which I am so completely not doing."

"Your love life isn't over, Rain."

"Please." She rubbed her belly. "My love is going in one direction now. Well, two. Thing One and Thing Two, and neither one of them will be named Charles. I mean, she didn't just make a joke about that, Raina. She announced, 'One will be named Charles!' What if this man, who evidently has some weird hold over me, insists on it? Makes some deal or persuades me that it's the right thing to do? What if she lives four more months and I have to name a baby Charles?"

Rose lifted a shoulder. "When you think about the fact that our mother was Charlotte? It's not the worst name if you have two boys and want to honor her."

Raina shot her a look. "*Charles?*"

"Charlie Wingate! How cute is that? Even for a girl."

"Whose side are you on, Rose?" Raina added a playful flick of her fingers on Rose's arm.

"There are no sides," Rose told her. "But if there were, I would be on yours first, last, and forever, and I think you know that, womb-mate." When Raina smiled, Rose inched a little closer. "I think you're doing something kind, noble, and beautiful. He says she has months left and you are sending that woman to heaven with a smile on her face."

"Where she'll arrive, look down, realize the mistake, and instruct the gatekeeper to lock me out."

Rose chuckled. "I actually think the opposite is true. I think whoever is up there checking qualifications will guarantee entrance to a person who would selflessly give joy to a dying old woman."

With a grunt, Raina let her head fall back. "Well, the good news is the event space is spectacular. Right on the beach, big enough for a sit-down dinner for whoever we invite, and he's giving it to us at cost."

"Now all we have to do is plan this shindig," Rose

said. "I really hope Suze is happy, even though she said small and private."

"The ceremony will be, and right on the beach," Raina assured her. "And you and I won't be lured away by butterflies."

"Just the owner of the resort," Rose teased, getting a dark look in response.

"I am not attracted to him," she said. "So don't put that out there in the universe."

"Too late," Rose said, pushing up. "It's out there. And if you don't mind me kicking you out, Raindrop, I have to call my husband and tell him how much I love him."

Raina looked up at her. "You think the problem with Zach is solved?"

"They talked tonight, so we'll see." Leaning over, she planted a kiss on Raina's head. "Sorry, but I kind of love Charlie Wingate. Boy or girl."

Raina just glared at her, but they both went inside laughing about it.

Chapter Eleven

Chloe

Maybe this hadn't been the best way for Chloe to spend her day. But by the time she left the last county shelter, she was feeling beyond blue. A call from Travis did a little to lighten her load as she tugged two leashes and a heavy heart outside of the noisy kennels to talk to him.

"What's wrong?" he asked the minute he heard her less-than-enthusiastic hello.

"Oh, Travis. There are *so* many dogs that need love. It's sad."

"What brought that on?" he asked.

"I can't give up on He Who Cannot Be Named, so I decided to visit the shelters on Amelia Island to see if anyone has been looking for him and leaving flyers in case they do. Now, I'm at the Humane Society, which is my fourth stop. No luck so far."

He laughed softly. "Give the dog a name, Chloe."

"I can't. I'll get too attached."

"Like that hasn't happened already."

And he didn't even know that the stray had slept on her bed last night. Even Lady Bug had given up trying to make him get down, and they all snoozed rather peacefully together. "Nah. I'll wait until I've exhausted every possibility."

"Speaking of being exhausted, you should come home."

The way he said it made her frown. "Come? Are you at my bungalow?"

"I am and I'm working on a surprise. How long until you get here?"

"I wanted to stop at one more place, but...what are you doing?"

"You'll see. And, Chloe, don't spend too much time looking for the owner. The dog's obviously abandoned and he's yours now. Name him and claim him."

She looked over at the pooch in question, who'd found a slice of shade on the concrete. He lay flat on his belly, tugging the extendable leash as far as it would go.

Not so Lady Bug, who flitted around his head on the end of her leash, occasionally barking, but he didn't get up. Finally, Lady Bug flopped down next to him in surrender.

"I promise you'll be glad you did," Travis added, enough of a secret message in his tone that she instantly knew what he was doing at the bungalow.

"Are you building a fence?" she asked.

"How did you know?" He sounded genuinely disappointed. "It was going to be a surprise."

How did she know? Because he was amazing like that. "Sorry, but I could see the look in your eyes when we talked about the fence my dad suggested."

"Hey, I told you on our first date how I felt about picket fences."

She smiled, remembering how he'd admitted he wanted to live in a cozy house with a wife, some kids, and an utterly cliché white picket fence. "You're sweet, Travis, but Lady Bug doesn't need that kind of enclosure."

"Are you kidding? She'll love this."

"Are you sure my dad wants that around the bungalow? It's his property and..." She frowned, hearing a man's voice in the background. "He's there, isn't he?"

Travis chuckled. "Supervising with a cane and a can-do attitude."

She had to laugh, knowing exactly what that meant. The project would be done quickly, efficiently, and perfectly—and done *today*—because...Rex.

"I can't wait to see it," she told him. "But I made myself a promise that I'd go to every shelter in the area. I have one left."

"Is it far?"

She tapped the Notes screen on her phone and glanced at the address. "It's off Eighth Street, a place called Rocky's Rescues. After that, I'll be home to cheer you on."

"By then, we'll be done and drinking beer under the awning I've already installed."

"God bless you, Probie," she said warmly. "I'll join you— Oh...I'm getting a call."

"And I'm getting a look from Rex. It says 'no dilly-dallying.'"

"I know that look so well. Talk soon." She read the name on the screen and winced.

Gil Huxley from the bank, no doubt arranging that last interview before making an offer.

Just as she prepared herself to answer, both dogs barked impatiently, and she let that be a sign.

"Later, Gil. Later."

While the call went to voicemail, she gathered up the dogs for the drive to the last shelter, thinking about the small fenced-in area around the bungalow. These two dogs would love that, but how long could she stay in a guest house that belonged to her parents?

You're almost thirty, a voice in her head reminded her as she glanced back at...Count Chocula. Yes, she adored him, but...

She had to have her life together, starting with a real job and then a real place of her own, before she could take on that kind of responsibility. Because if she had both of those, she'd keep this dog and name him...*something*. Plus, she could let herself get closer and more serious with Travis. And they could sit under an awning like the one he was building and watch the dogs run around in a fenced yard and be so stinking happy she'd think she died and went to heaven.

Except then she'd also be the newest investments

marketing manager for Lighthouse Bank, so maybe she'd think she died and went...to the other place.

"Has anything ever sounded so boring?" she asked Lady Bug, who, instead of looking out the window like she usually did, turned in the passenger seat to check on the behavior of the dog in the back.

Sometimes, Chloe thought Lady Bug absolutely hated that dog. Other times, she sensed a real maternal instinct. And every once in a while, like last night when her legs were trapped with Bugger on one side and No Name on the other? She knew they were all bonding to the point of no return.

She rubbed the little pup's head. "He's okay, Lady B. Harmless, I'd say. Do you want to keep him?"

She looked up with a wary gaze.

"You could use a friend," Chloe continued. "Especially if I have to go to some dreadful office at eight in the morning and stay until five doing whatever marketing managers of investment departments do."

Lady Bug dropped on the seat with a heavy sigh.

"Exactly. They do nothing...fun. I know, I know, life can't be all fun."

The GPS interrupted her sad train of thought with instructions, and Chloe followed the turns until she pulled up to a small tree-lined driveway in front of a clapboard-covered house that had seen better days. Next to it, there was a sizeable enclosed lawn where at least seven dogs ran wild around a woman who seemed to be having as much fun as the animals.

"Well, this looks lively," she mused, squinting at a faded sign that said, "Rocky's Rescues" with a little squirrel wearing a weird helmet and goggles. "Maybe they'll let you guys play."

She parked on the street and grabbed her bag, the last of her flyers, and let both dogs out. Instantly, they ran toward a large pen to join the others as the woman, wearing jeans and a T-shirt, came closer to greet her.

"I hope you're not bringing them in," she called. "We're full and not taking any new dogs."

"I'm not. This handsome boy here is a stray and I'm going to local shelters to see if you've been contacted by his owners." Chloe put a hand on his head. "Is there someone I can talk to who might know?"

"Me. I'm Rocky Zotter." She opened the gate and slipped out, brushing back some hair that could be pure silver or dyed blond, depending on the light. "And he is a handsome boy." She beamed at the dog. "And the little one? Trouble wrapped in precious and covered with joy?"

Chloe let out a laugh. "Yes, you've nailed Miss Lady Bug. She's mine, forever and ever. But we picked up this guy on the beach a few days ago and are in search of his owners. He just doesn't feel like a stray to me. I'm Chloe."

"Hello, Chloe." The woman held out her hand, offering it and a warm smile that crinkled a few lines around blue-gray eyes. "Sorry if I looked panicked that you were bringing in two more. I'll never close this place if I keep taking in more."

"You're closing?"

"As soon as I can find good homes for those kids," she said, angling her head toward the pen. "My daughter just had a baby up in South Carolina. I need to go be a grandma, stat." As she talked, she came closer to...No Name, holding her hand out, making eye contact, testing him.

After a second or two, she crouched in front of him, giving his head and neck a few strokes. "What's your name, gorgeous?"

"No clue," Chloe admitted, knowing that dog people often talked to the animal and expected the human to answer. It was a weird and sweet little thing that always drew Chloe to people who loved animals like she did. "And I haven't given him one."

She squinted up at Chloe. "Don't want to get too connected, huh?"

Chloe laughed. "Guilty."

"That's smart. You name 'em, you own 'em. But if he were mine, I'd call him...Yogi. Like the bear." She tipped her head to the weathered sign. "Obviously, I like the cartoons. I can't tell you how many dogs leave this place named Bullwinkle."

She had no idea who Bullwinkle was. "Sweet. It sure would be nice if you posted this flyer for anyone who comes looking for him."

"I will," she said without looking up. Instead, she studied the dog intently, lifting his lips to check out his gums. "Clean teeth and he's at least five years old."

"So he has an owner," Chloe said.

"Exactly. No chip, huh? I suppose you took him to a vet to check."

"I did," Chloe said. "No chip, no collar. Also, no illness or bugs, and housebroken."

"Definitely not a stray," Rocky agreed.

"Although he's a bit of a chewer."

"That's the boxer in him. His eyes are alert, too. He's got a good brain in there." Rocky settled on her backside, her full attention on the dog. Instantly, Lady Bug meandered up to her and stared right at her, one bark of warning.

"I'm not going to hurt him, Miss Protection Pants," she joked, giving Lady B a rub. With a remarkably gentle touch, she eased Lady Bug to a sitting position but kept her gaze on the other dog. "I certainly haven't seen anything on the rescue groups about this one being missing, but you never know. Maybe someone just let him go and hoped he'd find you."

"Oh." Chloe pressed her hand to her heart and dropped right to the ground next to her, scooping up Lady Bug just at the thought of simply abandoning a dog loved enough to train and have their teeth cleaned. "Who would do such a thing?"

"You'd be surprised. Maybe. I'm not. People can really be awful or just not in a position to take care of him. You know, they lose their jobs or their homes and they have to let their buddy go. Right, handsome man?" Rocky rubbed her nose against his and let him lick her chin. "What a sweetheart he is."

Chloe sighed. "He's a good boy."

"Why don't you just keep him?" Rocky asked.

"Because I'm..." *One of those jobless, homeless people.* "I'm in kind of a transition place," she said instead.

"Ah, the great transition place. So many people live there. Not that there's anything wrong with that," she said quickly. "Obviously, I'm a resident myself, with this place ready to close and my daughter pestering me to get on up there already. But transition shouldn't keep you from giving this guy a home. Not that I am meant to have an opinion, but I got a lot of them anyway."

"I could keep him," Chloe said, thinking of that new fenced area and how nice they all snuggled last night. "I wanted to be certain he didn't belong to anyone else. I'll leave the flyer and take...Bullwinkle."

"Scooby is another good name for him."

"Oh, now that's a cartoon character I know." Chloe stroked his head. "Scooby-Doo, where are you?"

"He'd like to be home," Rocky said softly, rubbing his ear with a magic touch that made his tail wag like the two body parts were connected. "I can see that in his eyes."

Chloe fought a whimper and looked around. "What's going to happen to this place when you leave?" she asked.

"My neighbor is putting together an offer to buy the place."

"And keep it as a rescue?" Chloe asked hopefully.

"Fat chance," she scoffed. "Not with the value of real estate around here. A row of townhouses, I think. It's fine. I got my use out of it. Lived here since my divorce in '96 and basically thought I died and went to heaven."

"Oh." Chloe let out a soft exclamation at the echo of her own thoughts. "And you saved a lot of dogs."

"Hundreds," she said, glancing at the pen. "There's a happy vibe at Rocky's Rescues, but all good things must come to an end."

"Your grandchild will thank you."

She pushed up, still smiling. "Yeah, I can't wait. Gonna be the best grandma ever. Here, I'll take your flyer, Chloe. You take...Dennis the Menace."

Chloe laughed and handed her the flyers, then shook Rocky's hand. "Thanks. Really nice to meet you. This is a great place." She looked around again, taking in the tall trees and the rundown house that was more of a cottage, at best. "How'd you get started? Was it already a rescue?"

"Nah, it was just a house and not a very nice one. I got it for a song, and then built some outdoor kennels so I could live in my own version of paradise, which is to be surrounded by dogs. Also, the occasional cat, but they live inside. And one rabbit, who's in the back. And a deer who visits every morning."

"Wow." A wave of envy rolled over her. "I guess you knew the color of your parachute."

She laughed. "Whatever color a sucker for a lost dog is. Like you, sweet little man." She gave the dog one more loving stroke. "My advice? Keep the dog, Chloe. Give him a name and a home. If not for you, then for little Lady Bug. She's attached to him even if she has a strange way of showing it."

Wow, she was good. "Thank you." Chloe gave her a spontaneous hug, which she returned with no hesitation.

A minute later, she climbed into the car, letting the dogs assume their favorite seats. She glanced in the rearview mirror and made eye contact with...him.

"If I had a job," she whispered, "then I could have my own place and I could keep you. And then you could have a new home and new name. Would you like that?"

He got up on all fours and stared at her, cocking his head like he knew she'd asked a question.

"You would, wouldn't you?" she asked, reaching her hand back to run her fingers through his fur.

With the other hand, she picked up her cell phone and tapped the voicemail to listen to the message.

"Hey, Chloe, Gil Huxley here. I have you tentatively on my boss's calendar for next Monday, which would only be a formality. Assuming that goes well, I've got an offer letter with your name on it. Gimme a call, okay?"

"Okay," she whispered on a sigh, tapping the call back button. She got his voicemail and confirmed the appointment, holding the gaze of the dog in the backseat the whole time she spoke.

She tapped the red button to end the call and set the cell down, looking from one dog to the other, both of them seemingly captivated by her decision.

"Well, what do you say we go home..." She reached for the brown dog, her gaze shifting past him to the weathered sign and the squirrel with goggles. "Rocky."

He barked so sharply, it startled her.

"Rocky?" she asked on a laugh, never seeing that reaction before. "Is that your name?"

His tail whipped from side to side and his whole body seemed to vibrate with happiness.

"Rocky it is!" She leaned back and gave him a kiss, then reached over and scooped up Lady Bug. "You got a brother and his name is Rocky!"

The louder they barked, the better her decision felt.

Chapter Twelve

Madeline

"Okay, we're doing this, Madeline? Right now? You to Dad, me to Suze? Simultaneously telling them we are taking over the anniversary surprise vow renewal...thing?"

"Mmm." Madeline stared out the window, vaguely aware that Rose had asked her a question while they drove together to their parents' beach house.

"You're not going to tell him anything, just that we got this vow renewal thing figured out, right?" Rose pressed.

How long could Madeline sit in this car and not tell Rose that Sadie was hiding out—*hiding out!*—at her house in town? Not much longer.

"What is wrong with you, Madeline?" Rose's hand landed on Madeline's arm, yanking her out of her thoughts.

"What? Yes, Rose. We're talking to them."

"But you are not talking to *me*. What's going on with you? You've been on another planet since you came to the flower shop."

"I'm not..." She shook her head, not wanting to say anything that would break her promise—stupid, stupid promise—to Sadie. But that was all Madeline wanted to do! She wanted to scream Sadie's secret out loud and get the poor girl some help and support.

The only problem? She still didn't know what Sadie's secret was. She didn't know what help she needed. She didn't know anything except she'd given her word to her sister not to breathe anything to anyone.

"It's the dress," Madeline said, grabbing onto the first thing that popped into her mind.

"The Ginger Rogers dress?" Rose asked. "I cannot wait to see it. I know Suze is going to love it. Oh, of course." She snapped her fingers. "That's what bothering you. You don't know whether to have her get fitted for it or be surprised on the morning of the vow renewal ceremony."

If only it were that simple. But Madeline took the lifeline Rose had thrown and clung to it.

"Exactly," she said, maybe a little emphatically. "If she sees it, she might think it's too much for the small beach event she thinks we're planning and ask me to come up with something else. If she doesn't see it, I won't know if she loves it."

"She'll love it, but I know you're a perfectionist and the idea of a dress without a fitting is appalling to you."

What was appalling was the fact that Sadie Wingate was, right this minute, holed up on Amelia Island and no one knew that and Madeline didn't know why. It was killing her.

"I could make two dresses," she said, forcing her brain to focus. "I could make something beachy and light for the ceremony and then she could change into a dancing and reception dress. Lots of brides are wearing two dresses these days."

"Except would Suze want to do that?"

"I don't know," Madeline said, unable to keep the exasperation out of her voice. That got her another hard look from Rose as she turned onto the beach road. "It's all the subterfuge, Rose. It makes me crazy."

"Subterfuge?" Rose's voice lifted. "I think it's called a surprise, nothing...nefarious. And, hey, if you want subterfuge—"

"I don't, that's the thing."

"Talk to Raina, who is now carrying Chase Madison's babies, or at least that's what his dying grandmother believes."

"What?" Madeline blinked at her with a gasp. "You're kidding, right?"

"No, but I think it's really sweet. Listen to this." As Rose told her the story, it really did manage to get Madeline's mind off Sadie. Because Raina being a "fake mom" for Chase's sick old nonna was slightly beyond belief.

"That's insane," Madeline said, shaking her head as she imagined Raina agreeing to fool the old woman. "Also, is it...the right thing to do?"

"Now you sound like Raina. Who gets hurt? The woman goes to heaven happy. Chase isn't trying to claim to the world the babies are his, and I probably wasn't even supposed to tell you." Rose tapped the brakes as they reached the gate in front of the house. "But we Wingate girls don't keep secrets."

And Madeline's heart dropped down to her belly with a thud.

"Oh! Look at that!" Rose exclaimed, pointing to the bungalow.

There, a brand new white fence was being installed on the sandy lot next to the tiny guest house.

"That's Travis," Rose said. "He must be doing that for Chloe's new dog."

"I didn't think she was keeping it." Madeline peered at the fence and the young man installing it, but her gaze shifted past his shoulder to another, much more familiar man. "Is that Dad?"

"Oh, my gosh, it is!" Rose pointed to their father, parked in a comfy beach chair under an umbrella, using his cane to direct Travis's every move. "Isn't it wonderful to see Dad back in action again?"

Despite her worries and heavy heart, Madeline had to smile. "It really is."

"And he's going to be so happy when you tell him he's getting what he wants, but the details are being handled by us." Rose pulled into the driveway in front of the beach house. "I don't see Chloe's car, though. This must be a surprise for her."

"Don't we have enough of them for one family?" Madeline huffed out the question with a frustrated breath, earning a sharp look from Rose.

"You sure you're okay?" her sister asked softly. "Is it really the anniversary event that's bothering you, Madeline? There isn't going to be a lot of planning and Raina seems to have the whole venue and dinner under control. We'll get together and make a guest list..." Her voice faded out. "Madeline, honey, I'm worried about you. I'm the one who should be preoccupied and unhappy."

"I'm not..." She closed her eyes, knowing it wasn't true. She *was* unhappy. She should never have promised secrecy to Sadie. "I just have a lot going on these days."

"We all do, but I'm here for you. We all are. And Tori will be here for the big event and..." She wrinkled her nose. "I'd love to say Sadie, but that girl is more elusive than—"

"She'll be here," Madeline said, the words popping out before she could stop herself.

"You talked to her? Thank God. It's been so long since I've heard her voice. Is she okay? Or traveling the world and sampling chocolate? That girl does have a life, doesn't she?"

For once, Madeline was happy Rose was chattering away, barely leaving time for a breath, let alone an answer. That saved her from lying.

"Oh, yes, she has a life," Madeline agreed. It happened to be taking place in Madeline's living room at the moment, watching Netflix and wearing pajamas, but it was...a life. "I'm going to talk to Dad."

"Okay, but you're sure about Sadie? You told her about the event and she'll be here?"

"Yes." Again, not a lie. Madeline had told her all about it and Sadie would be on Amelia Island. Unless she took off—it *was* six weeks from now. "I mean, she'll try to be here."

"That's awesome!" Rose exclaimed, coming around the car. "I have to call her tonight. Okay, you go give the news to Dad. This is perfect, because I don't see Suze out here, so I bet she's in the beach house. Our plan is working!"

With Rose's playful nudge, Madeline set off to the bungalow, admiring the new, nearly completed fence.

"Look at this fancy addition to the real estate," she called as she got closer.

"Maddie!" Dad waved to her from his seat. "Look at what we're doing for Chloe."

"Hi, Travis," she said as she passed him, slowing her step to nod at his craftsmanship. "This looks awesome."

He glanced up from the post he was hammering into the ground, his handsome face beaded with sweat and a little dirt. "Hey, Madeline. Go chill your dad out for me, will ya? Rex is a hard taskmaster."

"Welcome to Wingateworld." Laughing at his eyeroll, she headed over to Dad, who sat under a new oversized awning in front of the bungalow. "Hey, Daddio." She planted a kiss on his ballcap, appreciating that he reached up and squeezed her arm with his left hand—six months ago, that hand couldn't move. "What's this all about?"

"Well, Chloe has that new stray dog and we all know she's not going to let him go."

Madeline opened up another folding canvas chair that was probably for Travis, who didn't dare take a break under Rex Wingate's watchful eye. "So you're making him room to play. I love that." She squinted in question. "Does she not know about this?"

"I told her to have Travis do it and he came looking for her this morning while I was walking around. One thing led to another, which led us to Home Depot, and... this bungalow has a fenced-in yard. Can only help resale."

She stared at him. "Not sure what's throwing me more here, Dad. You went to Home Depot or...you're thinking about selling this property?"

"Travis drove me and Susannah gave her blessing on Home Depot," he said. "I'm not selling, but I still think like a real estate man, Maddie. Always have, always will. Now, what is new in your life? Tell me everything."

She swallowed. Not *everything*. "I have very good news about your secret mission on November 11th."

"You do?" His whole face brightened, lifting Madeline's spirits for the first time that day. "When and where and how many people?"

She laughed. "Two of those things are TBD, and one —where—is a surprise. But trust us on this, Dad. You are going to love it and so is Suze."

"Us? Your sisters know? Never mind, don't answer that. I know you gals have no secrets."

She adjusted herself in the seat, really sick of being reminded of that today.

"But Suze doesn't know?" Dad asked. "You're sure?"

"Nope. She doesn't know what we're planning." Again, not a lie. But all this deception was making her nuts. Lying, not keeping promises, being untrustworthy—

all well out of Madeline Wingate's wheelhouse, along with being late or leaving unfinished tasks on a To-Do list.

"Well, tell me about it," Dad insisted. "What's the headcount? Menu? I guess Rose is handling the flowers, so—"

"Let's not discuss another aspect of this," she said, holding her hand out to stop him. "We all want you and Suze to be blown away with the perfection and leave the planning to us."

He considered that, slowly nodding. "Okay, I see where you're coming from, Maddie. I'll just show up in a tux. Feel free to use my credit card for anything you need, though. Promise me that."

"Okay, I'll promise you that." Leaning her head over to rest it on his shoulder, she sighed. "Thanks, Dad."

"I do have one more question, well, a request for the event."

"Sure, anything you want—especially with that credit card on the table," she joked.

"This is something money can't buy." He reached his hand to take hers. "I'd love Sadie to be here."

And her whole body froze.

"I'll do my best," she finally said.

"Thank you," Dad said with a satisfied smile. His gaze shifted to Travis, who was struggling with the last section of fence. "Do you think he passed the test?"

She bit back a laugh. "The 'is he worthy of Chloe' test or the 'can he build a fence in an afternoon' test?"

"Both."

"Fence looks good and..." She looked out as Chloe's hatchback came rumbling over the stone driveway. "You might want to ask her about the worthiness factor."

They sat quietly for a moment, watching Chloe jump out of her car. Well, the dogs jumped; Chloe climbed out with a slightly uncertain look on her face.

"I can't believe you did this..." Her words floated over the beach toward the house.

Travis dropped his tool and walked toward her, arms outstretched at first. But then Lady Bug scrambled toward him, her fluffy tail swooshing with joy.

"Lady Bug approves," Madeline said softly.

"Mmm."

Madeline took her eyes off the two of them to glance at her father. "Are you not sure about this young man, Dad? Think it's too soon after leaving Hunter at the altar?"

"I'm sure. And Chloe..." He watched them give each other a hug, then Travis put his arm around Chloe and walked her toward the fence to show her his work, the new dog prancing around like he had no idea what to do with himself.

"What about Chloe?" Madeline asked.

"She just has to figure it out," he said.

"Figure what out? Travis?"

"Oh, he's figured. Same with the dog. She's keeping both of those boys." He chuckled and glanced at Madeline.

She inched closer, definitely not following him. "Then what are you testing?"

"I'm just waiting to see how long it takes for Chloe to figure out what she was meant to do with her life. She's so close, you know? I can feel it, I can see it, but...can she?"

"Well, Dad, if you can feel it and see it, why don't you just tell her? She's kind of lost these days and really stressed about not having a professional direction."

"I don't tell my girls what to do." At her look, he gave a sharp laugh. "I know you think I do, Maddie, but I don't. You've all picked your own path. I just tell you how to follow it."

"With their whole heart and soul," Madeline said, a recipient of that Rex lecture many, many times.

"Yep. But what it is? Well, that's up to them to find."

They both turned and watched Travis and Chloe, the two of them crouching down to love on the new dog, who suddenly bolted into the fenced-in area and rolled on the sea grass and sand.

"Go, Rocky, go!" Chloe called.

"Ah, she named him." Dad grinned. "We're getting there."

"Getting where?" she pressed.

He smiled, still watching Chloe and the dog. "I learned long ago with you Wingate women that sometimes you have to go about things in a way that's a little less obvious."

Madeline considered that as Chloe came jogging over, announcing that she was keeping the dog. While she settled in to talk to Dad, Madeline's mind went back to Sadie.

Maybe Madeline had to go about things in a way

that's a little less obvious. Maybe she had to come up with another way to get Sadie to talk and show her face. If only she knew what it was.

"HEY, YOU HERE?" Madeline called when she stepped inside her townhouse, looking around and seeing no sign of her sister.

As it had been since Sadie arrived, the shutters were closed, making it way too dark for a corner unit. Sadie acted like spies were lurking outside the brownstone building, peering into windows trying to find her.

On a sigh, Madeline opened the shutters, filling the room with light, which only showed that Sadie had cleaned up, and disappeared.

"Sadie?" She glanced into the den and office on the first floor, then headed upstairs to the guest room her sister was using. She glanced into her own bedroom, which looked as neat as when she'd left it, then walked down the short hall to the other room, which was empty.

Bed wasn't made, but that might be asking too much. What mattered was...Sadie left the house? This had to be the first time since she arrived a few days ago.

Taking out her phone, she wandered back downstairs and texted a quick, "Where are you?" to Sadie.

Twenty minutes passed without an answer and by then, Madeline was growing anxious. Sadie didn't have a car, so how far could she have gone? Downtown Fernandina Beach was just steps away and she could certainly mingle with the tourists, but would she risk being seen by a friend or family member?

Maybe Sadie was done hiding, Madeline decided. Maybe she'd get a call any second from Raina who would say, "You won't believe who's standing in my office!" or Grace or—

The door opened and Sadie walked in, wearing sunglasses and a hat, impossible to recognize except that the hat belonged to Madeline.

"Did you manage to not get seen?" Madeline asked, remarkably calm considering her racing heart.

"I think I did," Sadie said without an ounce of humor.

In fact, Sadie's seriousness was one of the weirdest things about this. She'd never been that serious about anything. Sadie liked to joke and tease and see the lightness in every situation.

But all that seemed to have disappeared and it broke Madeline's heart.

"Where have you been, Sadie?" she asked flatly.

"I had an appointment." She slid off a sweater that she certainly hadn't needed on a warm day like this.

"What kind of appointment?"

Sadie's eyes shuttered. "It's personal, Madeline. Where have you been?"

"To see Dad."

Once again, her eyes closed, but this time they stayed that way, as if the words had hurt.

"You've been home for days and haven't seen him, Sadie," Madeline said, stating the obvious and not liking that her sister winced. "I'm sorry, but...why? Can I even ask why?"

"You can ask but I don't have to answer."

Her throat tightened in frustration. "Honey, if you are in trouble, you have a huge, loving, and supportive family that would do anything for you. Please let us."

She blew out a breath, brushing back some wild locks and heading into the kitchen. Without a word, she filled a glass with water and gulped it down.

"I forgot how hot it is here, even in October," she said, talking about the weather as if she didn't have a care in the world.

"Did you also forget that your father nearly died six months ago? That your mother was broken and scared, that your sisters gathered and missed you?"

"I came for the wedding that wasn't," she said, a hint of a spark in her golden-green eyes as they peered over the rim of the glass. But the spark faded. "And please save your guilt trip for someone else. Do you think I don't want to see Dad?"

"Then see him or at least tell me why you won't."

"Madeline." Her voice cracked as she turned away and put the glass in the sink. "You can't help me. The person I just met with can, though, but it's going to take some time. Until then..."

"Until then what?"

Sadie didn't answer for the longest time. She kept her back to Madeline, put the glass in the dishwasher, and wrung her hands as she stared out the window. Finally, after an eternity, she turned.

"If I let the family know I'm here, would everyone agree to keep me off social media completely?"

Madeline blinked in shock at the request. "Of course. Who cares if you're on social media?"

"Well, some people do."

"People...who are looking for you?" Madeline ventured.

"People...from my old company."

"Your old company?" Finally, an actual fact. "They would want to find you?"

"I don't know what they want," she said. "I'm sure I'm *persona non grata* now."

"What did you do? Steal a chocolate recipe? Give trade secrets to a competitor? Eat all the inventory?" She tried to laugh on the last one, but Sadie's sad expression eliminated all chance at humor.

"I know, you did something dumb, honey," Madeline continued, adding tenderness to her tone. "What? How bad could it be? Did you hurt someone? Did you break the law? See something you shouldn't? Is there a man involved?"

Her eyes closed again and Madeline sensed she was right over the target.

Still silent, Sadie slid onto a counter stool next to Madeline. "I hurt myself, okay? I wrecked my life and...I don't want to talk about it. I want to fix it and undo my mistake, which is happening while I lay low right here. But the person I saw today, who is going to help me, said I'm probably fine if I don't show up on social media. However, if I ask that of the family, they are going to inundate me with questions and I just cannot talk about it."

Madeline huffed out a breath. "I don't think we have to worry about someone putting up a Facebook post, Sadie."

"Kenzie?" she scoffed. "The queen of TikTok?"

"She's in Boston with Tori and they won't be back until the anniversary party. Oh, and by the way, my number one job, according to Dad, is to get you to that event."

"I'll be there. As long as—"

"I know, social media." Madeline's brain was whirring with ideas. "How about if we make it an unplugged event, and that will include our niece? So can you tell everyone you're home?"

"But what if someone accidentally gets me in a picture or—"

"You only need to see the family. Say you're on a hiatus from work, which is true."

"A long, permanent hiatus," Sadie murmured.

"And we'll just be super careful. No one is going to see you here."

"What about at the beach house?" Sadie asked.

"There's no one lurking with cameras. Why?"

Sadie looked up, tears in her eyes. "I love you, Madeline. And I love staying here, but I want to see Mom and Dad so much. I know the guest suite is open and I just want to hole up at the beach and be there with them, but I cannot be asked questions. You know how Dad is! He'll want to know everything."

She thought about her conversation with her father today and slowly shook her head.

"Not necessarily. For one thing, Dad's a lot more mellow since the stroke. For another, he'll be so happy to see you, all you have to do is say you'd rather not discuss details, and he'll be on board." Madeline reached for her. "Please, Sadie. Let everyone know you're here."

"Maybe," she said. "I need to hear something from the attor—" She slammed her mouth shut. "Just give me some time."

She'd seen *an attorney*? She *was* in legal hot water. How? Why?

Instead of asking, Madeline reached for her little sister and folded her in a hug. "Okay, thank you. I can't stand keeping this secret."

"I know," Sadie whispered, pressing a kiss on Madeline's hair. "I know you can't. Just give me a little time."

"Okay." Madeline leaned back and eyed her. "And now, as your special gift, I will share a shocking story that I will call 'Raina and the Nonna.'"

"Excuse me?" Sadie sputtered a laugh. "Please tell me this story comes with wine."

Madeline was up and at the fridge in seconds to get the bottle, her heart lighter than it had been since Sadie showed up.

Chapter Thirteen

Raina

The swipe of the windshield wipers not only cleared her vision but gave Raina a perfect view of the Mercedes parked to the side of The Sanctuary's driveway. The luxury coupe was being drenched in a downpour. Heck, if she owned that car, she'd want to keep it dry and there was a garage ten feet away.

But her roommate, she'd discovered after this brief period of sharing some space and a few conversations, was nothing if not considerate. He'd left the garage for Raina, which was exceedingly kind, especially since she told him that morning she'd be with her sisters and had no idea when she'd be home after work. But those plans had changed and she certainly hadn't even thought about letting him know.

Points for the nice man who had her lying to the old grandmother but made sure she was dry in the rain. At least she'd come to terms with the nonna decision, she reminded herself, thanks to Rose's relentless insistence that it was the right thing to do.

As soon as she opened the car door, she heard a loud

noise coming from inside the house. What was that sound?

Not able to hear over the rain, she walked to the door and pressed the garage door wall switch, frowning as it dropped and the noise inside got louder.

Not *noise*, exactly, but music so dramatic and deafening, Raina drew back. He was listening to *opera?*

Good heavens, Chase Madison was certainly full of surprises.

Slowly, she opened the kitchen door and stood frozen at the assault on all her senses. The high-pitched soprano voice echoed a plaintive wail through the whole house, practically vibrating the French doors. The tangy scent of tomatoes, garlic, and onions sizzling on the stove filled her head on the first inhale and launched every tastebud to life.

But it was the visual that captured her—the sight of Chase Madison in profile at the counter, wrist-deep in a bowl of flour, a plain white chef's apron covering a dress shirt with the sleeves rolled up, his eyes closed, head back, lost in the music. A glass of red wine was on the counter in front of him, along with an array of ingredients that made her kitchen look like Julia Child was at work.

"Um...hello?" she called, loud enough to be heard over the opera.

Instantly, he whipped to attention, blinking at her like he'd been transported to another world.

"Raina!" He reached to a portable speaker on the counter, tapping the top to silence the music. "I wasn't expecting you. Didn't you say you were doing something with your sisters?"

"We rescheduled for tomorrow at Rose's shop. Sorry."

"No, don't be. I'm the one taking over the place." He put down a brown egg she hadn't realized he cradled in his palm and shook his head. "I had a hankering for *Norma* and thought I'd be alone."

"Norma?" She lifted her brows. "Another grandmother you're keeping from me?"

He laughed at that, visibly relaxing in front of her eyes. "*Norma* is the name of the opera. And"—he gestured toward the flour—"*Pasta alla Norma* is a Sicilian treat." He wiped his hands on the apron, regarding her with a smile that seemed to grow the longer he looked. "I hope you'll have some with me."

Based on the aroma in the air, only an insane woman would say no. A pregnant one? Not a chance she'd turn down whatever he was making.

"I would love to," she said. "I'm going to change, get out of these heels—and possibly throw them into the ocean—and then I'll be down for some water and pasta Norma, which I've never even heard of but am happy to eat."

"Eggplant and pomodoro over homemade fettuccini, which I was just about to start."

"Stop." She let out a soft grunt, dropping her head back, then peeked at him from under her lashes. "Wait. You're really making your own pasta from scratch? Like, no blue box with an Italian name?"

"Please don't let my nonna hear you say that," he joked, gesturing toward his bowl. "She'll expect our kids to know how to do this by the time they're seven."

Her chest tightened unexpectedly, maybe because of the uber-casual way he referred to her babies as "our kids." That would have to stop.

But she didn't want to argue with a man up to his apron in homemade pasta and pomodoro.

"How is our sweet Analucia?" she asked instead.

"Good." He beamed at her, gratitude and warmth in his dark brown eyes. "I stopped over today and she wanted to be sure you're eating right."

Raina laughed and tipped her head toward the pan on the stove. "I think I'm about to," she said. "Be right back. And please..." She pointed to the speaker. "Play the opera."

"Maybe with just a little less volume," he said.

She heard much softer strains of the music as she headed up to her room, closing the double doors and kicking off her shoes the very second she could. For a moment, all she could do was drop onto the bed and rub her feet, letting out a long sigh of emotions she didn't understand.

She certainly wasn't unhappy he was here. All her concerns about having her space invaded by a stranger were gone, replaced by different feelings. Feelings of...guilt.

Yes, that's what had her heart at the moment. *Why?*

Well, the nonna lie, to begin with. But it was more

than that. Why did Chase's very presence make her feel guilty?

Closing her eyes, she let the image of him at the counter come to life again, easily able to remember every detail—like the dusting of dark hair on corded forearms and the lost expression as he channeled the passion of the music.

Oh. That was why. One look at the man and she was feeling things she didn't want, didn't need, and really shouldn't have. He was nothing more than a platonic acquaintance, a rent-paying roommate, and a nice guy who could cook a... What had he called it?

A Sicilian treat.

The food, Raina, not the man.

She pushed up and went to the closet, changing into comfy sleep pants that pulled up over her basketball belly and a massive T-shirt that had the Wallace & Wingate logo on the front.

Running a brush through her hair and tying it back with a scrunchie, she added some fluffy socks to an outfit that should certainly scream, "I'm not trying," loud and clear. Then she headed back downstairs, inhaling the heady, pungent, delicious smell that permeated the whole house.

"I put your sparkling water in a wine glass, if you don't mind." Chase held out a crystal goblet filled with the Pellegrino she'd been drinking since the day she found out she was pregnant.

"Festive. Thank you." She took it and tapped the red

wine glass he held in his other hand. "Here's to *Norma*, opera and pasta."

"I'll drink to that anytime." He took a sip of wine and set his glass down, gesturing toward one of the bar stools. "I also took the liberty of waiting on the pasta, because if you've never made it, I thought you might like to watch."

"I'd love to." She settled in with the water in front of her, looking at the ingredients. "Is it complicated?"

"Not the way my grandmother and mother taught me. I'm just going to drop three eggs in this flour, then one more yolk, knead the dough, roll it out, and send it through that pasta roller. The whole thing will take forty minutes."

"It sounds awesome and I'm a captive audience."

He smiled and got to work, giving her every excuse to just look at him, studying his strong fingers as he dug them in the flour mix and started to blend by hand.

"So, how was your day?" he asked, pulling her back to reality and away from his work.

"A little crazy, but good. I have a retail space right on Wingate Way that's coming open after the holidays, if you're interested in opening a little pasta store."

"Wingate Way? I thought that was all sisters on that street."

"Many sisters, not all. It's the ice cream parlor where I first pitched your business. Silas Struthers and his wife are moving and I have to find tenants, but I can't put just anything smack dab between Madeline and Rose. It has to be perfect to protect the vibe of Wingate Way."

"I get that." He formed a ball and dusted the countertop with flour. "You want something family-friendly but with good income potential so it's there long term. Plus, you can't directly compete with tenants who've been loyal for years. Or, in your case, who are family."

"Exactly." She sipped the water, regarding him over the rim. "Like a little Italian restaurant maybe?"

He laughed and shook his head. "That I don't want to do."

"Just hotels and houses?"

"Eh." He lifted a hand in a move so classically Italian, she almost laughed. "I don't know."

"You don't? What's your career and life plan after this hotel is done?" she asked, genuinely interested.

"Right now, my career and life plan is to stay here, get Ocean Song up and running, guide my grandmother to her final resting place, and then...I don't know. I might build another hotel, I might buy more rental properties. Heck, I might move to Italy."

She inched back, surprised by the last one. "Really? I guess it's in your blood."

"I have a home there. Well, my mother had a home and I inherited it. It's on the water just outside of Palermo with the most beautiful garden. I use it as a personal getaway, but..." He gave a dry laugh. "I've been too busy to get away."

"It sounds lovely."

"Oh, it is. And so's this dough. Let's see how it kneads, because that's the real test." He used the heel of his hand, flattening and folding as he worked the dough into something pliable and soft. "The more you work it, the better the pasta."

"I bet you can't teach that," she said, watching him work.

"If you want to learn, I will."

"But it looks...instinctive."

"True. A lot is done by feel, sensing where the tension in the dough is and evening everything out with a gentle touch. It's really a dough massage."

"Oh," she laughed. "That's exactly what I dream about doing to my feet when I take the devil's heels off every night."

"I can—" He caught himself and gave a wry smile. "I can*not* understand why you wear them."

"Habit. Also, they make me feel powerful when I'm negotiating a deal."

He shot her a look. "I've negotiated with you. You don't need heels, Raina."

"We didn't negotiate. I offered the asking price on this house, and then I let you rent." She leaned in, smiling at him and the pasta. "And I'm pretty sure I got the better end of that deal."

He laughed, holding her gaze for a moment as a warm, comfortable sensation rolled over her. Maybe it was just the familiarity of coming home to someone who could talk business and make her laugh. He was easy enough to talk to, like a friend she didn't know she needed.

"So what happened to the plans tonight?" he asked as

he pulled a metal contraption out of a cabinet under the island. "I left this here and I see you haven't moved it."

"I'm not sure I looked in that cabinet. Does that make the pasta?"

"I make the pasta. This rolls it out." He screwed it on to the side of the counter, then used another flat tool she didn't know she owned to cut the ball into quarters.

"Oh, tonight," she said, remembering the question. "Life, work, sport schedules. Madeline refusing to let everyone come to her house, so she must have left a drawer open or a piece of fabric on the table." She rolled her eyes. "We changed it to an early morning breakfast at Rose's flower shop so we can create a guest list and invitations and all the things involved with our anniversary event. Speaking of, I'm sure their first question will be, are you sure the space will be ready? Can I give the girls a positive report from Ocean Song?"

He blew out a breath. "I twisted some arms and elicited some promises and basically called in all the favors I have left."

"Oh, Chase, thank you."

He lifted a brow. "Anything for the mother of my children."

Heat rushed to her cheeks.

"Sorry," he said quickly. "No room for humor on our deal?"

"Always room for humor," she assured him. "It's just...only your grandmother, right? No one else thinks..."

"No one, you have my word. I told her nurse, Paul,

the truth, because she's already asked him to knit booties—"

"No!"

He laughed. "Yes. But he is the only person she sees or talks to. Her family is all gone or quite distant. There's really just me. And..." He dropped his gaze to the counter that hid her pregnant belly. "And Charlie One and Two down there."

They both laughed, holding each other's gaze as they shared the ridiculous secret.

"My sister actually likes the name," she said.

"*You* told someone?" He inched back. "I'm surprised."

"No secrets from my twin. Not from any of them, to be honest. The general consensus is that I'm doing an act of mercy, should not be punished in this life or the next, and that I made a fair exchange so we could have the only remaining beachfront venue on Amelia Island."

He angled his head and lifted his wine glass in a mock toast. "I fully agree. Now, would you like to hold the dough or crank?"

"Me?"

"It's more fun if two people do it. Come on."

She got off the stool and slipped around the counter as he held the flattened dough over the metal contraption.

"Just turn that crank and I'll feed the dough."

She followed instructions, deeply aware of how close they stood, of how he smelled like spices and soap. She managed to turn the handle over and over again, and each time, after he adjusted a dial, they stretched the dough longer and flatter.

"But how does it become noodles?"

"Patience, *cara mia*." He took the crank out and moved it to another hole in the pasta maker. "Now comes the fun part. I'll crank and you catch."

He hadn't been kidding about the fun. With each turn, they produced flawless fettuccini noodles that came out in one long bunch, which he "nested" on a baking sheet. After they finished, she couldn't deny the sense of satisfaction the process had given her.

"That really beats a box," she said, getting an "are you kidding" look in response.

While he took the noodles to the stove, she put her elbows on the counter, a question about him kind of bothering her. "Can I ask you something personal?" she ventured.

"Of course."

She appreciated that he didn't hesitate. "Well, you really do seem to love the idea of having children and we all know your family certainly wanted you to. I'm so curious why you never did."

He nodded, quiet as he found the plastic wrap and pulled a long piece over the glass bowl, tightening it neatly around the edges.

"I guess you could say the wives were stacked me against me," he said.

"Excuse me?"

"You remember I told you I've been married twice."

"I do and, well, asking about that *is* a gross overstep."

"Not at all." He took another drink of wine, then walked to the stove, stirring the savory concoction bubbling on the front burner. "My first marriage happened when we were both barely twenty years old. She was my high school sweetheart, also a good Catholic Italian girl, and she got pregnant." He chuckled. "So maybe not that good or Catholic, but definitely Italian."

"Hey, things happen. But what about the baby?"

"We got married right away in a tiny civil service, mostly because her parents insisted and, oh, my grandfather was not pleased with me. And one thing I didn't want was an angry Sicilian grandfather who'd given up his life in Palermo to raise me in the States. Marriage was really the only option."

Raina propped her chin in her palms, fascinated by the story.

"So anyway, we got married before she was three months pregnant and then..." He winced as though whatever he had to say would hurt. "She lost the baby."

"Oh." Raina groaned and closed her eyes, the punch hitting her hard.

"I know you've experienced miscarriages."

"And now I understand why you were more sympathetic than my own husband."

"It's really hard," he conceded. "Krista was relieved, I think, but I had mixed emotions. It hadn't been hard to psych myself into being a father, missing my own as I did. I admit I was sad. And married."

"You broke up?" she asked.

"We stuck it out for a few more years, struggled

through college, then…" He shook his head. "It was never going to work. We split up very amicably after six years, and are still friends to this day. She's happily married, with a couple of kids, and lives in Philadelphia."

"Huh." Raina considered that, nodding. "And Wife Number Two?"

He gave a mirthless smile. "Not as amicable, not still friends. Gabby worked for me when I was well on my way up the success ladder. She set her sights on being what she liked to call a trophy wife—not a term the least bit endearing or attractive. Plus, I was only thirty-eight, and she was ten years younger, so not a huge age difference and I wasn't looking for a trophy, but a partner."

She frowned, doing some quick math. "So you were single from, what, twenty-six to thirty-eight?"

"Married to my ambition," he admitted. "There were a few relationships, but nothing…perfect."

"Gabby was?"

He gave a soft snort. "Gabby was in the right place at the right time. I loved her company and she made me believe…" His voice faded out and he put down the wooden spoon and turned to her, crossing his arms and leaning against the counter. "It didn't work out."

"What happened?" she asked, too invested in the story to worry about whether or not that was polite. Anyway, he knew *her* dark divorce story.

"She lied," he said simply. "She told me she wanted kids but when it came time to try, she always, always had a reason to postpone. Fact was, she didn't want kids, she wanted money and status and friends and to be arm candy. Honestly? She really didn't even like kids but I got fooled. Once she admitted it, there really wasn't enough to hold us together. She had her own friends and I had work and..." He shrugged. "She filed for divorce and it was final about two years ago. She didn't get what she wanted—which was a fat alimony—and neither did I. So..." He gave a humorless smile. "Long story, but no kids."

"There's still time."

He looked doubtful. "I'm turning fifty. I don't want a thirty-something wife, Raina. It's not what I'm interested in. I have Ocean Song—"

"Your legacy."

He nodded. "And maybe I *will* build another. Maybe I'll start a chain. Or maybe I'll go retire in the Sicilian sun and make pasta and drink wine in my poppy's garden, but..."

But there wouldn't be kids, she thought, sensing that was the thought he couldn't finish.

For a long time, she just looked at him, realizing that for all his sense of personal power and head-turning good looks and success, this man was...lost.

Maybe he'd never recovered from his parents' deaths, or that long-ago miscarriage, or the life he thought he'd live, but Chase wasn't nearly as wildly *together* as she'd first thought.

That made him...a problem. And Raina, the ultimate fixer, could—

No.

She erased the thought before it took hold, pushing off the stool.

"The rain let up," she said quickly. "I think I'll get some air while you finish. Feel free to turn the music up."

"Sure." He nodded and smiled, but there was something sad in those dark Italian eyes.

Something someone else would have to fix. Lying to his grandmother was enough for one forty-three-year-old, still married, five-months-pregnant woman, thank you very much.

Chapter Fourteen

Rose

Saturdays at Coming Up Roses were always crazy, but with the party planning meeting now scheduled for the hour before she opened, Rose had to move at warp speed. She had all four kids here, because Zach could help load up deliveries, the girls wanted to see their aunts and play with Nikki Lou, and Ethan certainly wasn't going to stay home alone.

"Wait until I have my license in a week, Mom," Zach said as he scooped up a lily arrangement for the van. "I can do these and you won't have to pay Hank on Saturdays."

"Hank has done my Saturday deliveries for years, Zach," she said, tapping the speaker on the store phone so she could hear the message one of her distributors had left.

"Not looking like we can deliver tulips, Rose," the caller said. "At least not that weekend, sorry. We've got Gerbers galore and plenty of sunflowers, calla lilies, and mums because, hey, it's October."

"I know, but this bride needs tulips," she muttered as she clicked off the message and moved on to the next one.

"Hello, this is Polly Simmons from Florida Floral Wholesalers returning your call about the tulips in two weeks. We can get them, but they'll have to be shipped in. We can send them to Port Canaveral, but it will be cutting it close to your deadline."

"Not Port Canaveral," Rose groaned, frantically taking a note. "We need them up here." She jotted down Polly's phone number, abandoned the messages, and turned to Zach. "When you're done loading, can you call Florida Floral and make arrangements to have those tulips sent to the Colonel's Island Terminal, not Canaveral? And why are you grinning like a loon, Zach?"

"Because you need me."

"Was there any doubt?"

"Well, there was when Dad made me get back on the soccer team."

"And the way you played last night?" She reached for his arm. "I'm so glad I had Dad on FaceTime when you kicked that goal."

He gave a humble tilt of his head, like it had been no big deal, but she knew better. And despite the meeting cutting into her busy Saturday, she was grateful she'd canceled plans with her sisters last night to be at Zach's game. And doubly grateful she'd had Gabe on the line to share the experience.

"But you do need me, Mom. So, according to my deal with Dad, I can be here all day today and the days I don't have soccer practice."

"Or have to meet for National Honor Society," she added, recalling all the stipulations Gabe and Zach had worked out.

Her son rolled his eyes. "Yeah, yeah, but I'm not running for office this year. Next year, I promise."

"And Tiffany?" she asked, cringing a little, because he did not like it when she pried too deeply into the situation with his girlfriend.

"We're talking but taking things slow." He lifted a massive bouquet of roses. "Dad convinced me that was best for now."

Based on what Gabe had told her, Rose agreed, and she felt like the Zach crisis was mostly averted.

A crash from the other side of the room made them turn.

"Avery!" Alyson cried out, throwing her arms toward a pile of acrylic vases that had been stacked for a wedding pick-up. "I told her not to try and take one out of the pile."

"I got this," Ethan announced. "We'll pile them up again, Mom."

"I didn't mean to do it!" Avery whined, instantly getting a hug from her older sister.

"Don't cry, Ethan will help us," Alyson assured her.

"And I'll finish loading," Zach said. "Then I'll return your tulip call. And watch the rugrats while you meet with your sisters."

For a moment, Rose looked across her spacious back room, past all the flowers, vases, and accessories, from one dear face to another. They really all did have her back, and were willing to do everything to help during these long months without their father. She'd needed last night at the game, with Gabe on the phone.

Today, she felt better and stronger than ever.

"Thank you," she whispered to Zach, giving him a hug. "You are your father's son."

He beamed like she'd given him the best possible gift.

A few minutes later, the deliveries were out, the vases were re-stacked, and she had the conference table clear for a meeting with her sisters—including Tori, who was going to join them on video. Ethan went down the street to get food from the Riverfront Café and the girls were playing quietly.

But still no word from Sadie.

On impulse, Rose grabbed her phone and clicked on Sadie's name, hitting the Call button. She was a little stunned when her sister actually answered.

"Oh, my gosh, Sadie! It's been so long since I heard your voice," Rose exclaimed. "How are you?"

"I'm...okay," Sadie said, sounding tentative and uncertain. "Where are you?"

"At the shop, but the real question is, where are you?" Rose asked. "What glamorous city have I found you in?"

"Oh, I'm in..."

Rose laughed when Sadie didn't finish the sentence. "See? You can't even remember. If it's Saturday, this must be Paris."

Sadie gave a laugh that sounded forced.

"I hope all is well wherever you are," Rose said,

sensing something was still a little off with her. "We all feel like it's been forever since we talked, so if—"

"I'm leaving!" a woman's voice called in the background of Sadie's end. A woman who sounded American and...familiar.

"Was that *Madeline?*" the question popped out, sounding ridiculous as soon as she asked it. "I mean, that sounded so much like her."

"Um, no, I have a new...um...assistant," Sadie told her. "And we're swamped today, Rose, so I have to go."

On a Saturday?

"Did you hear me?" the woman called again. "I'm leaving."

Yes, that definitely sounded like Madeline. Which was impossible.

"I'll call you back, Rosie!" Sadie said. "We are in the middle of a big chocolate symposium and my team needs me. I'll call you later, okay? Bye!"

Before Rose could even respond, the call disconnected, leaving her frustrated and perplexed.

"What the heck is going on with that girl?" she mused.

"What girl?" Raina cruised in with a coffee in one hand and a banana in the other. "Don't judge," she added. "I stopped by the café and got my decaf and morning temptation. I saw Ethan picking up your order— he would not accept help or money, that little sweet pea— so I figured this party is covered."

"He's getting muffins for everyone and I have a pot

brewing but no decaf, so I'm glad you got that." Rose stood to greet her sister. "You look beautiful, Raina."

She inched back at the compliment. "My new room-mate made me the most insane pasta. I think it left me smiling for days."

"The pasta or him?"

Raina shot her a narrow-eyed look, utterly devoid of humor. "Don't," she said. "Life is complicated enough and I don't need any more problems. Who were you griping about?"

"Aunt Raina!" The girls came running over, arms out to hug her.

"Are the babies moving?" Alyson asked, putting her hand right on Raina's stomach. "Can I feel them?"

"Can I have a bite of your banana?" Avery asked, dancing on her little toes.

"You can have half." She handed the banana to Avery. "And they just woke up, so keep your hand right... here." She guided Alyson's little hand to the side. "And say hello to Thing One."

"It could be Thing Two," Alyson said, smiling up at Raina.

"I think he's over here." She patted the other side. "Kicks like a soccer player."

"We went to a boring soccer game last night," Avery informed them.

"Wait, Aunt Raina!" Alyson shrieked. "You know one's a boy?"

"I don't know," Raina said on a laugh, putting her cup

down so she could pull Alyson in for a hug. "Would it matter?"

"We don't like boys," Avery announced, breaking the peeled banana and handing half back to Raina. "We only like girls."

"That'll change," Raina said dryly. "And I came over early just to talk to you." She bopped Alyson on the nose. "Got a minute?"

"Me? Yes!" Alyson glanced at Rose with surprise and pride. "Aunt Raina wants to talk to me."

Rose smiled at her, then Raina. "Everything good?"

"Yes." Raina sat down at the table and pulled out a chair for Alyson.

"Don't you want to talk to me, too?" Avery asked, making them laugh.

"Of course, Ave, I always want to talk to you. But I'm on a mission with Alyson."

Rose inched closer, intrigued. "A mission?"

"Sort of." She eased Avery onto her lap but her attention was on Alyson. "Do you remember when that boy fell off the monkey bars and broke his arm a while back?"

"Josh Pinkerton? Yes. He's back now but he will only let boys sign his cast."

"See why we don't like them?" Avery chimed in, cracking up Raina and Rose.

"Well, I met his father." She looked up at Rose. "He's a carpenter at Ocean Song."

"Oh." Rose grabbed the other chair and sat down. "Is the little boy okay?"

"He is, but I think there's some issue with insurance,"

Raina said. "And they're trying to find out exactly what happened that day. I remember you said you saw it, Aly."

Her lip curled. "His bone was sticking out of his skin, Aunt Raina!"

"Eww!" Avery shrieked and stuck her head into Raina's chest.

"Seriously," Raina agreed, patting Avery's back and making Rose think one thought: *Raina is going to be the best mom.* "But before the bone, did you see what happened?"

Alyson nodded. "Yes, because I was next in line to go across. Well, not next in line," she corrected herself. "Cody the showoff was before me and of course he was rushing Joshua off the bars."

"Is that why he fell?" Raina asked.

For a moment, Alyson didn't answer, but looked at Rose with a question in the blue eyes behind her glasses. "That's why Miss Sherman said he fell. I mean, she said the boys were 'roughhousing,' which is what boys *always* do."

"So true," Raina agreed. "Is Miss Sherman your teacher?"

"She's the assistant. Mrs. Hilliard is my teacher."

Raina nodded. "Did you see that other boy, Cody, push him or cause the accident?"

A little color drained from her face. "No."

"Did you see anything?" Raina pressed, glancing at Rose with a concerned look. And Rose understood that... Alyson wasn't being completely forthcoming.

"You can tell us, honey," Rose said, putting a hand on

her daughter's arm. "You can tell Aunt Raina and me anything."

She squirmed in the chair. "I don't want Miss Sherman to get mad at me, I'm one of her favorites. Actually, I am her favorite."

Rose leaned closer. "Your teacher's assistant wouldn't get mad at you for telling the truth."

Alyson stayed quiet for a moment, looking from Rose to Raina. "Cody didn't push him. The bar broke and that's how Josh fell. Right after he fell and started screaming, my teacher—Mrs. Hilliard—came running over and she was with Josh. That's when I saw the bone." She pointed to her forearm. "It was all bloody and sticking out like—"

"We know," Rose said gently. "But why do you think Miss Sherman would get mad at you?"

"'Cause Mrs. Hilliard said something to her and she came back to the monkey bars and fixed the broken bar. She pushed it back in place and no one saw her except me."

Rose gave Raina a questioning look. "Is this why you're asking?"

"I honestly don't know," Raina admitted. "Chase said there was some issue with the insurance and it might have to do with how it happened. Are you absolutely sure you saw this, Alyson?"

"Yes, because I had my old purple glasses and I could see perfect with them. Not these." She tapped the pink rims.

"We're waiting for her new glasses," Rose explained. "The old ones broke."

Avery looked up at Raina. "They broke on purpose."

Raina made a shocked face, sending Avery into giggles, but not Alyson.

"I said I was sorry!" she scolded her sister.

"But you are still playing on those monkey bars?" Rose asked, ignoring the discussion as she realized how dangerous that was.

"No, no," Alyson said.

"They put a sign up and we can't climb them," Avery added.

"Well, that's a relief," Rose said, looking at Raina. "But do you think that Josh's father needs to know?"

Raina shrugged. "I honestly don't know what the situation is, but if you are absolutely certain you saw this, Aly, would you be comfortable telling that to someone you don't know?"

"I guess."

"And I don't want you to say anything you aren't one hundred percent positive you saw," Raina told her. "Could the teacher have been doing something else to the monkey bar? Are you sure she fixed it?"

Alyson nodded. "I saw her do it."

"So the school's liable," Rose said. "I wonder if that's what this is all about."

"I don't know." Raina eased Avery off her lap and leaned closer to Alyson. "But you are a hero for telling the truth."

Her eyes flashed at Rose. "Can I get contact lenses now, Mommy?"

Rose shook her head. "Your new glasses will be ready next week and you are not getting contact lenses."

Alyson stuck her bottom lip out just as the back door opened and Madeline came in, exactly at eight a.m. on the nose. The girls ran to greet her and Rose stood, too.

"I just talked to Sadie," Rose said, reaching to give her sister a hug. "And I would have bet money I heard your voice in the background."

Madeline just stared at her, looking a little bit like Alyson when pressed about the monkey bar incident. "My voice?"

"Yeah, I guess she has a new assistant who sounds just like you. But the bad news is she's too busy with a chocolate symposium to join us."

"What's that?" Avery asked on a gasp.

"No idea, but it sounds like a good time," Raina quipped.

"She didn't sound like she was having a good time," Rose said.

"How...did she sound?" Madeline looked like she was scared to hear the answer.

"You know, distracted and busy. Like Sadie." Rose shrugged, having a hard time finding anything positive about how much Sadie seemed to be avoiding them. "Everything she does is important and takes priority. She certainly isn't joining us today, but Tori is."

Madeline put her laptop at the head of the table and started pulling notebooks and lists from a bag, bringing the conversation to a stop. "Glad to hear it, because Tori's supervising the menu. I brought a list of action items, dates, and names for who's responsible." Madeline gestured them to the table. "We better start. I have a bride coming in for a fitting at nine-thirty."

"If it's Melissa Havensworth, tell her I might have her tulips," Rose said as Ethan came in with bags from the café followed by Chloe and the dogs, then Grace and Nikki Lou.

Before long, the back of the flower shop was noisy and alive and all the sisters—except Sadie—were gathered around the table laughing and planning what Madeline called the VR Event.

Whatever they called it, the party would be great, Rose decided, because of the ladies around this table, who knew the only thing that mattered was that they celebrated Rex and Suze and the legacy they'd built.

THE DAY DIDN'T SLOW up until late afternoon when Rose finally finished the last arrangement, took a final order, and happily closed shop. Grace had taken the girls to play board games with Nikki Lou at the inn, Ethan had gone to a friend's house, and Zach was at the conference table finishing a paper for his AP English class.

At least she thought he was. As Rose locked the cash register and front door, she heard him laughing on the phone in the back.

That's what she wanted to hear more than anything,

she realized. More than the keyboard of his laptop, more than the sound of him humming while he put flowers in the cooler, more than him teasing Ethan with affectionate nicknames.

She just wanted to hear him laugh.

"I guess I could make a movie tonight," he said, his voice soft enough that Rose knew he was talking to Tiffany. "As long as my mom doesn't need me."

"You're free to go," she called, sailing into the back room. At his shocked look, she realized he thought—well, *knew*—she'd been eavesdropping. "To leave here, I mean. Now. This afternoon. You're done with your unpaid job, Zachary. Thank you!"

He smirked. "Right, okay, Mom." He added a soft laugh into the phone. "Sure, I'll tell her. Tiffany says hi."

"Hi, Tiff! How is she?"

"Fine. We're, uh, thinking about going to see a movie. Over in Yulee. Would that be okay if she drove?"

It wasn't a long drive, but off Amelia Island. Tiffany had had her license for a month now, and had passed her test the first time. Rose had seen her father in town a few weeks ago and he'd been bragging about what a great driver she was, so...

"Of course," Rose replied, already giving it too much thought. It was Saturday night, they were great kids, and this was exactly what Rose wanted from Zach—for him to have a life. "You worked here all day and did homework when you weren't busy. You go and have fun. Take her to dinner and I'll pay."

"Wow, thanks, Mom." He laughed again at whatever Tiffany had said. "No, it's not guilt money."

"It certainly isn't." Rose made a face. "Maybe a little."

"Well, thanks and Tiff says thanks, too. So, pick me up at six?" he asked, standing to walk outside and finish his conversation without his mother listening.

Utterly pleased with how this week had gone since she and Gabe had talked, Rose started the process of cleaning up the back room, sweeping up flower clippings and petals, and...

She frowned at something under one of the chairs, leaning over to see what it was.

A notebook? Was that Madeline's? She lifted the small leather book, flipping it open to the first page to see MW. Yes, it belonged to her sister. She flipped another page and instantly knew what she had. Madeline had dropped the book that held all her passwords.

What was it with people who didn't keep those somewhere electronic and safe? Madeline would be frantic if she realized this was gone.

Holding the notebook, she stepped outside to give it to Zach so he could run it to Madeline, but he was deep in conversation, laughing with Tiffany. The poor kid had been her personal assistant all day.

"Hey, Zach," she called. "I'm running over to Aunt Madeline's."

He gave a thumbs-up, and she jogged toward Madeline's shop, crossing the ice cream parlor parking lot and heading to the back door. It was locked, of course, and she knew the code, but if Madeline wasn't there, she might set off an alarm.

So, she hustled up the alley between the two businesses, hoping it wasn't too late to get in by way of the salon. But that was locked, too.

Grunting in frustration, Rose stood for a moment trying to decide what made more sense. She didn't have her phone with her, but by the time she went back to the shop and got her phone, she could have walked this notebook to Madeline's house—where she might be searching high and low with no idea where it had fallen, no doubt when she'd unpacked her bag.

It would take two minutes to get to Madeline's townhouse. Without taking one more of those minutes to think about it, Rose hurried toward the row of brick townhouses, bypassing small groups of shoppers and tourists, waving to Sarah Beth, who was locking up her little boutique. As she made her way through the heart of her town, she realized that her usual smile and uplifted heart were firmly in place for the first time since Gabe left.

They could do this, she thought with a boost of confidence. They could navigate distance and separation, the kids and the business, life and his new path—because even apart, they were together.

She turned onto Madeline's street, pausing for a car to pass, then crossed to the rowhouses, taking the sidewalk to the last unit, a little out of breath when she rang the bell.

When Madeline didn't answer, she reached for the

keypad, touching the first button just as the door opened a crack.

"Rose?" Madeline peered out. "What are you doing here?"

Rose laughed softly at the unfriendly greeting. "Uh..." She lifted the tiny notebook. "Saving your backside from fretting about losing this."

"Oh, wow." Her eyes widened in horror. "I had no idea I lost it!"

Rose fluttered it. "Well, you're welcome."

"Yeah, oh, yeah. Thanks." She eased the door open no more than an inch, reaching her hand out. "I'll take it."

For a second, Rose thought she must be kidding. "Do I need to know a secret password for you to open the door?" she joked. "Because I'm pretty sure it's in this book. Under L for let-me-in-dot-com?"

Madeline just stared at her. "I can't, Rose."

She...*what?*

Rose blinked at her, trying to make sense of that. "Are you...not alone?" A flash of shock and awareness and even disbelief rocked her momentarily.

Madeline sighed and gave the door one more inch—barely. "It's complicated. Can I have the book?"

"Is there a *man* in there?" Rose whispered.

"You don't have to act like UFOs landed, Rose. Please. I'd like my privacy, if you don't mind."

Her jaw dropped. "You are seeing someone and didn't tell me? Madeline, I—"

"I'm not," she ground out. "Please, don't make this difficult."

Who was making anything difficult? What was she hiding? And why?

"Okaaaay," Rose said, handing her the book through the six-inch opening. "I don't know why you're being so weird. I mean, it's me. Your sister."

Madeline took the book and muttered, "Thank you."

Before Rose could even respond, the door closed in her face, leaving her confused and mad and really, really curious.

Chapter Fifteen

Madeline

"Sadie!" Madeline barked on a strained whisper. "I'm going to kill you!"

"Shhh." Sadie popped out from behind the kitchen counter where she'd hidden, no doubt hearing the whole conversation. "She might be lingering out there."

"You think? You think our sister might be standing out there in shock and fury after I lied to her, didn't invite her in, and slammed the door in her face?" Ire skittered up her spine. "This has gone on too long. I'm done."

"Madeline, please." She came around the corner, her hands in a prayer position. "Just a little while longer. I'll get an answer from the attorney soon."

"Oh, now you're admitting you saw an attorney?" Madeline threw her hands up. "Well, what do you know? An actual fact in a sea of vague answers and thinly veiled lies."

"I'm not lying to you," Sadie said.

"Well, *I'm* lying. To *my own sister*!" Puffing out a breath, Madeline walked deeper into the living room and plopped on a chair, frustration rocking her. "Keeping a secret is one thing. Not breaking a promise is another. But lying? To Rose? I cannot do it. I won't. You have to come clean."

Sade took a few steps closer, perching on the sofa across from Madeline. "Please understand that I simply cannot tell you."

"I don't care what you did, Sadie! I don't care if you committed a crime or saw something you shouldn't have or got involved with the wrong people or...or whatever. Nothing you have done could make me—or anyone in this family—love you any less. Don't you realize that?"

"It's not about...this family."

The way she said it, with the most subtle emphasis on "this," made Madeline inch closer. "Is it about another family?"

Sadie pushed out both hands, palms forward. "Stop, Madeline. I am not going to tell you. All I can say is I was in a...situation, okay? I got into a situation that I...I shouldn't have been in. I'm getting out of it, but it will take time."

"And a lawyer."

Sadie lifted a shoulder. "And time."

"Is money involved? Bad people? A man? Oh, God, a married man."

"Stop it!" Sadie exclaimed.

"Did someone hurt you, Sadie?" Madeline demanded. "Because if someone—"

"No one hurt me," she said, pushing up. "And if you don't stop this, I will disappear as easily and unexpectedly as I arrived."

"Don't threaten me, Sadie."

"I'm not. I'm sorry," she said quickly. "I don't mean that as a threat, but I'm just telling you what the consequences of this will be. I *have* to stay quiet. I have to. Okay? I need this refuge. Don't take it away."

Madeline groaned, and sighed, and tried to remember the last time she was anyone's refuge. "I don't have a choice, but I don't have to like it."

After a moment of sitting in silence, Sadie stood and went into the kitchen, getting a glass of water from the fridge door.

"You actually have a physical password book?" she asked. "That's so...old school."

"I'm forty-nine, Sadie. My school is old and I can't be bothered with some complicated app. I write my passwords in a book the way most baby boomers do and I guess it fell out of my bag when I was at the flower shop."

Sadie snorted. "Madeline, I've known you my entire life. You've never, not once, lost something. But I'm sure you knew Rose would bring it here."

Madeline bristled at the charge. "I didn't know that, Sadie. Please don't accuse me of a ruse when you're the one who needs a lawyer and won't tell me why."

Sadie sighed and closed her eyes. "Do you want water?"

"I want answers."

With a grunt, she came back into the living room. "Let's try something else, shall we? How was your meeting at Rose's?"

"Fine."

"What did you all decide about the party?"

Madeline stared at her for a moment, her brain whirring with questions, but she knew she'd get nowhere asking them. "We came up with a guest list."

"How many people?"

"We capped it at one hundred, just to keep it intimate and not invite everyone on Amelia Island."

"Smart."

Madeline stiffened, mostly because Sadie hadn't been there and her input would have been valuable. And fun. And they would all be planning the party, not just six out of seven.

"Tori's working on a great menu," she said. "She's already been in touch with the chef at the hotel. Rose is doing all the décor, and Chloe's renting chairs and an awning for the beach wedding...well, vow renewal. She has a few contacts from her wedding."

Sadie leaned closer. "She's all recovered? Every time I talk to her, she seems like she's lost."

Madeline didn't answer, but looked down, biting her lip to hold back the sharp retort she wanted to fling because she was so angry and frustrated.

If you care, why don't you see her? But she managed not to say a word.

"Madeline," Sadie whispered. "I know this is hard for you. But you know why I picked you, of all the sisters, for help?"

"Because I live alone and you had the best chance of getting away with this?"

Sadie closed her eyes. "Because you are like another

mother to me. Because you are so wise and reasoned and deeply caring."

"Thank you, but Raina is smarter, Rose cares more than anyone about everything, and Grace is probably the most reasonable. Chloe's up to her eyeballs in trying to grow up and Tori's in Boston. That left me."

Sadie slipped off the sofa and sat cross-legged right in front of Madeline. "You missed the first part. You are like another mother to me. You were fourteen when I was born, Madeline. I thought you were an adult, and you were always...gentle."

A lump formed in Madeline's throat as she looked into the depths of Sadie's ever-changing eyes. Today they were gold, glimmering with unshed tears, and as honest as anything she'd ever seen.

"You were special," she said softly.

Sadie smiled. "You called me 'Sadie, Sadie, tiny lady.' Do you remember?"

Madeline nodded, her eyes misting at the memory.

"When Grace and Chloe were born," Sadie continued, "they were the next exciting things in the family and I was as stuck in the middle as a kid could be. I was just silly Sadie with wild hair and a hankering to go places. But you always...saw me."

"I loved your hair," Madeline said, reaching a hand out to touch one of those curls. "And I loved you. Still do, tiny lady."

"Please, Madeline, don't be mad at me."

"I'm not."

"You are," Sadie corrected. "And I don't blame you.

But I knew of all the Wingates, you were the one who I wanted to trust. And I do. I know I've put you in a bad situation and you had to lie to Rose. I'm so sorry. But I'd do it for you. That's all I want you to know. I would because I love you so very, very much."

"I love you, too," Madeline whispered, wiping a tear. "And that's why I want to help you."

"Then just trust me." She leaned in and took Madeline's hands, squeezing tight. "I don't want to lie, either, so that's why I'm not saying anything."

Madeline squeezed her hands back, examining Sadie's face. "Please tell me this will all be over by Suze and Dad's anniversary and you'll be there, in a pretty dress, not a shroud of secrecy."

She took a deep breath. "I promise you that even if it isn't over, I'll be there. Until then, let's just agree to keep that shroud of secrecy draped all over me."

Madeline sighed. What else could she do? "Okay, Sadie, Sadie, tiny lady."

Sadie leaned back and grinned. "Tiny lady wants pizza tonight. Can we order?"

Madeline just laughed. "Of course."

Once again, Sadie had won the round and Madeline knew absolutely nothing more than she did when they started.

At nearly two a.m., Madeline threw back the covers and let a rare case of insomnia win the battle. Without making a sound, she put on her slippers, tugged a bathrobe around her, and stepped into the hall.

Something Sadie said had stuck in her head and would not let her sleep.

"It's not about...this family."

Then what family was it about? The Saint Pierre family? The business where Sadie worked was family owned, and all Madeline knew was that they were darn near royalty in Brussels. Famous for chocolate and...chocolate.

She knew nothing about them. Were they criminals? Had they roped her into something nefarious?

In the kitchen, she tapped the under-counter light and opened the pantry door in search of tea, but all she could see were ancient memories that threatened to come out of their locked compartments.

Who knew better than Madeline what greed and lies and a complete lack of a moral compass could do to a company or a person's career? She stared into the cabinet, but didn't see the plastic containers or coffee and tea. Instead, she saw...sleek dark hair, the intelligent eyes, and the completely innocent smile of a talented woman who Madeline once thought could do no wrong.

And yet all dress designer Elana Mau ever did was...*wrong*. Wrong enough to send her to prison.

But Sadie? It seemed impossible that she'd be involved in anything like that. What could be illegal about chocolate?

Well, what could be illegal about *wedding dresses*? A

person with access and brains and a need for money could steal from any company.

Shaking off the memory, she found some chamomile, brewed a cup, and cradled the warm ceramic in her hands for a few moments. Just as she started to walk toward the stairs, she heard Sadie's voice again.

*It's not about...*this *family.*

She pivoted and headed into the darkened den, straight to the antique parson's table where she kept her home laptop. Why hadn't she thought of this before? If something was going on at a large company, wouldn't it be in the news?

She quietly pulled out the chair and opened the laptop, bringing it to life as she sipped her tea.

She started with a simple search of the company, Chocolat de Saint Pierre. Wasn't that the official name of the candy most people called Saint Pierre? Madeline always thought of the company as "like Godiva, but smaller," and not nearly as iconic.

Sadie would hate that, since her job was to make the brand a household name, but the process was a slow one and she'd only been doing marketing for the company for a few years.

Madeline bypassed the company website, which probably wouldn't be advertising bad news like Madeline was in search of, instead looking through pages of news stories, none of which seemed terribly troublesome. And most of them were in languages Madeline didn't speak, like Dutch and French.

She went back to the website and found her way to a

brief history of how the Saint Pierre family started a candy company after World War II and the oldest son studied to be a chocolatier, and then his sons took over the business. One article described the family as "Belgian royalty" and another described its deep heritage.

Was this the family Sadie was referring to? What did—

"What are you doing?"

Madeline whipped around at the sound of Sadie's voice, stunned that she hadn't heard her come into the den. Her hair was disheveled from sleep, but her eyes looked...dull. Broken. Betrayed. And focused on the screen with the great big Saint Pierre logo across the top.

"I'm...reading about your company."

"Why?"

Madeline didn't answer. Instead, she stood and reached out both hands, an apology and explanation— and twenty more questions that would go unanswered— forming in her head.

Sadie backed away, refusing Madeline's touch, her gaze still on the screen.

"You won't find anything about me on the website. I'm in charge of the people who design and update it— well, I was—and no one but the family and top chef chocolatiers are mentioned. We keep it product-focused."

Madeline sighed and nodded. "I don't know what I was looking for. You said it wasn't this family you were worried about—"

"I didn't say I was worried about anyone," she shot back. "I didn't say anything, honestly. This is merely..."

She flicked her hand at the laptop as she walked closer to it and dropped into the seat where Madeline had been. "Conjecture."

Madeline expected her to slam the screen closed, but she didn't. Instead, she clicked on a link, revealing a full-sized picture of a group of people on a hillside in front of what looked like a palace.

Silent, she stared at them.

"The Saint Pierre family?" Madeline guessed.

She nodded and pointed at a sophisticated woman in a pale blue gown. "That's the mother—Cecile. She's a classic matriarch. Controls everything, including her kids. That's her husband, the CEO of Saint Pierre, Gregoire."

The man next to Cecile was handsome, likely in his sixties, with a sparkle in his eye.

"Greg has no less than three mistresses at any given moment," Sadie said.

"So Cecile doesn't control *him*."

She shrugged. "She's well-compensated for keeping her mouth shut and eyes closed where Gregoire is concerned."

Madeline leaned over Sadie's shoulder to get a better look. "Sounds like a great guy."

"He's not."

"And the others?" Madeline asked, skimming the faces of a few men, women, and small children.

"That is the oldest daughter, Isabella, an absolute wretch of a woman married to this guy, Leandre Valoire, who has an IQ of six. There's the older brother, Olivier, and his wife, Jeanne-Marie. Ollie is smart, and has a heart somewhere in that chest. Jeanne-Marie is sweet but in way over her head with this crew. Ollie's in line to be CEO after Gregoire dies. Those are their three beastly children who, if they are our future? We're in trouble."

Madeline snorted a laugh. "You really don't like these people."

"I liked some of them," she said quietly, clicking off the screen without providing any names or dirt on the others.

That brought up the list of news stories Madeline had been reading.

"Really digging, eh, Madeline?" Sadie asked with a wry laugh.

"Just trying to see if I can help you."

"You can't," she said, clicking the first link. "Oh, this was from Isabella's wedding last year. I was there."

"Let me see," Madeline said, inching closer. "Are you in any of the pictures?"

"Maybe." She scrolled through some of what the magazine had posted, clicking one after another. "Oh, there. I'm kind of in the background, but you can see me."

Madeline squinted at it, trying to make out Sadie's face in the crowd, but her gaze shifted to the left when something caught her eye. Not something—*someone.*

It was the hooded eyes. The crooked smile. The cleft in a chin and an imperfect nose, misshapen by...

Nah, not a punch, Maddie. The loom hit me and broke my nose.

It was like his voice slipped out from a crack in the

compartment where Adam Carpenter had been locked away for two and a half decades.

"Oh my God," she whispered, pressing her hand to her lips. "It's not possible."

"What?" Sadie asked on a laugh. "I straightened my hair. I thought it looked good that night."

She actually felt a little dizzy as she stared. Dizzy and shocked and...unable to look away from his face. Yes, he was twenty-five years older—so was she—but he looked exactly the same. Older but...yes, that was Adam.

"What is it?" Sadie asked, looking up at Madeline.

"Who..." She almost couldn't breathe as she lifted a trembling finger and pointed to the screen. "Who is that man?"

Sadie squinted and zoomed in, focusing on...on him. It *had* to be him. It had to be.

Sadie leaned in. "Oh, that guy. Adam—"

"Carpenter," Madeline finished. "Adam John Carpenter of Altoona, Pennsylvania."

"What...tuna?"

"That's where Adam Carpenter was born, and..." She could practically feel the box where she stored the memory of Adam opening, threatening to drown her with vivid recollections and sweet promises and...the feeling of the rain drenching her hair the day she waited and waited and...*waited*.

"No, no. Not Carpenter," Sadie replied, tapping the screen on the man's tuxedo. "Logan. He's American. Do you *know* him?"

She leaned in, putting her hand on the mouse to zoom in. "I think so. What was he doing there?"

"He's a contract security analyst for the Saint Pierres. How could you possibly know him?" Her voice rose in disbelief as if it was preposterous that Madeline, a dress designer who rarely left the confines of Fernandina Beach, would know this good-looking man wearing Armani at a wedding of near-royalty in Brussels.

But she did. At least, she thought she did...once.

"Years ago, when I was in New York," Madeline said. "When I worked for Elana Mau—"

"The embezzler?" Sadie asked with a snort.

"The dress designer who was my mentor," Madeline corrected, hating that the great Elana Mau was reduced to a nasty footnote in history. "He worked at a fabric manufacturing company in the fashion district." She shook her head and turned to Sadie, trying to put a puzzle together but way too many pieces didn't fit. "What do you mean, security analyst?"

"His job is to protect the family. Internet protection, physical protection, doing their bidding, whatever it might be."

"Like a bodyguard?" Madeline asked, her voice lifting in disbelief.

"A little more complicated than that. Are you sure you know him?"

"I think...it really looks like him. And his name was Adam."

Sadie considered that. "Yeah, not the most unusual

name in the world, but most of the guys in that job are former law enforcement. Was he a cop?"

"Not even close," Madeline scoffed. "He ran the loom at a textile house."

"It's probably not the same person, then."

"But..." Madeline said. "Those eyes and that smile. It's twenty-five years later, but I would recognize him anywhere." She got even closer to the computer, then turned to Sadie. "Do you have any other pictures of him?"

Sadie gave a soft laugh, probably at the sheer desperation in Madeline's voice. "You'd have to look all through the internet, but..." She put her hand on the mouse on top of Madeline's. "You're shaking! Who is this guy?"

"Just...no one. Someone I knew, but...it was nothing."

Sadie lifted her hand and narrowed her eyes. "And now who's not telling the whole story?"

Madeline closed her eyes, trying to decide how much she wanted to share.

Very, very little, she decided.

"There isn't a story to tell," she said. "I liked him. A lot. I thought..." She swallowed the rest, ashamed to admit what she'd thought. She thought he loved her...and she *knew* she loved him. "Anyway, one day, he disappeared and I never heard from him again."

"Madeline Wingate!" Sadie jabbed her arm. "I have gone my entire adult life thinking you never even had a boyfriend. And you've been hiding the loom guy all these years?"

"I haven't been hiding him," she said, turning back to the image. "He's the one hiding—in Brussels."

"But who was he to you?"

"It was...a relationship, until it wasn't."

"What happened?" Sadie asked, clearly fascinated by this turn of historical events.

Madeline narrowed her eyes. "Shall we make a deal? I tell you and you tell me...everything?"

"No," Sadie said simply. "Mine's fresh and other people are affected. Yours is from the literal last century."

So, in other words, no deal. "Well, maybe this isn't him, but who knows? His name's Adam Carpenter, not Logan."

"How did you break up?" Sadie pressed.

"We didn't," Madeline said. "He just didn't show up for our date."

"*Oof.* Stood up. The worst. Did you hunt him down and make him pay?"

Madeline shook her head. "He disappeared and the company where he worked had no idea where he went or even where he lived. I might have looked for him, but the next day, the office was raided and Elana was arrested. My life was kind of upside down then."

"That's interesting." Sadie leaned back, crossing her arms. "And you don't think those two things were related? His disappearance and her arrest?"

"No, he didn't work for my company. He didn't even know Elana Mau. I met him running fabric errands in the fashion district."

Sadie looked dubious. "Was it serious?"

Madeline looked at the screen one last time, not sure how to answer Sadie's question. "It felt serious," she said. "I...I..." She swallowed. "I fell in love with him."

"Madeline." Sadie breathed her name, reaching for her. "I didn't know that. I'm sorry you lost your loom guy."

She laughed softly. "It's fine. It was a long time ago. It's just that seeing him..."

"Are you sure that's him? Because I'm almost certain Tristan said that guy was..." Her voice trailed off. "Well, never mind. I can't help you find him now because..."

"Who's Tristan?" Madeline asked.

"One of the family," she said. "The other son in that picture. And, no, I am not asking him if he knows anything about Adam's past, so don't even—"

Madeline held a hand up at the vehement response. "Oh, no. No. I'd never want you to ask...anyone. I was just wondering." Blowing out a breath, she took one more long look. There was no way that wasn't Adam Carpenter, or at least his doppelganger.

"Have you ever considered that his disappearance was related to your boss's arrest?" Sadie asked, yanking her from the image.

"No. I told you, they didn't know each other."

"You sure? Is it possible he was working for the government trying to sting her operation and he used you for access?"

Madeline felt the blood drain from her face.

"I mean"—Sadie added a serious look—"I'm pretty

sure that Adam Logan guy was former FBI, but I could be wrong. Or it's not the same guy you knew."

"Former..." For a moment, Madeline couldn't speak. Her whole body felt boneless and weak. Had Adam been an undercover plant trying to learn more about Elana Mau? Had he just *used* Madeline for information?

Because that ripped this old wound wide open.

"Hey, hey." Sadie took her hand, pulling her back to the moment. "It's ancient history and doesn't matter, right? Aren't some secrets better left buried, Madeline?"

She smiled at her sister's implication, then nodded. "You're right, Sadie." She straightened and closed the laptop, locking up that old compartment and digging for fresh Band-Aids. She had no desire to relive the pain of Adam Carpenter. "You're absolutely right."

It didn't matter why he disappeared. It didn't matter why "the loom guy" made her think he loved her. None of it mattered twenty-five long and lonely years later.

"That's enough secrets for one night," Madeline whispered.

"Yeah, talk about payback," Sadie joked, pushing up. "You come digging into my life...and find your own."

The irony was not lost on Madeline.

Chapter Sixteen

Chloe

"Thank you, Mr. Lynch." Chloe stood when the bank executive did, taking the hand he offered and returning his smile. That was the hard part—looking as enthused as she should be after a brief but very complimentary meeting where he'd simply raved about what a tremendous addition she'd make to the Lighthouse Bank team.

Gil hadn't lied about it being a perfunctory meeting—she obviously had the job.

"I hope you'll be able to start next week, Chloe," the CEO named...something Lynch said.

Was it a bad sign she couldn't remember his first name?

"We're excited about our investments division," Mr. Lynch said, "and really think that with the right local marketing, we'll be a destination bank for our community."

"I'm sure you will be," she said, letting go of his hand to pick up her bag. "Thank you for taking the time to meet with me today."

"Oh, thank *you*," he gushed, gesturing to his door. "Gil's out there waiting to get your offer letter, so let's put him out of his misery, shall we?"

Sure enough, the man who would be her direct boss was lurking in the reception area outside of his boss's office, ready to pounce.

"How about you spend a few minutes with the head of HR, Chloe?" Gil asked as they walked down a wide hallway to his office.

"Oh...today? Wouldn't I meet with HR when I start?"

"Why waste time on your first day when you can bone up on everything this week before you start?" he asked. "Maryann can get you loaded up with the onboarding packet."

"That sounds...nautical. Part of the lighthouse theme?" she guessed, gesturing to the window that offered a perfect view of Amelia Island's landmark.

He laughed. "See? You're so clever, Chloe. You're going to bring such creative energy to this job. But, in all seriousness, an onboarding packet is what we give to new employees."

Of *course*. "What is it, exactly?"

"Chock full of import," he told her, his voice so serious. "It contains the complete employee handbook with our company history, mission statement, and the internal systems. And the P&P—policy and procedures—manual, and, of course, we're a financial institution, so there's a mountain of compliance and confidentiality paperwork to sign."

She stared straight ahead, not trusting herself to

respond to how awful it all sounded, despite Gil's genuine enthusiasm.

"Oh, and get this," he added. "We give all new employees blue-light glasses because you will be on the computer a lot, I'm afraid."

She gave a smile she was certain didn't reach her eyes, which, up to this point, hadn't needed any protection from blue light because she spent as little time as possible in front of a screen.

"That's...nice," she managed.

"You'll find nothing but nice here at Lighthouse," he assured her. "Great people from the mailroom to the executive suites. It's why no one ever leaves once you join our team."

Ever? The idea of never leaving Lighthouse Bank was...no, she actually didn't want to think of growing old at this place, despite how *nice* it was.

He paused at a doorway and peeked into an empty office, and let out a sigh of disappointment. "Too bad. Maryann must be at lunch. And I have an appointment—"

"That's fine, Mr. Huxley."

"Please, it's Gil."

"You've spent a lot of time with me today, so I'll let you get back to your work." She took a step backwards, trying not to look like she wanted to run. But, wow, she wanted to run.

"You don't have the offer letter," he said. "And Maryann does have to put her stamp of approval on it, so I guess I'll just email it to you."

"That's perfect," she told him. "I'll look for it and call you."

He drew back, lifting one brow behind his glasses. "Don't break my heart now, Chloe. I'm sure you're in demand and I don't have any other candidates as strong as you."

"That's very kind."

"And...don't tell anyone, but..." He looked from side to side like someone might be in earshot and he was about to divulge state secrets. "I've added five days PTO to the offer. No one starts with two full weeks of paid time off at Lighthouse," he said. "Most people work here two years before they get that. It's just my way of saying we want you on the team."

"Wow, that's...great. Thank you, Gil." This time, when she smiled, she meant it. He was the nicest guy and really did want her for the job.

He had no idea she woke up in a sweat at two in the morning over the idea of working in a bank. Or maybe that was because Rocky liked to sleep smashed against her.

She finally managed to end the meeting, promised to call him after she got the letter, and breezed out of the corporate offices into the sunshine like a woman being let out of prison.

Immediately, she heard the bark of her two favorite dogs and saw the smile of her very favorite firefighter, who'd taken Lady Bug and Rocky to Egin's Creek Park, across the street from the bank and within view of the lighthouse it was named after.

She gave a wave and jogged across the street to join them.

"Well?" Travis asked when the dogs stopped barking and jumping for her love.

"Well, the job is mine along with five extra days off every year and my own blue-light glasses."

Travis searched her face. "You don't seem happy."

Blowing out a breath, she reached down and lifted Lady Bug from the ground, snuggling her for the comfort the dog always gave to Chloe. "Are you sick of the park or can we walk a little more?"

"I don't think these two ever get sick of the park and my shift doesn't start until five. Come on." He gave Rocky's leash a tug and they all walked to the grassy area and walking trail that ran the perimeter of the park.

Some kids and moms were under the shade trees, resting after time on the playground, passed by a few runners and other dog walkers. Chloe put Lady Bug back on the ground, and, happy she wore flat shoes, they followed the trail to the long dock that jutted into the waterway that meandered through the center of the island.

"Did you like the CEO?" Travis finally asked.

"I liked everyone," she said honestly. "The place is the polar opposite of *A-List Access* in that regard. Every person I met was warm and friendly and so excited to have me work there. You'd think I actually understood the banking business."

"You understand people, you're smart as a whip, and

they know that when you put your mind to it, you'll come up with ideas that will attract new customers."

Why did that sound so unappealing?

She answered with a sigh, staring out at the water. "I don't know what color my parachute is, Travis, but I have a feeling it's not...lighthouse blue."

He didn't say anything but guided them to a bench where they could sit and let the dogs rest.

"So, you're not taking the job?" he asked.

"I didn't say that."

"You don't have to. I can tell you'd rather run off that dock and jump into the water."

"I've done that," she said, a smile lifting her lips at the memory.

"Seriously? Don't think that's legal."

"It was a Senior Stunt in high school. About twenty of us did it and then went back to fourth period soaking wet." She laughed softly. "Good times."

"Especially for the guys in your fourth period class," he said with a wry smile.

She elbowed him. "Ha-ha, very funny."

But he wasn't smiling. He was regarding her with a very serious expression that she couldn't interpret. "What's wrong, Travis?" she asked.

"Nothing's wrong, I promise. I want you to be happy. I want you to be settled. I want you to..." He gave a self-deprecating laugh. "I want you, period. I mean, for my... person. But all of that—your happiness, you being settled, you being mine? It all feels really far off right now."

"I know." She leaned into him. "First of all, I am happy. I'm home and near family, I'm not out in L.A. or with Hunter or striving to be in a place I don't belong. Settled? Well, once again, I'm home and near family. Not only do my parents like me being in the bungalow, my father approved you building my dogs a pen."

"That leaves one last thing," he said. "You, Chloe Wingate, as my girlfriend."

She gave him a shaky smile, surprised at the thrill the words gave her. "You need an official label?"

He lifted a shoulder. "I need to know where we're going."

"Would it change anything?" she asked.

"It would give me peace and a direction and a sense of—"

"*Rock Starrrrr!* Oh my God, Rock Star! It's you!"

Chloe and Travis whipped around to see a man running toward them, shoulder-length curls flying in the wind. Instantly, Rocky leaped, yanking the leash as he barked and howled with the same volume as the man.

"Rock Star! Baby, I found you!" The man fell to his knees in front of them, both arms out for Rocky, who jumped up on the man's chest, licked his face furiously, and wagged his tail so hard it had to hurt.

But not as much as Chloe's heart as she stared at what had to be a reunion of two creatures who knew and loved each other very, very much.

≈

FINALLY, she knew his real name—Rock Star. And his owner, who was kind of a rock star himself. Five minutes after meeting Fritz Dunedin, she knew she was looking at the person she'd been searching for since the day she found Rocky...well, Rock Star.

"I can't even believe this," the man said, shaking back his insane waves and beaming at them from the ground where he still sat, holding his dog like he'd never let him go. "I literally came down here first, the minute I got back, as soon as I found out he was gone, to post these flyers."

He waved a stack of papers with "Missing Dog" handwritten across the top and a big picture of Rocky in the middle.

"This is Rock Star's favorite park in all of Fernandina Beach." He hugged the dog and kissed his brown head. "Dude, I thought you were history!"

"We've had him for more than a week," Travis said, still studying the man like he simply didn't trust him. "Where have you been?"

"Canada, mostly. And a couple of gigs up in Washington State." He cuddled Rock Star into his lap, letting the dog lick at the huge holes in his jeans. The sweet puppy had never looked happier, which was really the only consolation for Chloe. "I'm in a band called Xanadu Rising and we're getting kind of legit. Our manager is finally coming through with a decent tour schedule."

"And you just left your dog?" Travis asked, his disdain hard to hide.

"Oh, no, man. Never. I let my 'sort of not really official but she's hot' girlfriend watch him but..." He dropped his head and kissed the dog. "Now she's my ex."

"What happened?" Chloe asked.

"She lives in a van," he said, as if that explained it.

"And?" Travis pressed.

"And she left the door open at a gas station—like a moron—and Rock Star took a walk."

"Did she report him missing?" Chloe asked. "I had his name and picture at every shelter and all over Facebook's local rescue pages."

Fritz's eyes shuttered. "Please. She was ticked off he ate a cushion in her van and I don't think she cared he got out, if you catch my drift. She didn't tell me because she knew I'd blow a gasket. I got back early this morning, and her van was gone. She left a note letting me know that she took off after Rock Star did."

Chloe recoiled in horror. "Are you serious?"

"And that's why she's my ex," he said, adding another kiss on the dog's head. "I don't know how to thank you guys. You found him on the beach? It's his happy place. This park and the beach. I'm sure he was looking for me."

Chloe was sure of that, too, which left her with all kinds of emotions from sadness to relief. These two belonged together. She stood up and got closer to the dog, who looked at her with no small amount of guilt. Like he'd known he was going back to his owner all along.

"Rocky," she whispered, getting down on the ground with him. "I'll see you again, bud. I love you, you know that?"

Fritz beamed at her. "Bet he sleeps on your bed. The whole spoon thing?"

She laughed. "Guilty."

"Yeah, that's my boy." He gave the dog's head a rub. "You even gave him the right name, which I bet he told you."

"He kind of did," she admitted. "Every name I'd try, I got a look like, 'Are you kidding me?' until I hit on Rocky, which I guess was close enough."

"He's a great communicator," Fritz said. "And don't you worry, Rocker Man. I don't have another gig for a month."

"Then what will you do with him?" Travis asked.

"I'll keep him!" Chloe offered before the man could speak. "I love him."

"Seriously?" Fritz looked more than interested. "Hey, yeah, if you can take care of him, I'll pay you."

"Oh, that's..." *Not a bad way to make a living,* she thought. Only it wouldn't pay what Lighthouse Bank was offering. "I'd love to watch him for you," she finished. "Let me give you my number and I'll take him any time, day or night." She glanced over her shoulder. "We kind of jumped the gun and built a pen for him."

"Wow." He pushed his hair back and pulled out his wallet. "Cool, man. Really nice of you. Let me pay you."

Lady Bug came over to nuzzle Rocky, as though she sensed what was going on.

"Not necessary, please," Chloe said, holding out her hand. "The pleasure was mine. And, as you can see, Lady Bug's."

"Did you make a boyfriend?" he asked, leaning down to put his face right in front of Lady Bug's. "I can see why he likes you." He tapped her little black nose. "You're a cutie."

Lady Bug swished her tail at the compliment and got a little closer to Rocky.

"And to think you didn't like him when we first got him," Chloe teased, trying to keep her voice light when her heart was anything but. "I honestly got very used to the idea of keeping him."

Fritz smiled at her. "Like I said, I'm on the road a lot. If you and your husband don't mind—"

"Oh, he's not—"

"We don't mind," Travis said quickly. "He's really a great dog."

"Thanks." Fritz pushed up to a stand. "Oh, new leash and collar, huh?"

"And I have bowls, and some toys, and a blanket he really likes." Chloe stood, too, scooping up Lady Bug more for the comfort of holding her close while they said goodbye.

"You keep them," Fritz said, reaching into his pocket to produce a phone. "Here, put your number in and I promise he's yours when I'm on the road."

Relieved, she gave him her number, then bent over and gave Rocky one more kiss. "You were a good boy, Rock...Star. Come and see us, okay?"

He wagged his tail, but stayed very close to Fritz, as if he didn't trust her not to grab and run and take him home.

"Thanks again." Fritz reached out a hand and shook hers, then Travis's. "You guys are life-savers. God only knows what could have happened to this guy. C'mon, Rocker! Let's get home, boy!"

They took off with a wave and a few happy barks, and some not so happy ones from Lady Bug.

"Oh, wow," Chloe whispered, her legs surprisingly shaky. "I can't believe that just happened."

"Talk about being in the right place at the right time," Travis said.

"Or wrong, although he seemed really happy to find his owner." Chloe bit her lip, watching the man and dog disappear into the parking lot. "One of us should be."

Travis put his arm around her shoulder, pulling her into him. "I'm sorry, Chloe. I know you loved that dog." He kissed the top of her head, and rubbed Lady Bug. "You, too. Now who you going to boss around, Bug?"

She just barked and snuggled deeper into Chloe's arm.

"Poor baby. She's sad. So am I. But not for Rocky. He's happy and that's all that matters."

"You want to go home?" Travis asked.

"Yeah, I guess." But home would seem so empty now. "We can run around the pen that we didn't need."

"You can get another dog."

"I already have to leave the one I have with my parents when I go off to work...at the bank." She winced. "Ugh. I don't like the sound of that."

His arm still around her, he guided her down the path toward the parking lot. "What about that other thing we were discussing before you had your beloved new dog ripped out of your arms?"

She looked up at him, knowing he meant the conversation about their relationship.

"Or you could maintain your current status," he said. "And continue on as my... what did he call her? A 'sort of not really official but she's hot' girlfriend."

She snorted at the echo of Fritz's description, then sighed.

"No?" Travis asked.

"One major life change a day," she said, easing Lady Bug to the ground and sliding an arm around Travis's waist.

She felt his gaze on her as she looked ahead, half waiting for the long-haired musician to come running back to say he'd changed his mind.

"What?" she asked, looking up at Travis when the sensation lasted too long.

"Nothing. I just think I might have fallen hard for a commitment-phobe."

She slowed her step, considering that. "I was ready to commit to that dog."

He chuckled softly. "Okay, Chloe. We'll take it at your pace."

Was she a commitment-phobe? She was the unemployed runaway bride living on her parents' property. She really, really wanted to change all of that.

She wanted to be Travis's girlfriend. She wanted to be gainfully employed. She wanted to be living on her own. She wanted all of that.

But wanting it wasn't enough. She had to make it happen.

Chapter Seventeen

Raina

When she arrived at Ocean Song, Raina had to admit things seemed to be moving along at a great clip. Walking into the sun-drenched lobby, she no longer felt like she was in a construction zone. The reception area was complete, although no one stood ready to welcome guests.

The lobby had furniture, even if some pieces were still in plastic covers. And the wall of glass to the outside gleamed, showing off the view of a pool that not only had been tiled but was being filled with water that very day.

This was progress, Raina thought, turning to walk toward the management offices to find Chase. He'd told her to come by so he could introduce her to his brand-new event manager, who'd be her hands-on coordinator for the vow renewal ceremony and reception. But first, she wanted to find Josh's father, the carpenter, and relay what she'd learned from talking to Alyson.

She spotted the man as soon as she rounded the corner, on his knees touching up paint on a baseboard.

"Jeremiah?"

He looked up, plucking a wired earbud out and smiling as he recognized her. "Hello. It's Raina, right?"

"It is. Do you have a moment?"

He stood and wiped his hand on overalls, extended it, then thought better. "Nah, it's got paint on it," he said on a laugh. "Hello, again."

"Things are really coming along here," she said brightly.

"Mr. Madison is determined to stay ahead of schedule," he told her. "He's moved things up by a month."

"My fault," she admitted. "We're trying to host a big party here in mid-November. But I wanted to chat with you about your son's accident."

His eyes widened. "That's right. Your...niece, was it? Alyson? Joshie told me he knows her. Said she's very smart."

"She is, and observant. It turns out she was at the monkey bars when it happened. She saw everything."

"Was it Josh's fault?" he asked without a second's hesitation. "Or did another kid cause him to fall? Because, look." He huffed out a sigh and shifted from one foot to the other. "This is kind of embarrassing, but if someone who was at fault could at least cover the cost of the hospital? Well, that would be great, because I have terrible health insurance and they don't want to cover much at all."

"Oh, dear." She imagined how scary that must have been for him.

"I'm a contract worker and it's expensive to get the good stuff."

"I know it is," she said, her mind spinning over what Alyson told her. "It wasn't Josh's fault."

"She—your niece, I mean—knows that for sure?"

"Based on what Alyson saw, the cause wasn't Josh or another kid. It was the monkey bars themselves. Alyson saw the teacher go back to the very spot where he fell and fix a broken bar, and then they stopped letting kids use the equipment. If you're looking for someone to blame, I suppose you could go after the monkey bar manufacturer or...the school."

"Aw, man." He grimaced and dropped his head back. "I don't want to sue anyone. But I do want to get Mr. Madison some of his money back."

"Excuse me?" she inched closer. "Did you say Chase—"

"Oh, I'm sure he'll deny it, but I know who paid the bill. I was having a full-blown freakout when they called and not just because my kid broke his arm. I mean, accidents happen, but I knew what a hospital can cost. Then Mr. Madison came by, heard what happened, and drove me to right there." He grinned. "Like a bat out of you-know-where in that fancy convertible of his."

She had to smile. "He said he was there that day."

"He was more than there," he said. "I never got a bill. I was sweating bullets waiting for it. When it didn't come, I followed up. They said an anonymous donor paid the ER walk-in fee and asked for the bill to be sent to him. I know who it was. That man is made of goodness, but you probably already know that."

She didn't, but she was sure starting to find out.

"I can't sleep at night knowing I didn't try to get him some of that money back."

Searching his face, she thought about the predicament and how Jeremiah was made of goodness, too. It would be so easy to accept the gift and move on, but he clearly had integrity.

And the school? Maybe they were terrified of getting sued, but someone needed to address the issue with them.

"I'm not sure how you fix the problem, Jeremiah, but I think I'd start with the school and see how they respond. They may not want to get lawyers involved at all. I also think my sister would allow Alyson to come forward and say what she saw. I can put you in touch with her."

He ran his hand through his hair, considering that. "Thank you, ma'am."

"You bet." She smiled at him. "And if you'll excuse me, I have a meeting with Mr. Madison now."

He frowned and shook his head. "He ran out of here an hour ago, ma'am. Something with his...grandmother."

"Nonna?" Her heart dropped. "Is she okay?"

"Julia knows," he said, nodding toward the offices. "You should ask her."

"I will. Thank you."

As she rushed away, Raina said a quick and silent prayer for Chase's sweet, sweet nonna, hoping this wasn't...worst-case.

She found Julia at her desk just on the other side of the management office door.

"Oh, Raina, I'm so sorry! I was supposed to call you, but—"

"Is Nonna all right?" she asked, her breath trapped in her throat.

"I don't know," Julia said softly, pushing back some silver locks. "Her nurse called and said her blood pressure went sky high. He'd already called 911. Chase took off and I haven't heard a word."

Raina put her hand to her lips with a soft grunt of worry.

"But the new event manager is here," Julia said. "I know Chase wanted to introduce you. Would you like to meet her now?"

Raina's mind whirled as she took a step back. "I'd like to..." Her voice trailed off as she finished the sentence in her head. She'd like to fix the heart of the man who was... how had Jeremiah described him?

Made of goodness.

"I'd like to reschedule," she finished. "Would that be okay?"

"Of course," Julia assured her. "I'll tell him."

Or Raina would. After saying goodbye, she walked out to her car and sat in the driver's seat for a moment, imagining him dealing with Nonna's death. Maybe he'd followed the ambulance to the hospital or maybe he...

She didn't know.

But nothing could stop her from driving to the small house not far from the beach to try and help in any way she could.

∽

Raina passed an ambulance when she turned onto the street where his grandmother lived. An ambulance that wasn't speeding or flashing or moving like it was taking a dying woman to the hospital.

Was that a good sign or not?

Swallowing, she spotted his car in the driveway and parked in front of the house, anxious for news. Good news, she hoped.

She hadn't even knocked when the door was opened by a man who looked to be in his late thirties wearing scrubs.

"Paul?" she guessed.

"Yes, hello." His gaze dropped down, lingering for a quick second on her stomach. "You must be Raina."

She put her hand on the bump. "It's a giveaway. I just came by to—"

"Raina!" Chase appeared in the hallway behind him, a huge smile on his face, which instantly gave her hope.

"Julia told me and I..." She winced a little. "I don't want to overstep my bounds, but..."

Paul stepped aside as Chase came closer, reaching a hand out. "Overstep? Are you kidding? You're the best thing in the world for her."

Then she was still alive! "That's wonderful." She took the hand he offered to guide her in. "I saw the ambulance and..."

"She had an incident," he said, shooting a warm look at Paul. "This man, the world's greatest nurse—"

"Hardly," the other man interjected dryly.

"—called for backup," Chase finished.

Paul gave a shrug. "Just doing my job, Mr. Madison."

"And doing it well," Chase assured him. "They gave her some medication and the BP is right back where it is supposed to be. All other vitals are okay, though she's a bit shaken up. Would you like to see her, Raina?"

"If that's okay."

"She'd love nothing more."

With a light hand on her back, Chase ushered her toward the hall and she noticed that this time, sunshine was pouring in through the kitchen. The whole house seemed lighter and brighter.

"Really sweet of you to come, Raina," he said softly. "I know I blew off our meeting—"

"That's not why I'm here."

He laughed softly. "I know that. You're here to see...*Bisnonna*."

At the word, she threw him a look. "Like a biscotti?" she guessed.

"Only sweeter," he volleyed back. "*Bisnonna* is great-grandmother. That is, if you'll keep up our little...game of pretend."

"Of course," she said without hesitation.

He added a little pressure on her back and dipped an inch closer to whisper, "Thank you." As a few chills rose on the nape of her neck, he stepped away, into the bedroom doorway.

"Nonna, you have a special visitor," he said loudly. "It's Raina."

"Raina!" Even in the hall, Raina could hear the joy in the old woman's voice. It was all she needed, really, to know that not only had coming here been a good idea, the whole ruse about the babies really was for a fine cause.

"Hello, Nonna," she said as she came into the room.

Like the rest of the house, it was bathed in sunlight—maybe the EMTs needed that to do their job but it also gave Raina a better look at the tiny, wrinkled, ancient woman under the comforter. She looked like Hollywood had cast a "little old Italian lady," from her feathery white hair to her nose-forward features.

"Come, come." She patted the bed, but her hand was unsteady and slow. "Talk, *cara mia*."

Raina sat on the side of the bed and took Nonna's gnarled hand in hers. "How are you?" she asked.

"Me? Eh." She flipped her hand. "Old and dying. The question is, how are you? How are my babies?"

Raina smiled and squeezed her hand. "Moving, growing and making my feet swell. But they are each about seven inches long right now, and one of them craves all the healthy food and the other would be perfectly happy if I ate nothing but ice cream."

She groaned but it sounded like joy, not pain. "Let me feel."

Raina glanced at Chase, who lifted a shoulder as if to say, "If you don't mind." She didn't.

Taking Nonna's hand, she laid it on her baby bump just like she did when Alyson or Avery wanted to "feel the babies move."

"Oh, you're healthy," Nonna said.

"I'm eating well." She leaned and added, "Your son is quite the cook, you know."

"Ahh!" Her face almost lit up. "What did he make for you?"

"Pasta...Norma?"

Her old eyes shuttered. "Eh. Mine is better."

That made Raina laugh. "Then it must be amazing."

She sighed, looking tired but refusing to move her hand from Raina's belly. "The garlic is good for the babies," she finally said. "And oil. Lots of oil."

"I'll remember that," Raina said, putting her hand over Nonna's. "You scared us today."

She just sighed. "It's almost my time."

"No, no," Raina said. "You need to...stay healthy. Like me."

With a soft grunt, she tried to push up, and instantly Chase came closer.

"What do you need, Nonna?"

"When..." She struggled to breathe and fell back. "When you marry?"

Raina drew back at the question, her eyes wide as she looked up at Chase. Nonna thought they were getting married? How far did he want to take this pretense?

Silent, he gave a tight smile.

Far.

"Soon?" Nonna pressed. "Before..." She pushed lightly on Raina's stomach. "Before Charles is born."

Chase stayed very still, a visible battle playing out in his expression. He was torn...between his love for one woman and his respect for another. For some reason, that touched her just like Nonna's sweet heart.

All Chase wanted to do was make people happy,

Raina realized with a start. Cook for them, sell them their dream house, pay for their kid's hospital bill, send them off to heaven happy.

He really *was* made of goodness.

"When?" Nonna demanded, the light dimming in her eyes with each passing second.

Chase sighed. "Um, Nonna, we're not—"

"November eleventh," Raina whispered, cutting him off.

"Oh!" Nonna's eyes widened. "When is that? I don't know what day it is."

"Less than a month," Raina said, letting out a breath before she dared to glance at Chase. But when she did, the look in his eyes nearly knocked her off the bed. Gratitude. Affection. Awe. Pure, pure...admiration.

This whole charade might be worth the lie just for him to look at her like that.

"The eleventh of November." Nonna let the words roll around like she was testing them out. "Carlo," she said, lifting a knotted finger toward him. "Get the limoncello."

"Excuse me?" he asked on a laugh.

"In the freezer. The bottle you made. We drink. Three glasses. We toast the wedding."

"That's so sweet," Raina said. "But I can't drink anything alco—"

"*Sì! Sì!*" She flipped her hand in the air like she was swiping a fly away. "The limoncello is good for the babies. One sip. One toast. We drink to your happiness because..." She gave a sad smile. "I won't be here."

"Nonsense," Raina said. "You will and..."

"I won't," Nonna insisted. "Limoncello. *Adesso!*"

Chase lifted a dubious brow. "She wants it now."

"Okay. If that makes her happy, I'll have a sip."

He looked at Raina for a beat, and even though she couldn't quite interpret the message in his gaze, something sent a shiver up her spine and a splash of warmth in her chest.

"Thanks," he whispered, then smiled at Nonna. "Limoncello it is."

When he left, the old woman exhaled noisily. "That Carlo," she said on a moan. "He's just like my Carlo."

"Your husband sounds like a wonderful man."

"Like your husband." Nonna gave a toothless chuckle.

But Raina clenched her teeth, refusing to respond. Not only would Chase never be her husband, the one she had—legally, at the moment—was anything but wonderful.

"Such a kind man, so caring and true," Nonna murmured.

Raina didn't know if she meant her own late husband or her grandson, but it didn't matter. Chase was all those things, and she imagined the older Carlo had been, too.

"He deserves a good woman," she said, giving Raina's hand a squeeze and taking away any doubt over which Carlo she was talking about. "I have prayed for you, Raina."

"Thank you," she said softly. "I really appreciate your prayers."

"Prayed he would find you," she continued. "He has been unlucky in love. Too young the first, too..." She rolled her eyes. "Not so nice, the second."

Raina smiled. "He told me."

"But you...just right."

"Like Goldilocks," she said, trying for lightness even though a lump was forming in her throat.

"You have a true...*anime*." She frowned, shaking her head. "I do not know the word."

"*Anime*? Like..." Raina was at a loss. "I'm sorry, I don't know."

"The spirit. The soul." She lifted her hand and pressed it to Raina's chest. "It matches my Carlo. You belong together. I know."

For a few seconds, she looked into Nonna's foggy eyes and tried to remember this dear old lady had no idea what she was talking about. She didn't know they were lying, but still, the words reached in and grabbed her heart.

"You belong together," Nonna repeated. "Never question that. My Carlo, he told me when he died and went to heaven, he would find you for our grandson." She nodded a few times, staring at Raina. "He did. He found you. He brought you here from..."

"Miami," she whispered when Nonna didn't finish.

"He brought you to Carlo," she said. "And now, you marry, you have babies, and Carlo and I will dance in heaven when we are together again."

Raina felt her eyes shutter, at a loss for how to respond to that. Whatever she said, it would only be one more lie, so she simply stayed quiet while Nonna closed her eyes and smiled.

"All right, Nonna." Chase came into the room carrying a tray with a large glass bottle with a few inches of yellow liquid in the bottom. "Limoncello and three glasses."

"We toast." She tried to sit up, but started coughing.

"A tiny sip for you," Chase said, setting the tray on the nightstand and putting his arm around Nonna. "Just a drop on your tongue or we'll have the ambulance back here."

"Mmm." She let herself be pushed up.

"Can you pour?" Chase asked Raina as he arranged pillows behind Nonna so she was sitting.

"Of course." She stood and opened the bottle, drizzling less than a teaspoon into each of the three ornate red glasses she assumed were from Italy. She handed two to Chase and held the other one. "We'll toast in Italian?" she asked.

"Nonna, you toast," he said. "I'll hold yours for you."

Nonna lifted a trembling hand and touched the glass with one finger on the rim, as if blessing it. "Raina and Carlo," she whispered. "*Per sempre.*"

Raina had no idea what that meant, but she tapped her glass to the other two. "*Per sempre,*" she repeated.

Chase just smiled and held one glass to Nonna's lips for a sip while Raina took one of her own, barely letting the icy cold liquid touch her tongue. Even with the minuscule amount, she could taste the tangy, sweet, lemony flavor that she imagined packed a punch if she had any real quantity.

After the two women sipped, Chase lifted the glass to his lips and held Raina's gaze, his dark eyes penetrating her...what had Nonna called it? *Anime*. Her soul.

Without a word, he knocked his back, then closed his eyes.

"Now we have toasted your marriage," Nonna said on another deep sigh. "I sleep and dream of Carlo, who is smiling down from heaven."

Raina leaned over and kissed the silky white hair on top of Nonna's head. "Sweet, sweet dreams, Nonna," she whispered.

The old lady smiled and mumbled something in Italian, letting Chase remove a pillow and make her comfortable.

"I'll take this back to the kitchen," Raina said, giving them a moment alone as she picked up the tray.

There, she found Paul sitting at the table, working on a crossword puzzle. He looked up and lifted a brow at the limoncello.

"For the record," he said, "I did *not* see booze go out of this kitchen and into my patient's room."

She laughed. "For the record, she barely sniffed it. Me, too."

"How far along are you?" he asked as he pushed his chair back from the table and stood.

"A little more than halfway," she said. "The babies are due the last day of January."

He crossed his arms, regarding her intently for a

moment. "Chase told me about your, uh, little white lie to Nonna."

She felt her cheeks warm as she faced the counter to put the tray down. "It's not so little or white," she said, feeling guilty. "And now she thinks we're getting married in November."

"Really? What a great gift to her."

She turned from the counter to look at him. "You think?"

"I'm her private nurse," he said. "I *know*. She isn't long for this world, and you have made her final days incredibly happy."

She sighed as tears threatened behind her lids. "I'm glad I could ease her pain in any way I could."

"You have. So, every time you feel guilty for lying to a little old lady, remember me telling you it was the best medicine you could have given her."

"Thank you, Paul. I appreciate that."

Chase came in then, and gave a rather sheepish smile. "It seems we get in a little deeper every time you come over here, Raina."

"I know," she agreed, glancing at Paul. "But it's okay."

"More than okay," Chase agreed. "She's a different woman than the one the EMTs treated two hours ago. In fact, I'm going to head back to the hotel and get some paperwork I'll work on here. Paul, would that be okay? I'll be back quickly."

"I'm not going anywhere," the nurse promised.

"Raina, do you want me to call the new event manager? You can meet her right now."

The truth was, all she wanted was to recover from the gut punch of the last few minutes. "Can we reschedule?" she asked.

"Absolutely. I'll walk you out."

After she said goodbye to Paul, she followed Chase to the door, but he walked with her down the driveway to her car, both of them silent.

"A mere 'thank you' doesn't seem adequate," he finally said. "But I really do want you to know how much I appreciate this."

"It's not a problem," she assured him. "Paul just absolved me from my sins, convincing me we're administering medicine."

"We are," he agreed. "And I won't be home tonight." Glancing over his shoulder, he gazed in the direction of the ranch house. "The EMTs confirmed what we already knew. It won't be long now. I'm just going to crash here until..." He swallowed. "I want to be with her at the end."

"Oh, Chase." Without thinking, she reached for him and they hugged, trembling as they shared an emotional embrace. "She's such a dear. I'm sorry you have to say goodbye."

He gave another squeeze and eased back, his dark eyes misty as he gazed at her. "You really helped, Raina. More than you'll ever know. You made the transition from this life to the next so much better for her."

That lump formed again and she just nodded, unable to talk.

He gave her another quick hug, then reached for the

car door to open it for her. She slipped by him, then into the car.

"Don't worry about the event, or about the meeting," she said, looking up at him. "I can get over there on my own and sit down with your new manager, and we are really rolling along on the planning. You've done everything possible to get the hotel ready, and I don't want anything to pull you away from Nonna."

With one hand on the door, he looked down at her, suddenly so big and masculine and close it was a little daunting.

"Thanks, Raina. If it's not running smoothly, I can crack the whip from here and I have lots of great people onsite," he told her. "We'll talk soon."

"Okay." She nodded and just as he was about to close the door, she held up her hand to stop him. "What did we toast to, by the way? *Per sempre?*"

"Forever," he whispered.

As her jaw loosened, he just smiled and closed the door. She sat in the car long after he disappeared into the house, the single word echoing in her head.

Forever.

Chapter Eighteen

Rose

"Mommy, I'm scared."

Rose looked into the rearview mirror and pinned her gaze on Alyson's sweet face. "You don't have to be, baby girl."

"But I've never been called to the principal's office before. I'm not a bad kid."

"You most certainly are not," Rose agreed. "And you haven't been called in for anything but a chance to say exactly what you saw the day Josh broke his arm."

Alyson sighed and looked out the window as Rose pulled into the school lot for the second time that day. She'd dropped off Avery earlier, and had driven Ethan to middle school.

But she'd gotten a call from Mr. Holland at Franklin Elementary last night, informing her that Josh Pinkerton's father, Jeremiah, had asked for a meeting regarding the playground accident. Raina had told Rose that the man's insurance hadn't covered much, and he was seeking a way to pay back his debts for the hospital costs. Alyson's account of the incident did truly place blame on the school—or the equipment—so she was asked to relay her memory of it.

That was stressful for a child, but Rose would be there with her. If Gabe were here, he'd be holding Aly's other hand during the whole thing.

As if on cue, the dashboard lit with a call from him just as she parked.

"It's Daddy!" Alyson exclaimed, reading the name. "He told me last night when we did prayers that he'd call."

Smiling at that, Rose tapped the button on her steering wheel.

"Am I too late?" Gabe asked before either one of them said hello.

"Not at all," Rose assured him. "Aly and I are just getting here and we have ten minutes before our appointment."

"Are you still feeling nervous, Aly-bear?" he asked, his strong voice an immediate comfort as it filled the car.

"No," she said, although she underscored that with a look that said the opposite. "Mommy said the same thing you did. Just that I tell the truth. But I'm scared I'm going to get Miss Sherman in trouble and I love her."

"You won't get anyone in trouble," Gabe said. "But you might help Josh's family and save another kid from having the same accident. You know what you saw."

"I do, Daddy," she said. "The teachers replaced the bar and then closed the whole thing, and no one pushed Josh. He wasn't being crazy, either, just climbing."

Gabe gave her a little more of a pep talk and told a

few bad Dad jokes that made her giggle, then he lowered his voice and asked, "And how's my favorite florist?"

Rose knew that was a cue to take him off speaker and pick up her phone for one precious moment of semi-privacy.

She did, pushing back her hair and pressing the phone to her ear, wishing with everything she had that it was Gabe in the flesh and not just his voice over the airwaves.

"I'm good," she told him. "Guess who drove himself to school in my father's car today?"

"Oh, I know. I told Zach to text me the minute he pulled into the lot. First day driving himself to school and he's got Rex's expensive sedan."

Rose chuckled. "The first thing he wanted to do when he passed the test was drive to the beach house and show my father his license. I had no idea Dad would turn around and hand him keys to his car!"

"Oh, I did."

She inched back at Gabe's comment. "You did?"

"I was talking with Rex a while back and we were brainstorming ways to make your life easier and he suggested Zach use his car for a while. Rex isn't cleared to drive and, God knows, we're not in a position to buy the kid a car. A second driver can only help your schedule."

"Oh, Gabe." She put her hand to her chest, touched that her father and husband were colluding to make her life easier—and Zach's better. "I didn't know that."

"I'm sorry to keep you in the dark, but Rex and I

agreed that you might get too worried about Zach driving the car."

"A little worried," she acknowledged. "But he's a great driver and isn't allowed to leave Amelia Island with any kids in the car, so it *is* a huge help. In fact, he's picking them up from school today because there's no soccer practice. I have a bride who insisted on a three o'clock final pass meeting for her wedding on Saturday. I'm dreading it, too, because she's demanding. I can't walk out in the middle of that to pick up kids."

"Zach driving *is* a huge help to you," Gabe said. "Not quite what it would be if I were there, but..." His voice softened with a note of sadness.

"Hey, hey," she said softly. "What's wrong, Gabe?"

"Nothing. Everything. I'm currently buried in second-guessing, constant worry, and feeling...far. I miss you, babe."

"I miss you, too."

"I'm having a rough go, Rosie."

Her heart hitched at the painful note in his voice. "School's hard?"

"No. Life's hard. I feel really...distant."

She swallowed, knowing exactly how that felt. "I get it, honey."

"I know you have that wedding on Saturday and it's a big one, Rose, but how would you like a little company this weekend?"

She gasped as her heart leaped. "Yes!"

"Okay, don't say a word to Aly or the other kids. I want to surprise everyone. I have a lab Friday night, so I'll leave really early Saturday morning and will be there for lunch."

"I might not be home yet. This is a massive wedding and..." She rolled her eyes. "Tulips."

"That's okay. I'll surprise the kids and then we'll all come to the shop, help you get done early, and spend every minute together until Monday morning."

She let her eyes close on a sigh. "Heaven."

"It will be," Gabe promised. "I love you, babe. And I miss the living daylights out of you."

"Same, my darling."

"Mommy!" Alyson jabbed her shoulder. "I just saw Josh Pinkerton walk in with his dad."

"Then we better go. Love you, Gabe." She touched the speaker button. "Wish your little girl good luck."

"You don't need luck, Aly-bear. You just tell the truth, the whole truth, and nothing but the truth."

She giggled at the phrase. "Okay, Daddy. I love you!"

"I love you more," he said, the slightest crack in his voice giving away his real emotion.

After they hung up, Rose gathered her bag and took Alyson's hand as they walked to Mr. Holland's office.

All she could think about was the fact that Gabe was coming home and she needed to see him, hold him, kiss him, and love him.

But in the meantime, she had to do this whole thing alone and some days, like today, it was very, very hard.

∾

"I HEAR YOU HUMMING, Rosebud. That means you're happy."

"Raindrop!" Rose turned from the massive autumn bouquet she was making for the next delivery, one hand on the stem of a Morgana Red chrysanthemum, the other extended in greeting when her sister slipped in the back door. "This is a nice surprise."

"I turned in here when my entire body ached to go to the ice cream parlor, but I've reached my Rocky Road allotment for the week. That store can't close soon enough for my body."

"January first, but do you have a replacement for Silas?"

"Not yet." Raina dropped a kiss on Rose's head and gestured toward the nearly finished bouquet. "Glorious, girl. Wow, you have a talent. How is that possible? I can't put a daisy in a cup and you make otherworldly creations."

Rose laughed off the compliment. "I'm particularly happy today."

"That's what I like to hear." Raina eased into one of the other chairs at the design table, glancing at the sketches and the row of five different types of vases lined up. "And what's all this?"

"Difficult bride coming in at three. And wait until I tell you about Alyson!"

"That's why I'm here, but full disclosure," Raina said, holding up a hand. "I saw Jeremiah at Ocean Song—things are going swimmingly for the big party, by the way

—and that is a very, very happy man. He said Alyson was an absolute rock star."

"She was," Rose replied with a laugh. "She should grow up to be an expert witness—or an attorney. When the principal asked her if she had her glasses on that day, she not only could prove she had them on, she emphasized the fact that they were brand-new with an upgraded prescription that she got on September first at 10:15 a.m."

Raina snorted. "That's...specific."

"Exactly what the principal said, but she told him that Mommy and Daddy promised her contact lenses one year after getting these glasses and she had it marked on her little calendar with the time so that she can get her contacts that day next year."

Raina whimpered. "That angel. I love her."

"She's a lot like you."

"And Madeline," Raina joked. "Trust me, she'll be at the eye doctor at 9:14 that morning. You can put it on your calendar in ink right now."

"I will, because there's nothing she wants more than contacts."

"So get the girl her contacts, for heaven's sake." She picked up a flower stem and playfully jabbed Rose's arm with it. "She just got thousands of dollars for the Pinkerton family."

Rose inched back, her jaw loose. "She did? They settled?"

"Get this," Raina said, leaning closer. "After the meeting, the principal went with Jeremiah to the playground, examined the equipment, pulled out some paper-work, and discovered that it had been fixed by a custodian since Josh's accident."

"Really? Then the school is liable. And the teachers shouldn't have covered it up."

"Well, they immediately closed the monkey bars for all use and reported the accident. But"—Raina waved the stem—"Jeremiah said he won't sue and the principal is trying to arrange for the school district to cover all expenses. Now all Jeremiah has to do is get Chase to accept the payment to cover his anonymous donation."

"The man is a saint, Raina."

"Oh, yeah, except for the lies he's telling his poor old nonna." She rolled her eyes. "And I'll be with him down in the depths of hell because I told her we're getting married on November 11th."

Rose nearly choked. "Why did you do that?"

"She's so sweet and old and sick and it made her happy. Made Chase happy, too. Apparently, he likes it when I lie."

"The man has a good heart, Raina."

"Yep." After a beat of Rose staring at her, Raina lifted a brow. "So?"

"So...it's nice to find a man with a good heart. Mine's coming home this weekend."

Raina's whole face lit up. "How wonderful for you."

"He's surprising the kids, so don't say anything, and don't change the subject, which was Chase—good-hearted, good-cooking, and good...looking."

"Let it go, Rosebud," Raina said with an eyeroll. "You

know where I stand on men. I've picked up Chloe's man hiatus and shall carry on that strange family tradition until the day I die."

Rose stuck her lower lip out. "That's sad."

"Rose?" Lizzie poked her head into the back room. "Oh, hey, Raina. Uh, Melissa Havensworth is here and she brought her mother, two bridesmaids, and husband-to-be. They're getting some things from the car for you to incorporate into the arrangements and will be in here in five minutes. You better make room for a lot of people."

"And opinions," Rose said dryly. "Thanks, Lizzie."

"Sounds like trouble," Raina said. "I'm going back to—"

The back door popped open and suddenly the room was filled with all four D'Angelo kids, led by Zach, who swung a ring of car keys on his finger like a gunslinger.

"Family delivery, safe and sound," he announced.

"Mommy, Miss Sherman isn't mad at me!" Alyson exclaimed, running around the table to Rose. "She said I had in...in..." She glanced at Ethan.

"Integrity," her brother supplied.

"Yes, that! Will Daddy like that?"

Rose hugged her and showered kisses on her head. "He will love it as much as I do."

Avery pulled on Raina's arm. "Can I feel the babies, Aunt Raina?"

"Yes, but..." Raina got up, snapping her fingers. "Who wants ice cream?" As the chorus of happy responses exploded, Raina pointed that stem at Rose again. "I know, I know. I said the ice cream allotment was reached. But you are about to have a head-on collision with Bridezilla and company, so I'm treating."

"Thank you, sweet sister of mine."

"And then can I feel the babies?" Avery asked.

"You'll feel them do the Rocky Road dance," she teased.

"Rocky?" Avery danced on her tiptoes. "Like Aunt Chloe's dog who they took away."

"They didn't take him away," Rose corrected. "His owner came and got him."

"I miss him," Avery whined. "He was a cute dog. I want a dog. Mommy, can I—"

"Come on, kiddo." Raina grabbed her hand and waved for Alyson to take the other. "Let's soothe your soul with something chocolate and delicious. Ethan? Zach? Let's get to the ice cream parlor before I rent it out to someone who sells...not ice cream."

"Not me," Zach said. "I have to empty off that loading dock for Mom."

Raina tilted her head and sighed. "Speaking of saints, Zachary D'Angelo. You are one in a million. We'll bring you a cone when we're done. Mint chocolate chip, right?"

"You know me too well, Aunt Raina."

"Thank you, and have fun!" Rose called, blowing kisses, filled with so much love she could barely contain it.

The glow faded over the next hour, however, as Melissa changed her mind more times than Rose could count, bickered with her mother, mocked her bridesmaids, and essentially ignored her fiancé, who spent the time looking at his phone.

"Okay," Rose said after all the decisions had been made for the ceremony, sweetheart table, reception décor, and exactly how many petals would line the aisle. "There is a slight—ever so slight—possibility that the tulips, which are being shipped from another country, will not arrive on Saturday morning. They are scheduled to, but I strongly recommend a backup flower. If you take a look at this—"

"Don't even show it to me." Melissa flipped back a long blond braid. "My mother carried tulips—"

"I did," Mrs. Havensworth confirmed.

"In June," Rose reminded her, already having had this conversation on their first call.

"And my grandmother carried them," Melissa continued, ignoring her. "So did my two aunts and my little sister will. It's not negotiable. And you promised them."

Actually, she hadn't. Rose would never make a promise to a client she couldn't be sure she could keep. But this wasn't the time to argue with Melissa.

"I have done everything in my power," she said. "They are scheduled to be shipped, arriving at the nearest port early Saturday morning, and I will start the bouquets and table arrangements the minute I have them."

"And boutonnieres," Mrs. Havensworth reminded her. "Plus, my corsage and one for your mother, Jason."

He looked up from his phone. "Oh, yeah, sure. She'd love that."

"Any color is fine," Melissa said, as if that were a concession.

"Actually, any color isn't fine," Rose replied. "If they aren't pink, we'll have a problem."

Melissa lifted her shoulder. "The fact that they are tulips means everything to me."

"And if they're not?" Rose inched the laptop with a screen full of gorgeous fall flowers. "Maybe you should pick your backup."

"If they're not tulips, I don't want any flowers." With that, she stood and waved for her posse to join her. "See you at the venue on Saturday!"

Rose fell down into her seat with a huff when they left and almost immediately Zach popped out of the walk-in cooler.

"My heart breaks for that dude," he said on a laugh.

Rose smiled. "Brides can get...bridey."

"She wants her tulips."

"So bad," Rose agreed. "You made that call, right? You got them to change the port?"

"I did, I promise."

She gave him a smile, itching to tell him that his father would be home in just a few days. But she'd made a promise, too, and although she might not be home when Gabe walked in, she got a little shiver of anticipation over how happy they'd be to see him.

And once she got this wedding behind her, the rest of the weekend would be nothing but joyous.

"Thanks for working today, Zach," she said, standing

to put her arms around him. "You get the kid of the year award."

He just laughed and gave her head a kiss, reminding her so much of Gabe that her heart simply folded in half.

The only bad part about him coming home would be saying goodbye again—but she'd face that when she had to.

Chapter Nineteen

Chloe

I t was time to make the call.

Chloe stared at her phone, knowing that Gil Huxley had probably just arrived at his office this morning and was waiting for a response to the offer letter he'd sent the night before. Now was the moment to pick up her phone, call her new boss, and accept her new job.

Instead, she leaned against the fence that Travis had installed in the bungalow's yard and watched Lady Bug roll around, a sad slowness to her usual prancing paws.

"I know, I know," Chloe called. "I miss him, too."

Lady Bug dropped to the ground with a sigh, but almost immediately jumped up and barked, trotting to the other side of the fenced-in area. In a second, Chloe could see who had her attention—and probably a treat.

"Hey, Daddio," she called to her father, who was slowly making his way from the beach house to the bungalow, the cane he really didn't need offering support he didn't want. But if he'd left it at home, her mother would march over here in seconds.

"Good morning, Daughter Number Seven!"

She met him as he arrived, giving him a hug. "To what do I owe this honor?" she asked. "Is rent due?"

He chuckled. "Yes. Pay in coffee with a lot of cream and since Suze isn't here, give your old man some sugar. I'm feeling so dang housebound, I just had to come over and see you."

"Wonderful!" she exclaimed. "Where's Mom?"

"Having breakfast with the historical society ladies and I was lonely. What are you doing this morning?"

"Ah, the thing I do best: avoiding a commitment. Do you think I'm a commitment-phobe? Wait. Don't answer that, Dad. You are the man who walked the runaway bride down the aisle and watched her take off seconds later." She gestured to the two canvas chairs under an awning. "Have a seat and I'll bring you coffee with the secret works. I need to pluck advice from your brain."

He tapped his head. "The one that stroked out six months ago?"

"The one that is still the wisest in the world."

A few minutes later, they were settled next to each other, coffees in hand. Chloe read the entire offer letter to her father, who sipped his sweet, creamy coffee and gave every word careful consideration.

She didn't say so, but while he gathered his thoughts, Chloe looked to the puffy clouds hanging over the horizon, grateful she still had this amazing father to guide her through life. Not for the first time, she mentally praised the medical professionals, including her sister's main squeeze, for saving his life.

"Well, you may hate commitments, or think you do,

but they want to make one," he finally said. "It's clear they want you—and I mean *you*, not just anyone—in that job."

She nodded in agreement. "The irony is that at my 'dream job' in L.A.? All they did was remind me how expendable I was. It's nice to feel wanted."

"And the salary isn't awful."

She shrugged. "The work, though? Doing PR for an investment department?" She made a face, then added a fake smile. "Can I count on you for your support, Mr. Wingate?"

Chuckling, he took another sip. "Have you given up the dream of being a reporter for sure and certain, Chloe?"

"Yes. That job wrecked me and I just don't think the journalism field I learned about in the halls of higher learning is anything like real-life reporting. The industry has changed and there are scores of 'citizen journalists' who have their own Twitter and YouTube channels, but..." She wrinkled her nose. "The days of Barbara Walters are gone, and I think I'm going to tuck that dream into the memory box of my girlhood."

She kind of expected him to argue, and remind her of just how enthusiastically she ran a pretend news desk in the den as a kid, but he merely nodded. "On to the next dream, young lady."

"If only I had one." Sighing, she reached down to pluck a blade of grass caught in Lady Bug's coat. "You know I'm lost, Dad. I don't have a dream or purpose or anything I'm really looking forward to, and that scares me."

"Maybe dreams and purposes are overrated. Maybe you should just do something you're good at that gives you...bliss. There's not enough bliss in this world, I say."

She turned to him, blinking. "Are you telling me to turn down this job at Lighthouse Bank?"

"Are you good at it? Never mind," he said quickly. "You're so bright, you'd be good at anything you set your mind to. That's why Gil Huxley is throwing a decent salary and two weeks' vacation at you."

She stifled a groan. "Two weeks won't be enough. I'll dream of escaping the minute I sit at my desk every morning."

"Chloe." He put a hand on her arm. "If you hate the idea so much, you shouldn't take it."

"But am I just being super picky and dumb? I could finally get my own apartment and leave this place for guests, like it was meant for."

"You are our guest. Plus, we have the third floor of the house. I don't really want you to leave," he said with a soft laugh. "And Lady Bug?" He lifted his mug toward the little dog, who was scratching at the pen gate. "Wants to go into this nice little place we built her."

Just as she got up to open the gate for Lady Bug, Chloe heard the crunch of tires on the gravel, and sucked in a soft breath of surprise when she saw Travis's truck pulling in.

"Not expecting your man?" Dad asked.

"He finished a shift but had an all-hands meeting at ten, so, no. Maybe the meeting got rescheduled."

"I can leave so you two can take your morning walk."

"Don't you dare." She stood to go greet Travis and put her hand on her father's shoulder. "I love these moments with you, Dad. And no man is going to get in the middle of them."

He looked up and beamed at her. "One will, eventually. Maybe even that one. But I do love you, Chloe."

Smiling and holding that happy thought, she headed to the truck, wondering why Travis hadn't leaped out yet, as he normally did, to give her a thrill just to see him in his khakis and Fernandina Beach Fire Department T-shirt.

He was another reason she should take the job at Lighthouse Bank. She'd promised him that as soon as she was settled and employed and had her life on track, their relationship could be serious and official.

"Hey," he called from the driver's seat, the door open and only one leg out. "Brace yourself."

She slowed her step and glanced over her shoulder at Dad, who was watching from his chair. "What for?"

"Incoming." He finally climbed out and instantly closed the door, like he was trapping someone or something inside.

Frowning, she walked closer. "What's going on?"

"You can say no," he said quickly, looking strangely... serious. "I mean, feel free and I'll figure something out. But I don't think you will, so...Chloe. How would you like..."

Her heart stopped for a second. What was going on right now?

"To be the proud owner of..." He yanked the door open and a large tan dog the size of a small horse bounded out. "This lady right here?"

"Oh, my goodness!" She pressed her hands to her face, stunned as she watched the sizeable dog lope around, stopping to sniff and then crouching to relieve herself. "She's...huge."

"She was basically thrown out of a car in front of the station."

"No!"

"I hate people sometimes," he admitted. "She's a doll, though. Very docile."

"And...huge," she repeated on a laugh, vaguely aware of Lady Bug barking her fool head off from inside the pen.

"Well, she's, uh, in the family way."

"She's pregnant?" Gasping, Chloe took a few steps to the dog, who came closer, moving so slow she thought the poor dog might give birth any minute. "Hey, beautiful."

They met each other halfway, and Chloe didn't even need to bend down to stroke her big head and look into eyes that tilted up with the classic angle of a pitbull, reminding her of Rocky. Her whole body was the color of peanut butter except for a white snout and jade green eyes.

Instantly, the dog dropped to the ground, one paw stretched out, then she turned, announcing a submissive nature.

"Oh, baby girl!" Chloe carefully reached for her distended belly. "You look more pregnant than Raina."

"And probably has more babies in there."

"Travis!" She folded to the ground next to the dog.

"I know, I know. I just thought..."

"Who do we have here?" Dad ambled closer with a chuckle in his voice.

"Does she have a name?" Chloe asked Travis.

"No collar, no name. My guess is she's been used to breed and for whatever reason, they don't want this litter. I heard the sheriff is cracking down on some nasty puppy mills and scared owners might be vacating in a hurry."

With a groan of pity, Chloe reached down and wrapped her arms around the dog's muscular neck. "She smells clean."

"I hosed her down. Captain said the local shelters are full right now, which is probably why she was left at the station. Thank God they didn't just dump her in the woods."

"Oh!" Unwilling to let go of the dog, who seemed to love the affection, Chloe looked up at him. "You think I should take her...and her litter?"

"I think if someone took her to the shelter, they might keep the puppies, but..." He didn't finish, but made a disgusted face.

"You keep her," Dad said. "If that would make you happy."

Her heart pressed against her chest as it swelled with love for him. "Thank you, Dad, but it might be too much even for our new pen and the tiny bungalow. And when she has a litter? I'm not equipped, but oh, I wish I could keep you, Buttercup!"

The dog lifted her head and gave a swipe to Chloe's hand with her tongue.

Travis laughed. "She likes that name. Don't keep changing it."

"Nailed it on the first try, did I?" Chloe hugged her again, her whole body aching for the dog, who clearly craved love and attention. "Buttercup it is. But...I can't..."

"You might take her to a vet and find out how many are in there," Travis suggested. "Or just keep her for today. I have to get back to the station for the all-hands meeting, but I knew if I didn't get her, someone would deliver her to the shelter and..."

"And that would not be good for you, Buttercup." Chloe kissed the dog's big head, then looked up at Travis. "Can you grab Lady Bug? I want to introduce them."

He lifted a brow in question. "You think that's a good idea?"

No, it probably wasn't. Then she *and* Bugaboo would get attached to this sweet girl. "Yes."

As Travis walked to the pen, she looked up at her dad. "What should I do?"

"First, take care of the dog. Do you want to take her to your vet? Someone who could give you some advice and help? Maybe know how to place the dogs?"

She snapped her finger and pointed at him. "Rocky."

"He's gone," Dad reminded her.

"Rocky Zotter. She can at least give me some guidance, even if she's not taking any more dogs. She might know another safe no-kill shelter. I'll take this girl over there right now."

"Can I come with you?" Dad asked.

Chloe felt her face light up. "Of course!"

Just then, Lady Bug came bounding closer, her tail flipping, far more at ease with this dog than she'd been with Rocky. She gave one loud bark in Buttercup's face, then rounded the big dog, and snuggled in to smell her.

"You can come, too," Chloe said to Lady Bug as she stood, looking at Travis. "Thanks for the reprieve," she said.

"From what?"

"From calling Gil Huxley. I got the offer letter and I owe him an answer." She looked down at Buttercup, who was busy taking a sniff of Lady Bug. "But I need to take care of business first."

"Business, eh?" Dad said with a pointed look. "Now I see bliss on your face."

Travis's brows shot up. "And here I thought that bliss was for me."

She just laughed at them and went to get a leash for Buttercup.

As they drove to Rocky Zotter's house, Dad seemed to come alive. Maybe it was his bone-deep interest in the local real estate, or maybe it was the super sweet connection forming between Buttercup and Lady Bug in the backseat, or maybe the man simply needed to get out more.

Chloe wasn't sure, but she was happy he was with her.

"She's selling this?" Dad said as they pulled up to the property, greeted by the weathered sign and the flying squirrel logo for Rocky's Rescues.

Next to her, she felt him sit up straight and look around with a soft whistle. "Gotta be two acres, at least," he said. "I didn't know it was for sale."

She smiled at him. "You haven't been working, but I think the lady who owns it did a private listing. Is that what you call it? She sold to a neighbor."

"Pocket listing and whoever bought it made a smart investment."

"I guess." But the value of the land didn't interest Chloe as much as the few dogs she saw in the pen out front as she pulled into the long driveway. "I doubt she'll take a pregnant pittie, but maybe she can help me." As she parked, she let out a sigh that felt like it came from deep, deep inside. "I love this place," she whispered, not even realizing she'd spoken.

"What do you love about it?" Dad asked, sounding very...real estate-y.

Chloe took a long look around, taking in the towering pine trees and big lot. "I like the vibe. I like being here. And look at that pen with dogs! Who wouldn't like that?"

Although there were only three dogs today, so Rocky must be working her rescue magic and had found the others homes.

"It's a terrific location," Dad said. "Far enough out to feel country, but you're not five minutes from the beach and ten from town."

She understood that he saw property in terms of value, but she saw it differently. "True, but I like the purpose of the place, the way it's situated so the dogs get light but still can have shade, and the..." She narrowed her eyes, trying to come up with a word. "The earthiness of it. I know, I know. Not an earthy hippie girl, but... Oh, Dad. What a place to raise and rescue dogs, huh?"

She glanced at him, expecting him to have his phone calculator out, clicking up dollars-per-square-foot. But he was staring at her with a strange look on his face—the same expression Travis wore.

Like they knew something about her she didn't.

"What?" she asked.

"Nothing," he said.

"You don't look like nothing, Dad."

His lips lifted into a smile. "Ask Raina about what she calls 'home vibes.' She'll explain them to you."

Chloe gave a shrug, too concerned about the new dog to worry about Dad's real estate musings. "Okay. Well, for now, let's go see if Rocky's here."

Chloe came around and helped him out, then opened the back to let sweet Buttercup galumph her way to the ground. Good heavens, she could give birth any minute! Lady Bug leaped out, too, and all of them set off toward the house.

Buttercup stayed right next to Chloe, but Lady Bug darted over to the pen, barking at the other dogs, who looked at her like she was a fluffy, annoying gnat. *They weren't wrong*, Chloe thought.

Before they reached the door, it opened, and Chloe instantly recognized the silver-blond hair and happy blue eyes of the woman she'd met here with Travis.

"Rocky? I don't know if you remember—"

"Chloe," she said, reaching out a hand and glancing at Buttercup. "But you have a different furry friend." She added a smile at Dad. "And a different man."

Chloe laughed. "I did find Rocky's owner— Oh, I named him after you. This is Buttercup, and this is Rex Wingate, my father."

Her brows shot up. "Wingate like Wingate Properties? I almost called you to sell this place."

"You would have gotten my daughter, Raina," he said, extending his right hand. "She's running the business for me now. Hello, I'm Rex. Have you sold yet?"

She laughed. "Are you really here to solicit my business?"

"No!" Chloe said, shooting him a look. "Dad! I thought you wanted to give me moral support."

He lifted a shoulder. "I'm still a real estate man."

"How can I help you, Chloe?" Rocky asked.

"My friend, Travis, brought this lady home from the fire station, where she was abandoned."

Instantly, Rocky seemed to forget they were there, her laser focus shifting to Buttercup.

"Well, hello, dolly," she said, breezing by them to crouch down in front of the dog. "You're a sweet lady.

From one of the hellish puppy mills, I'm guessing by the size of this belly."

Rocky put both hands on Buttercup's stomach, then glided her hands up to cup the dog's face with ease and grace and expertise, holding her steady to exchange eye contact. "Baby, you've seen some rough times, haven't you?"

Chloe whimpered and put her hand to her lips. "Is she okay?"

"She will be after she unloads this litter. My guess is that'll happen in the next week or so." She stood and looked out at Lady Bug, who was still at the fence trying to get attention. "And there's the little white bird."

Chloe laughed at the apt description, but her smile faded as she looked down at the pregnant pup.

"In the next week? Really? I don't think I can handle them, or maybe even her. I know you're not taking rescues now, but do you have any suggestions for me that isn't the dreadful county shelter? I'm worried she won't survive that."

She huffed out a noisy breath. "I gotta think about that one. I might. Let me look in my Rolodex for some phone numbers—and don't make fun of me, I still use one of those. Sixty-five and proud of it."

Dad laughed. "I loved my Rolodex."

"You want to come in?" Rocky said, opening the door wider.

"Sure." Chloe turned and called Lady Bug, who finally gave up and ran to the door. "All of us?" she asked Rocky.

"Well, the big one's not leaving your side and the little one isn't going to threaten any of my cats. Come on in."

Inside, Chloe glanced around the small home, which was little more than a living room on one side, a dining room with no table but plenty of cat climbers on the other, and a hall that led to a large, bright, woefully outdated kitchen.

"Good bones," Dad said, looking around. "Could use a reno, but I love all the windows."

"I love the view," Rocky said, waving them to a Florida room that jutted out from the kitchen. "Check out my backyard. I'll get my Rolodex in my office."

"Look at all the pens!" Chloe exclaimed, somehow not expecting such an elaborate dog facility in the back. Both of the dogs went directly to the screened-in windows like they couldn't get enough of the pine-filled air.

"I used to board dogs here in addition to taking in rescues," Rocky told them. "It's not a job for a woman my age, because it's a hard day's work, but I'll tell you, it made me a pretty penny. Boarders paid for the house and everything I needed."

"How many dogs can you take in?" Chloe asked as she walked into the screened-in room and scanned the covered kennels, each with its own private pen, plus a massive fenced-in yard tucked into the trees, perfect for running around.

"I can house up to ten dogs, and people happily pay thirty dollars a day, forty for one the size of your big girl here. And I still had room for a few rescues. I took the 'unadoptable' ones from the county, and found them homes. Sometimes my boarders would come and get their dog only to find out he or she made a friend. Then they'd take two home." She chuckled. "It was a lovely and lucrative business, and a life I adored. But now..."

"How many acres?" Dad asked.

"Two and change."

"Bedrooms and baths?"

Rocky laughed. "Two and one. It used to have two baths, but I transformed the back bath into a dog shower and grooming center. You gonna make an offer?"

"I might."

Chloe sucked in a soft breath at the words. "Dad!"

"What? This is a rare find."

"Tell me about it," Rocky said, crossing her arms and following his gaze as though she was seeing the property through his eyes. "The buyer wants to put up a row of townhouses and it's taking a while to get county approval."

"Multi-family units can take forever," Dad said, speaking with the authority of a man who'd dealt with the county for many decades. "Plus, it could fall through."

"Trust me, I hope it does," Rocky said.

"You don't want to sell?" Chloe asked.

She sighed and shook her head. "I just hate to see Amelia Island lose a place like this in exchange for...*townhouses*." She dragged the evil word out as she opened the door and let Lady Bug and Buttercup out to the spacious yard, both of them darting toward sunshine.

"As you can see, dogs love it here. And I love it here, but... life changes. I gotta be a grandma now." She started out of the room. "Gimme a sec."

"But what if you could find someone who would continue your legacy?" Dad asked, bringing Rocky to an immediate halt. "Someone younger and ambitious..." He looked hard at Chloe. "Someone who loved dogs like you do and would bring this place back to its former glory, with rescues and boarders."

Chloe didn't say a word but stared back at her father, a cascade of chills rolling down her arms. "Dad," she whispered. "I can't..."

"You can't, but I can. And you can pay me rent. It's how I work every business on Wingate Way. None of your sisters own their buildings or land, but they make a good living from the businesses. The model works, believe me."

For a long moment, she couldn't speak, but suddenly felt dizzy with...desire. "Oh, my goodness, Dad."

Behind him, Rocky chuckled. "You two want to talk it over while I step out with the dogs?"

"Do we?" Dad asked.

"There's...nothing to talk about," Chloe whispered, tears welling. "This would change my life in the best imaginable way."

"That's exactly what I was thinking," Dad said.

"You would *keep* it?" Rocky asked her. "For boarding and rescues? The rescues are important, so—"

"Yes!" Chloe exclaimed. "I might...decorate it differently but not out there. I'd just...be so happy."

Rocky looked from one to the other, her whole expression transforming into joy. "If you're serious and you keep this place as a rescue shelter and dog boarding? I'll call my neighbor and return his down payment the minute you give me an offer."

"My grandson can bring one over from Wingate Properties this afternoon," Dad said with a wide grin. "And I won't need a mortgage, so we can do a thirty-day close."

"Hallelujah!" Rocky said, so loud both dogs ran to the door, barking.

Chloe just stared at him, speechless as a million thoughts exploded in her head. This was it! This was exactly what she wanted to do. A home, a business, and dogs!

"Dad," she managed to say. "Are you sure?"

He gave a single, simple nod. "You run the business and pay rent, get that firefighter and his buddies to fix up the kitchen, bath, whatever, and then you can live here, too. You know what that would be?"

She closed her eyes and whispered, "Bliss."

Laughing, Dad reached for her. "I'd say you can call that bank and turn down the job."

"Oh, Daddy!" Chloe sobbed the word, hugging him, so overwhelmed with love and certainty, she couldn't speak. "I love you so much. Thank you, thank you."

He patted her shoulder and stroked her hair, a sob shaking his shoulders, too. "I lived through that stroke," he whispered, "for moments like this."

When they separated and turned to Rocky, Chloe

wasn't surprised that tears were rolling down her cheeks, too.

She took a few steps closer and reached for Chloe's hand. "I'd say you were just rescued, young lady. I'm not surprised, though. That's what we do here."

Chapter Twenty

Madeline

A slow burn of panic had worked its way through Madeline all day and not just because the bride from hell, Melissa Havensworth, had demanded new buttons and lace for the bustle of her dress, throwing the entire day off-kilter.

But she couldn't blame Melissa. No, that honor went to Sadie Wingate, who'd left early in the morning before Madeline got up, leaving a note scribbled on a paper towel and on the kitchen counter. The ink blurred and spread, making the words nearly unreadable. But Madeline had read them, memorized them, and looked at the darn thing twenty times that day.

Seeing the lawyer today. Wish me luck. S

Madeline had texted when she found the note, and again many times throughout the day, but Sadie never answered. So she'd gone home at lunch and again at three, hoping her sister would be here, but no such luck.

Now, with the sun setting, she stood in her living room and felt like crying.

"Where *are* you, Sadie?" She ground out the question through unshed tears.

Why wouldn't she text back? Just one word? Was she hurt? In trouble? On a plane back to Brussels?

She pulled out her phone to check for a text she knew wouldn't be there, grunting at the time. She was late! Madeline "Never Late a Day in Her Life" Wingate was officially fifteen minutes late to meet her sisters at Rose's shop.

Late, disorganized, unprepared, and trembling. For Madeline, all those things were like an out-of-body experience.

She took a slow breath, looking around her townhouse with that vague sense that she'd forgotten something. Yes, she'd forgotten her common sense!

How could she go to Rose's flower shop, sit with all her sisters to catch up on their lives and plan the big party, when all she wanted to do was plead for help? How could she look from one beloved face to another and sigh with the others when they bemoaned the lack of Sadie's input and asked—not for the first time—why they never heard from her these days? How could she keep a secret when her sister was, for all intents and purposes, *missing*?

"Oh, Sadie," she whispered. "I'd kill you if I weren't so worried you're dead."

The thought sent ice through her veins.

Could Sadie be in *real* trouble? Like...life-threatening trouble? Of course she could be. Madeline had no way of knowing, because she was utterly and completely alone in this.

Except...was a Wingate woman ever alone? Not if she was honest, open, and risked the wrath of Sadie by telling her sisters everything.

They could help. They *would* help. Her sisters would move heaven and Earth to find Sadie, no questions asked.

Wait...scratch that. *Plenty* of questions would be asked and Madeline would tell them all she knew, which would take a total of one minute. Then, they'd dive into action.

Raina would be on the phone with every person at Chocolate de Saint Pierre to demand—and likely get—answers. Rose would calm them with positive thoughts that really would help right now, and Tori would make them laugh, keeping them sane.

And the younger Wingates? Grace would quietly pick up her phone and call all the local hospitals and police stations, and Chloe would put on her reporter's cap and find every attorney in a twenty-mile radius and start contacting them.

What about Suze and Dad? They deserved to know that their daughter was missing! How long did Sadie expect her to keep this secret?

No longer, she decided as she started to march with purpose. This was it. Sadie had either carelessly ignored all of Madeline's texts or she was in trouble. If it was the former, then she didn't deserve secrets and promises to be kept. If it was the latter, Madeline was the only person on Earth who knew and could help.

She had to tell her sisters. Tonight.

Holding firm to the decision, she walked to the door, then froze and pivoted back to the kitchen. Just in case Sadie came home and had...lost her phone. Unlikely, but no stone should stay unturned.

She ripped off a paper towel, found the same ink pen Sadie had used and wrote her own lame note.

I'm at Coming Up Roses for a 7 Sis meeting. xo M

Then she rushed to Wingate Way, slipped down the alley between Rose's shop and the ice cream parlor, and darted to the back door. Yanking it open, four familiar faces around the table—and one on a computer screen—stared at her in abject shock.

"You're late!" they seemed to scream in unison, followed by a lot of laughter and "has the world come to a stop?" comments.

Madeline opened her mouth to tell them exactly why but...nothing came out. Was breaking Sadie's confidence the right thing to do? Was it the only thing to do? Would it put her in more danger or trouble if they launched a full-scale search? Was Madeline overreacting?

"Are you okay?" Rose asked, coming closer after Madeline stood for a beat in complete silence.

"I...I am," she stammered. "I am late, I know, but..."

"Oh, I know. Melissa popped in here after you finished changing her bustle. Guess what? She demanded a whole different setup for the sweetheart table. Who does that two days before her own wedding?"

Madeline just gave a tight smile and nodded, accepting the excuse.

"Did you hear the news?" Chloe leaped from the table, coming to hug her. "I have my own business! A dog rescue and boarding place. I'm working out a rental arrangement with Dad."

"Who's still investing in property," Raina said, beaming. "That man is unstoppable. Oh, and I didn't get to tell him that I got a call from a broker representing someone who wants to rent the ice cream parlor for—get this—candy. My sweet tooth shall be happy, and so will Dad."

"He deserves to be happy, because he's the greatest guy who ever lived," Chloe cooed, getting a resounding round of agreement from the others. "I'm so relieved and excited, I could cry. I have, in fact. A lot. Also, I have a pregnant dog."

Madeline gave a soft laugh, not sure how to respond to that. "Awesome news, Chloe. I'm so pleased for you, but—"

"But that's not all," Rose said, giving Madeline's arm a squeeze as she guided her to a chair at the head of the table. "Gabe's coming home this weekend! It's a surprise, so don't tell the kids, but count me as another who is so happy, I could cry."

"I'm in that club!" Tori announced from the computer screen. "Want to hear my news?"

"Yes!" several of them replied with claps and cheers.

Oh, boy, this is a festive gathering, Madeline thought as she dropped into the chair and stifled a sigh. How could she ruin—

"We have a hearing next week and I really, truly think my ex is coming around to letting me have full custody with just holiday and summer visitation. Not only that, I have an offer on the house and Justin is coming up on Friday and staying the whole week."

"Hottypants lands in Boston," Chloe joked, her color high and her blue eyes bright. "You just have to get back here ASAP, Tori, so we can be all together. Well, all but Sadie."

Madeline's heart jumped as she leaned forward, ready to break the news and kill the mood.

"Oh, oh, hang on!" Raina said, holding up her phone. "I just got a text from the new event manager at Ocean Song and they have officially completed the final punch list on Magnolia Hall. There is no longer any doubt that the space will be ready for us on November 11th, which is, in case you haven't heard, also my pretend wedding date."

"What?" Tori choked.

"*Pretend*," Raina emphasized. "I upped the stakes with Chase's dear grandmother. I don't know what got into me."

"Sheer kindness and compassion," Rose said, smiling sweetly at her twin. "You're making her last days and weeks so blessed, Rain."

"I guess." Raina shrugged. "I hope it doesn't come back to bite me in the afterlife when I won't be blessed but...condemned."

They all laughed at that, giving Madeline a chance to take a deep breath and consider how to start.

"That's not the only good news," Grace said, her soft voice quieting them as they leaned forward.

"You and Isaiah are getting married?" Tori asked, making them all gasp, and Grace blush deeply.

"No," she said with a sly smile. "But he did say he loves me."

"This is not a surprise," Rose said, looking a bit smug over the relationship she took full credit for starting. "And did you say it back?"

Grace bit her lip. "I might have."

The reactions ranged from "awws" to "yays" to...a few misty eyes.

"Oh, Gracie." Raina reached for her. "You so deserve to find love again."

Grace hugged her and accepted another embrace from Chloe on her other side.

"I never dreamed it could happen," Grace whispered, her own eyes getting damp. "I thought I'd never love again after I lost Nick, but..." She blew out a breath. "It seems God had other plans."

"Isaiah has you singing his hymns, I take it," Tori said.

"And reading his Bible," Grace added. "It's a wonderful thing for Nikki Lou, who is thriving in her new program. Honestly, you guys? There was a time I thought I'd never laugh or love again and, boy, was I wrong."

Another round of celebration so loud no one seemed to notice that Madeline hadn't said a word. And how could she? How could she wreck all this spontaneous joy with a bunch of secrets and speculation?

"All right, all right—let's get down to party business,"

Raina said, but Rose held up her hand, her gaze on Madeline.

Of course it would be Rose who sensed something was off.

"You've been quiet, Madeline," she said.

"She's ashamed of her lateness," Tori quipped.

"She's been working on that fabulous dress for Mom to wear," Grace suggested.

When she didn't laugh, they all grew quiet and looked at her expectantly.

She cleared her throat. "I have to tell you guys something."

Every gaze in the room pinned on her, and before she spoke, she looked from one to the next. Yes, she was breaking her own personal rule of keeping promises, but it had been darn near twelve hours without a word from Sadie and this was now officially a serious problem.

No matter how much she hated to wreck their happiness—and Sadie's trust—she had to.

"I just don't want you to hate me."

The reaction was strong and came from every one of them—a chorus of, "We could never hate you!" filling the room.

No, they wouldn't, Madeline decided. But Sadie might. She swallowed, still torn over what was the right thing to do. Tell them and break a confidence, or stay silent and live with regret for the rest of her life?

"What is it, Madeline?" Rose urged.

"I don't know how to—"

A banging on the front door stopped her and made

Rose drop her head back with a grunt. "Does the Closed sign mean nothing to people?" she asked.

"Ignore them," Raina said, her attention on Madeline. "You don't know how to what?"

"I just want you all to under—"

"I know you're in there!" The muffled voice came all the way through the door and the front of the store, high-pitched and desperate.

"Pushy, aren't they?" Chloe asked on a laugh.

Rose stood. "I'll get rid of—"

"Hey, Wingate women! Your sister is out here!"

The shrieks, the screams, the gasps, and the sound of chairs being abandoned filled the entire workroom of Rose's flower shop. Four of them were up and rushing to the front, with Tori hollering from the computer screen.

Madeline, however, sat frozen in shock and disbelief, a wave of relief rocking her whole body as she realized—

"Sadie!" It was like they all screamed the name in unison.

"What is Sadie doing there?" Tori asked, almost to herself, since she didn't realize Madeline hadn't gone with the others.

Madeline didn't answer but pushed up and walked into the front of the store and absolute chaos, where the screams and greetings and kisses and far-too-brief explanations seemed to kick Madeline's shocked and confused heart.

"Wait. Wait. *Wait*," Raina insisted after it all died down and they dragged Sadie to the back to say hello to poor Tori, trapped in the computer. "Are you saying you quit your job in Brussels and don't have another lined up? That's pretty daring, Sadie. What brought this on?"

Sadie stole a nanosecond's glance at Madeline, who'd gotten nothing more than the same joyous embrace she'd given everyone.

"I just had enough of living over there," Sadie said casually, dropping into an empty chair and accepting a glass of wine Rose offered. "You know how I am."

"No moss grows," Tori cracked.

"Exactly. And that Belgian moss was bringing me down. So, I decided to come home for the big party and the holidays and figure out my life in the new year." She lifted the glass and swiped the air with it, including all of them in her toast. "Until then, I'm here and I'm yours. Tell me what's new and how can I help with the party?"

Once again, as each sister recited their latest news and then brought Sadie up to speed on the vow renewal ceremony, Madeline stayed quiet. Only this time, it wasn't fear or worry gripping her, but confusion and shock and no small amount of anger.

What was going on with her and why hadn't she had the decency to respond all day?

"We've all been trying to reach you," Chloe said.

"You never return calls," Grace added.

"Or texts," Madeline said dryly.

Sadie turned to her, the first real eye contact they'd had. "My phone belonged to the company and I really had to keep my personal communication to a minimum," she said. "And I had to give it back this morning."

Well, that was the first thing she said that made sense. Sort of.

"Where are you staying?" Madeline asked pointedly, daring her to be honest.

"I was thinking I'd take Raina's spot in the beach house," she said. "I'd have gone straight there, but I saw the 7 *Sis* group text last night and you were talking about meeting here. I didn't want to give Dad a heart attack on top of his stroke, so I'll go there tomorrow. Can I crash at your place, Madeline?"

In other words, could she get her stuff and elicit more promises to keep secret the fact that Sadie had been here for weeks?

Madeline opened her mouth to snap a retort but knew that whatever she said would be mean, mad, and not very sisterly. Did it matter now? Sadie was safe and here and out in the open.

"Of course," Madeline said softly, but couldn't resist adding, "I'd love to have some time alone with you."

"Madeline," Rose said. "What were you going to tell us? You were worried we wouldn't understand."

All eyes were on her again. "I was going to tell you..." She settled her gaze on Sadie and smiled. "I was worried Sadie wouldn't make the big event, but, well, that's a moot point now, isn't it?"

They only held each other's gaze for another second, but a lot was communicated in that instant. An apology, maybe. More promises, some secrets, and the bond of two women who were connected by blood and trust.

ALL OF MADELINE'S emotions had calmed by the time they finished, said all their goodbyes, and she stepped outside with Sadie. They walked for nearly a minute in silence, but when they were off Wingate Way and on the side street that led to Madeline's townhouse, both of them finally stopped and looked at each other.

"First of all, I'm sorry," Sadie whispered, the first real agony in her voice. "I honestly had no phone, I didn't get any texts—which I assume you sent—and I couldn't reach you. Do you know that without a phone, you don't have anyone's number? I never memorized your number."

"My salon's number is on the website," Madeline said softly. "And I don't care now that I know you haven't been murdered."

Sadie snorted. "My career's dead. Does that count?"

"Sadie. What—"

She got cut off by a swipe of the hand. "I legally can't tell you," Sadie said. "I have signed a non-disclosure that means I can never, as long as I'm alive, talk about what happened."

"But you are free to be out in public? Not worried about being seen or found or...whatever it is you were worried about?"

Sadie swallowed and nodded. "My whereabouts are no longer a secret," she said, the words sounding stiff and practiced. "My belongings are being shipped from my apartment in Brussels and I'm free to go about my life as if...this never happened."

"As if *what* never happened?"

"What part of an NDA don't you understand?" Sadie asked on a laugh. "A non-disclosure agreement means you cannot *disclose*."

At Sadie's look, Madeline laughed. "You can't tell *your own* sister?"

"That's exactly what it means," she said, slowing down as they reached Madeline's street. "And all I can do is ask you to keep this interlude we've shared to yourself. After that, I promise you, I give you my word, that I will never ask another thing of you."

Madeline felt her eyes shutter in silent agreement.

"But I will say this," Sadie whispered, taking Madeline's hands. "You have shown yourself to be the truest of the true, the most loyal and loving sister—"

"Not always loving," Madeline murmured.

"Always loving," Sadie insisted. "Of course you asked questions, of course you wanted to protect me, of course you've been frustrated by my...ambiguous non-answers. And of course you got angry with me, especially today, which was long and arduous and kind of sad."

"Sad?" Madeline squeezed her hands. "Did someone hurt you, Sadie?"

"I did it to myself," she said. "I made my own dumb mistakes and will always live with the consequences."

Her voice was broken enough to rip at Madeline's heart. She reached for her dear little sister and hugged her.

"Whatever happened is behind you now." She felt

Sadie nod enthusiastically. "You can stay here—with me or at the beach house or wherever—as long as you like."

"Well, I don't stay anywhere very long, as you know." She drew back. "But I'm going to enjoy the heck out of the next few months. Then I'll pick up the pieces and find another career and move on and...try to forget."

Madeline bit her lip, searching Sadie's face for any clue, but there was nothing in her delicate features but sadness and pain. That made her just want to love her more.

"Come on," she said, wrapping an arm around Sadie's waist as they headed down the street. "Let's put all this behind us and start life over in the morning."

"'Kay."

They walked arm in arm, the only sound their feet on the cobblestones in perfect unison.

"Oh, I should tell you," Sadie said as they reached the door and Madeline touched the keypad, "about that Adam guy."

Madeline's finger froze. Her whole body, actually, felt like it turned to ice. "Yeah?" She barely breathed the word.

"He was, um, involved today."

"What?" That word barely came out of her closed throat.

"It's a long story and it all falls under the NDA, so please don't ask questions. But I talked to him, and he is the guy you knew. I was right, too. He was undercover back then and he told me to tell you he's sorry and he, uh, hopes you're well."

Madeline just stood stone still with her finger trembling too much to press the code. She stared at the lock, unable to move or think or comprehend any of that.

Undercover. Sorry. Hopes you're well.

Twenty-five years of wondering and she got...five words. On a shaky breath, she looked at Sadie. "That's it?"

"I'm afraid so, hon. And I will never speak to him—or about him—again."

She really didn't know what to say, but Sadie kindly pressed the keypad for her and took them inside, both of them silent and sad and, ironically, still keeping secrets.

Chapter Twenty-one

Raina

I t was ten-thirty when Raina pulled into her driveway after she left Rose's shop, glowing from Sadie's arrival, but feeling well past bedtime for a pregnant lady. But when her high beams shone on a small convertible coupe pulled to the side, she was suddenly wide awake.

Chase was here? He said he wasn't going to leave Nonna's and he'd been true to his word. They'd talked a few times about the event, and she'd texted him to check on his grandmother, but she hadn't seen him since she'd left Nonna's house nearly a week ago.

Why would he be here?

She turned off the ignition and sat for a moment in the dark, peering at a house that was equally dark. He must either be on the back patio or in the guest room, neither of which could be seen from this angle. The living room and hall was dark, and he hadn't turned on the sconces by the front door.

Her heart, which had been so full of happiness to see Sadie and laugh all evening with her sisters, dropped to her belly with a thud. Could this mean bad news?

Taking a breath to brace herself, she walked to the front door and let herself in to a completely dark house. No light from the kitchen, hall, back patio, or his room.

Quietly setting down her purse and kicking off her shoes, she padded barefoot around the empty downstairs, guessing he was walking the beach. Although the French doors were closed and locked, so that could be wrong.

Perplexed, she walked toward the steps. He'd have no reason to be up there, where there was nothing but her bedroom suite and two smaller rooms.

At the top of the stairs, she looked into her room, startled to see the balcony doors wide open, a fresh ocean breeze wafting in and fluttering the sheer curtains she'd hung.

At any other time, she would have been alarmed, but everything in her said Chase must be out on that deck, in the dark. And there would be only one reason why.

"Chase?" she called in a soft voice as she approached the doors. "Are you out here?"

"Yes." His voice was flat and...dead.

She stepped through the doors and looked to the chaise, finding him in the moonlight. He was reclining, eyes closed, wearing shorts and a T-shirt.

"What are you doing here?" she asked as gently as she could, wincing when he took a breath to answer, already knowing what he was going to say.

"I came up here, hoping to find you," he said. "But then I came out here and...couldn't move. Sorry."

"No, it's fine. But..."

His eyes still closed, he lifted his hand, reaching for

her. She took a step closer and took his hand in hers, holding it tightly. "Is she..."

"Gone," he breathed.

"Oh, Chase." Without thinking, she brought his hand to her lips and sat down on the edge of the chaise, aching to comfort him. "I'm so sorry."

"No, don't be."

"I am! I didn't know her well, but..."

"She loved you." He finally opened his eyes and even in the moonlight she could see they were red-rimmed, his lashes wet with tears. The sight nearly took her breath away.

"Me? No, she loved *you*."

"You gave her the greatest gift, Raina." He managed to blink and push himself up on the inclined back, not letting go of her hand. "I can never thank you enough for that."

"You don't have to. I'm glad I was able to make her happy."

"You did." He closed his eyes again and lay back, their hands still joined. "She died happy at ninety-seven and I guess you can't ask for anything else from life."

"No pain?" Raina asked. "No EMTs or hospital?"

He shook his head. "I knew she was going. I let her drink a glass of limoncello and..." He let out a soft laugh. "And we talked about the babies."

Her heart did a flip but not with regret for the lie. Just joy that Analucia Cardinale had something wonderful to take with her.

"What did she say?" Raina asked.

"You don't want to know."

"Yes, I do."

He opened one eye. "I promised her...Charles."

"Chase!" She gave his hand a playful squeeze.

"Sorry. You don't have to..." His voice cracked. "I just..." He squeezed his eyes shut. "Unless you want to see a grown man cry, you better leave."

"I've seen grown men cry," she said gently, reaching to brush a lock of hair off his forehead because he needed tenderness so badly right then. "You've lost someone you loved very, very much. Feel free to cry."

He tried to swallow, then finally let go of her hand, using both of his to swipe under his eyes. "It's not like it was a surprise like...like my parents."

Her heart folded. "I can't imagine what that was like."

"It's what I'm reliving now," he admitted on a ragged whisper. "Not her. Of course I mourn her. I loved her. I *adored* that woman and am a better man because she was in my life."

Raina nodded, silent because she sensed he needed to talk, only half aware that she was very gently stroking his arm, offering comfort and sympathy.

"But losing them?" He grunted. "I was thirteen, Raina. You know any thirteen-year-old boys?"

"A few," she said, thinking of her two nephews, who were twelve, and another who just turned sixteen. All close enough for her to imagine the pain of losing a parent. Losing both? Unthinkable. "It must have been so hard, Chase."

"Agonizing," he said. "Impossible. I lived in a fog for a year, waking every single morning thinking it had to have been a bad dream, going to sleep every night so profoundly sad I couldn't breathe."

She blinked against tears forming. "How awful."

"My dad was the greatest guy," he continued, eyes closed as if the memories were washing over him. "He was smart and capable and funny and no one, no man *ever* loved a woman more than he loved his 'Magpie.'"

She smiled, remembering that his mother was Marguerita, and called Maggie. "That's sweet."

"And she was," he said. "The kindest, most loving woman. Never met a person she wouldn't help, a problem she wouldn't solve, a lost treasure she wouldn't drop everything for until she found." He smiled, obviously remembering something. "I was sick the day they went out fishing, and furious I couldn't go."

She inched back, not knowing this part of the story, only that his parents died in a boating accident.

"But I had a sore throat and strep was going around, so my mother made me stay home with Nonna and they went out with friends for..." His voice hitched. "It doesn't matter. They didn't come back."

Her hand stilled. "Then it was good you didn't go."

He looked like he might disagree, but he just huffed out a breath. "I became an orphan that day, which was the most gut-wrenching thing I've ever been through. Nonna swooped in and did everything in her power to fill that hole. Poppy, too."

"How wonderful that you had them."

He nodded. "But today? I have that feeling all over again. I know, I know—I'm almost fifty and have a life, a business, and..."

"It still hurts to be untethered from the people you've depended on since childhood."

He nodded, looking grateful she understood, silent for a long time.

"I wanted to honor them," he said softly. "I wanted to continue the Madison and Cardinale lines and be the kind of father my dad was, but..." He shook his head hard, as if he realized he'd gone too far. "Never mind."

"It's fine, Chase. If anyone understands longing for a family because you know how great one can be, it's me."

He opened his eyes and looked right at her. Through her. Into her heart. "You do understand. And look at what you're going through to make it happen." He glanced at her stomach. "All alone, too."

She was never alone, not with Wingates around every corner, but it didn't feel right to remind him of that.

"I'm just going through pregnancy. Oh, and a divorce." She gave a dry laugh. "People have been through worse." Her smile faded as she lightly pressed her hand on his chest. "You've been through worse."

For a long moment, their gazes locked as her heart beat to the same rhythm as his, just under her palm. She couldn't speak, held captive by the emotion in those brown eyes, the connection so powerful she was suddenly rocked by the bone-deep desire to lean forward a few inches and...and kiss him.

Not for comfort. Not for kindness. But in response to a longing so intense, she felt it from head to toe. She forced herself to stay very, very still and not give in to the ache.

He was just as still, his expression matching the thoughts in her mind, thinking and feeling—she had no doubt—exactly the same thing.

They needed...to kiss. They wanted...to kiss. They had to...

Stop.

She sat bolt upright and away from him. "I'm sorry," she whispered, breathless. "About Nonna. And your parents. And...I'm sorry."

She stood, catching a shadow of disappointment in his eyes, and then he sat up, too.

"And I'm sorry I invaded your, uh, space." He cleared his throat, grounding himself as he got up from the chaise. "I'll let you alone now, Raina, and go downstairs. I'm...sorry."

"Please don't apologize," she said. After all, she was the one who held his hand, felt his heartbeat, and thought about things a woman who was technically still married had no right to think.

"Paul and I dealt with everything but I couldn't stay at her house and I..." He looked around as if he was really seeing his surroundings for the first time. "I always loved it up here. The sound of the waves, the salt air, and just falling into bed."

And if she weren't still married and nearly six months pregnant? They might just be falling in it right now. And that would be so wrong, she couldn't even think about it.

"Yes, yes. It was a selling point for me, as well." She stepped back into the doorway. "I'm sorry I interrupted your...moment. I understand you need to mourn."

He looked down at her, silent for a beat too long, making her wonder what he was thinking and would he say it and what on Earth were they *doing*?

"I'm going to bed," he finally said. "Good night, Raina. Thank you again for giving my grandmother the greatest gift. It was nothing short of spectacular."

She just nodded and whispered, "Good night."

He walked out of her room and disappeared down the steps.

Raina didn't move for at least five minutes, until the vibrations in her body subsided and common sense returned.

She didn't know what just happened, but it... couldn't. It simply couldn't.

AFTER A SLEEPLESS NIGHT, Raina dragged herself from bed while the sun was peeking over the ocean, bathing the sky in peach morning light and promises of a gorgeous day on Amelia Island.

Pulled to the vista, she opened the French doors and stepped out onto her balcony, inhaling the first breath of clean, salty air. But her gaze instantly shifted to the chaise...the scene of the crime. Okay, not a *crime*, per se.

It wasn't wrong to comfort a man who'd suffered a deep loss, a voice in her head said.

But it wasn't right to nearly give in to the desire to close the space—physical and emotional—between them and discover exactly what it would feel like to kiss the man.

With a groan, she gripped the railing, needing support and another steadying breath of air.

Was it cheating to think about him that way when her divorce wasn't final? Did that make her just as bad as Jack?

No, obviously not. Her marriage was over, but...she was carrying another man's children. She was up to her eyeballs in restructuring her life, starting over as a single mother running a company that still belonged to her father. She was in no place to even think about a kiss or a man or a relationship.

And what was Chase thinking?

She closed her eyes and her lids burned with the negative image of the sunrise. But she could still see the look on his face when she'd stood up. Yes, disappointment, but maybe trepidation and uncertainty and, oh God, a glimmer of hope.

Where did they go from here?

There was no answer, but she heard a noise and wondered if he was planning to run off to work before she even made it downstairs. She couldn't say she blamed him, but they'd have to face this at some point, right? Or pretend that it was just her need to fix his broken heart that had them inches from a kiss.

She showered, dressed for work, and headed downstairs, not sure if she wanted Chase to be there or not.

Coming around the corner, she spied him on the deck, holding a cup of coffee as he stared at the same horizon she had...maybe thinking the same thoughts. The doors were open, so she made a little noise brewing a cup of decaf and chopping a banana, knowing that if he wanted to talk to her, he would.

"Hey."

His voice seemed to reach down to her heart, making her turn from the counter to meet his gaze. She sucked in a silent breath at the sight of his tousled hair, his handsome face, the long fingers wrapped around a thick white mug.

Her feelings had not disappeared overnight. They were, in fact, more intense.

"Hi, Chase," she managed, adding a smile. "How are you doing?"

He nodded, took a sip, and regarded her over the rim of the mug.

"You think you can work today?" she asked, rooting for the most neutral and natural of subjects for them to discuss. "I never told you that your event manager texted me last night to say the punch list for Magnolia Hall is complete, so all that's left..." Her voice faded as he shook his head. "Not complete?" she guessed.

"It is," he said, setting the mug on the counter. "And Laura is beyond competent, so you're in great hands. Julia, too, knows more about that hotel than I do, and my foreman has given me his word everything will be ready for you days before your event."

She blinked at him. What was he saying? Well, she knew what he was saying, but the bigger question was why did it hurt?

"You're leaving," she said, and it wasn't a question.

"I'm taking Nonna's ashes to Palermo so she can join Poppy and my parents in the Tyrrhenian Sea."

Her heart tumbled around her chest. "Oh. So soon?"

"In a few days."

An odd punch of relief hit her, along with a shocking realization. She didn't want him to go.

"But one of the suites is ready and furnished at Ocean Song," he added. "I packed my car this morning and I'll stay there until I leave. You can be the sole mistress of The Sanctuary, which is..."

Which is what? she thought when he didn't complete the thought.

"Best," he finished.

Best for...who? Well, obviously for both of them, but the fact that he chose that word told her that, yes, he felt what she felt last night and the thing to do was...leave.

Of course, of course. But why did that make her whole chest ache?

"Don't you think?" he added with a nearly imperceptible note of expectation in his voice.

She stared at him for a moment, not answering. She couldn't, because...she wasn't sure what to say. Should she admit to her feelings only to have him hold up his hands and say no, no, no? Should she scoff at the idea of...

what almost happened last night? Should she be honest or distant or *what*?

"I...guess it's best." Pathetic answer, but it was all she could manage

"I mean, under the circumstances," he said slowly. "With the hotel nearly done and my grandmother gone and you...you..."

"Will you be back on Amelia Island?" she asked, saving herself from whatever he was going to say.

He swallowed. "I'll come and go to see the hotel."

She worked not to look disappointed. "And the babies," she said with a teasing smile. "You know, sweet little Charles."

He laughed, looking grateful for the lightness when the room suddenly felt so heavy. "You don't have to hang that handle on one of your babies. Especially if they're two girls, and I know the science says your genes don't dictate that, but something tells me girls are on the horizon."

"I don't know." She lifted a shoulder. "My biological mother's name was Charlotte, so Charles might not be too far off. And then I can face Nonna if I meet her behind the Pearly Gates."

Still smiling, he leveled his dark gaze on her. "Let me know how your parents' surprise vow renewal goes."

It was getting harder to smile. Because...she wanted him at that party. She wanted to dance with him, laugh with him, introduce him to the people who mattered to her.

Which was so many levels of dumb, it took her breath away.

"I'm sorry you'll miss it," she said softly. "Since it's Ocean Song's inaugural event."

Very slowly, he took a few steps around the counter, coming closer, making her heart slam against her ribs.

"Raina," he said, his voice gruff. "I'm really..."

She stared at him, her breath caught in her throat, waiting for the rest.

"Really grateful I got to know you," he whispered. "Thank you for buying this house, for letting me stay, for...for..."

"For pretending to marry you and give you babies."

She waited for his easy laugh or at least a smile, but he just gazed at her, melting her with eyes as dark as the coffee that hissed in the maker behind her.

"For everything," he finally said.

They stood inches apart, looking at each other, that same blistering need building up in her to connect and kiss and hold and...start something.

This time, he was the one who backed away.

"Bye, Raina."

"Bye." She mouthed the word, staying stone still as he nodded and took another step backward, then another, never taking his eyes from her.

Then he turned and walked away, the only sound his footsteps, the door closing, and the pounding of her heart. Her poor, poor heart that she didn't want to give to him.

Except...*whoa*. It might be too late.

Chapter Twenty-two

Rose

Gabe's coming home.

Rose's first thought when she woke on Saturday morning was one of pure joyous anticipation.

Her second thought? *It's Melissa Havensworth's wedding today.*

Not such joyous anticipation. But with luck, timing, hard work, and focus, she should have all the arrangements done and delivered to the church and venue and then she could run home and fall into her beloved husband's arms for two solid days.

It was enough to get her out of bed early, dressed and ready to face the floral challenges before the great reward.

"Oh, hey, Ethan," she said, surprised to see her younger son as she came into the kitchen. "You're up early."

He looked up from a bowl of cereal, his eyes wide and...a little scared. "Yeah."

"Are you okay?"

"He's fine. Zach is fine and he doesn't want you to

worry but he wants you to know he's completely fine. He won't text you though. He knows the rules."

She recoiled at the words, which didn't make any sense at all. "He's not...in bed?"

Ethan shook his head, his color pale.

"Where is he?"

"Now that, I don't know. He woke me up at like, o-dark-forty, as Dad says. And he told me to tell you not to worry, he had this, and you will have your tulips for... Godzilla's wedding?"

He seemed unsure, but Rose wasn't. She knew he meant "bridezilla" and she knew why Zach had left.

He'd done exactly what Gabe would have—not trusted the port authority to put those tulips into a delivery truck and get them to the shop. Gabe would have gotten up at o-dark-forty and driven to the Colonel Island Terminal, which was an hour north but still the closest international port for these kinds of shipped deliveries.

She immediately reached for her phone, then thought better of it. Zach was under the strictest instructions not to answer a call while driving, and reading or sending a text would cost him his license for a month. That was an iron-clad rule she doubted he'd risk breaking.

Of course, there should be an iron-clad rule about leaving the house before dawn and making an hour-long trip up I-95 to Brunswick, Georgia. There certainly would have been one if Zach had come to her instead of Ethan and told her where he planned to go.

She simply would have never let him make that trip—and in the dark!

Trying to figure out what she should do, she got some coffee and checked his location on her phone, staring at the screen for a few minutes because...he was going *south*? Didn't he know where Colonel Island Terminal was? He'd been there a dozen times with Gabe on errands exactly like this.

She huffed out a breath and dialed his number, cringing while it rang three times and went to voicemail. Okay, he was following that rule but these were extenuating circumstances.

Oh, Gabe, why are you not here?

The thought echoed in her mind, erased only when Alyson came darting into the kitchen looking for breakfast, followed in short order by Avery, who was already crying because she stubbed her toe running after Alyson.

Lost in the normal Saturday morning chaos and trying not to think too hard about Zach, Rose checked the time and realized she had to get to the shop...but what about the kids? Zach wasn't here to watch them.

With one more grunt of frustration, she put out an SOS on the 7 *Sis* group chat hunting for one of her sisters to watch the kids while she handled the wedding...and had three responses in one minute. Raina, Madeline, and Sadie could all be there in fifteen minutes. But then Chloe chimed in that Buttercup was in labor, which sent the girls into a tizzy of wanting to go to the bungalow to meet the puppies.

In the end, Madeline said she'd pick up all the kids,

take them to the beach house so they could be near but not *in* the poor dog's face, and they could spend time with Aunt Sadie.

Her sister's unexpected arrival had brightened everything, especially Suze and Dad, who'd been so happily surprised and thrilled to have their always-distant daughter close by and staying in the third-floor guest suite.

By the time the kids were fed, dressed, and gone, Rose picked up her phone again to check on Zach, who was definitely going the wrong way to get the tulips. As her heart crawled into her throat, she called him again and this time he answered.

"Mom, don't kill me."

"That might be asking too much," she said dryly. "What in God's name are you doing, Zach?"

"Getting tulips. And I know I'm not supposed to answer the phone, but—"

"The port is in Brunswick, Georgia."

"Yeah, well, the tulips aren't."

"What?"

"I got a text at, like, five in the morning from the wholesaler."

"You did?" Rose frowned. "Why not me?"

"Because I was the last person to call them, remember? To change the delivery from down at Canaveral to Colonel Island? Well, they screwed up and the flowers are at Canaveral."

She gasped noisily. "You're going to Port Canaveral? It's three hours away!"

"It's fine. I'm not going to let you get ripped to shreds by that nasty bride. It's what Dad would do."

She closed her eyes, loving him for that but not happy at all. Not to mention that Gabe was in his car driving up from Miami this morning. He could have gotten the flowers on the way—he *passed* Port Canaveral. But that would have meant ruining the surprise and...her throat tightened with unshed tears.

It was all too much.

"Listen, honey—"

"I know, I know. Don't worry, Mom, I'll be— *Whoa!* What the—"

She heard a screech, a bang, then silence.

"Zach! Zach! Are you okay? What happened?"

Nothing. Not a sound. Just the deadliest, most horrific silence she'd ever heard.

She screamed his name again and again, nearly buckling to the floor as she realized he had to have been in an accident.

STAY CALM, *stay calm, stay calm.*

Rose dug for her most Zen inner self but was having a hard time finding it. Trembling, she called the sheriff's office, got passed around a little bit, put on hold, told her story to more than one deputy, and finally learned that there had been an accident on I-95 south of St. Augustine involving two cars and no fatalities.

No fatalities.

She clung to the words and barely heard the instructions to wait for a call from either the sheriff's office or her son, if he was the person involved in the accident. All she could do was get the mile marker number, call Lizzie and tell her to handle the wedding to the best of her ability, and get in the car to head to St. Augustine.

Only then did she call Gabe.

"Brace yourself, honey," she said softly. "I got some not-so-good news."

He was quiet while she told him everything, much quieter than she expected.

"I'll be there in a few hours," he said. "I'm just passing Vero Beach."

"Then we'll meet in St. Augustine. In the meantime, if he calls me, I'll call you." Her voice cracked with a sob she felt like she'd been holding in since she last heard Zach's voice.

"Babe, I'm so sorry. This would never have happened—"

"Stop," she said. "We don't know what happened yet. No hospital has called. We know there are no fatalities. We have no idea what's going on."

"This would never have happened if I hadn't left."

She swallowed, wanting to fling all sorts of positive platitudes at him, but none of them were easy to find. He wasn't wrong. But...his *dreams*. His great big wonderful dreams of being a doctor required sacrifice.

Except that sacrifice shouldn't include their son.

She choked back the tears and swiped her face. "I

have to drive. I have to concentrate. I'll call you the minute I know anything."

"Listen, Rose, I have to tell you—"

The dashboard flashed with an incoming call. *St. John's County Sheriff.*

"I have to go."

"Rose—"

She just hung up and pressed the button on the steering wheel, barely able to say hello or hear the caller's voice because her heart was pounding so hard.

"Mrs. D'Angelo? This is Deputy Janiece Starling with the St. John's County sheriff's office. Let me assure you that your son is fine."

"Oh..." It barely came out as a whimper.

"He's been in a fender bender and suffered no damage, with moderate damage to the car. Not totaled, but it had to be towed."

Another whimper, this one probably more of a prayer of gratitude.

"Unfortunately, he's not the owner of this car—"

"It's my dad's."

"Oh, I know. Rex Wingate, is it? Someone needs to tell him his registration has expired."

"No!"

"Yes. So we've impounded the car, and unfortunately, that was done while we were questioning your son and his phone's still in it. He's fine, and he's at the Lewis Speedway sheriff's station in St. Augustine."

"I'm on my way. I'll be there as quickly as I can."

She didn't breathe much for the rest of the trip, only

enough to call Gabe, get to where she was going, run into the pale stucco building where Zach waited, and finally wrap her arms around her son. She held him as tightly as she could for a solid five minutes.

"I NEVER HEARD Grandpa cry like that," Zach said as they hung up the phone and continued driving back up I-95 toward Amelia Island. "Dad was pretty wrecked, too. And you don't want to see your face."

Rose managed a smile, not bothering to look in the rearview mirror at her reflection. They'd all shed a lot of tears for one day. All but Zach, who'd been downright stoic from the moment she'd reached for him at the sheriff's office.

"Mom, I'm so sorry," he said, his voice pained as he delivered what had to be the hundredth apology.

"I know you are."

"I just wanted to..."

"Be like Dad," she finished for him. "That's been the problem all along, honey. You're just a sixteen-year-old kid, not a forty-three-year-old man. You can't be Dad, not yet at least."

When he didn't answer, she took her eyes from the road and her heart cracked in two as she caught his face melting into a sob.

"Hey, hey." She reached over and took his hand. "Don't cry."

"How can I not, Mom? I screwed up so royally, I...I...

let Dad down. I let you down. And, man, I let that bride down."

"She'll have to deal," Rose said, a little surprised that she'd completely forgotten about Melissa. "I should call Lizzie, but..." She shook her head. "It'll take care of itself. I'm just so glad you weren't hurt."

"Grandpa was sure I could drive that car. He checked insurance and everything."

"Well, he didn't check his registration, but it's completely understandable with his stroke. It's all done now. We'll get the new registration Monday and drive down to get the car to a shop. Maybe Raina can come with me, because your dad won't—"

He let out a noisy sigh and wiped his cheek. "How are we going to get through this, Mom? Two more years?"

She tried to swallow but the lump in her throat was too big. "We will. We can. We're the D'Angelo family and we can do anything. Isn't that what Dad always says?"

"Yeah, when he's here. I mean, come on."

"Honey, he's following his dreams," she insisted, even though the words felt as hollow as they sounded. "You have dreams, right? You'd want to be able to follow them no matter what age you are, and how many kids you have."

"I guess." He shifted in his seat with another agonizing sigh. "I can't do it, Mom. I told him I could step in and be the man of the family, but now I have to face Grandpa after his car's been wrecked."

"It wasn't your fault. That guy cut you off."

"I should have seen him."

"You heard Grandpa. He forgives you."

"And I should have checked the registration," he said. "Dad would have."

"Zach." She squeezed his hand. "Don't be so hard on yourself. You're alive and safe and that's all that matters."

"Yeah, well, don't forget—no tulips."

Rose made a face. "I'm sure I'll hear about it from our favorite bridezilla."

He didn't laugh, but leaned his head against the window, silent as she drove back up to Yulee and zipped over the bridge into town, realizing that she'd be just in time to take whatever flowers Lizzie had arranged to the wedding.

There, she'd face the wrath of Melissa, offer some kind of discount, and then wait for Gabe.

"What's Dad doing here?" Zach asked, sitting up when they pulled into the lot behind Coming Up Roses.

He was here?

"It was supposed to be a big surprise. He came home to see us. In fact, he was driving up I-95 while you were driving down, on his way, but..." She frowned at the sight of his pickup truck. "After I got you, I texted him to go to my parents' house and see the other kids. I wonder why he came here."

"Probably to let me know what a disappointment I am."

Rose shot him a look. "I doubt that."

Together, they got out of her van, walking toward the

back door just as it popped open. All she could see was...tulips.

A giant arrangement of bright pink tulips and greens held by Gabe. He eased the acrylic vase to the side and grinned. "I decided to make a detour to Port Canaveral."

"Dad!"

"Gabe."

He lowered the arrangement to the ground with one smooth move and stepped around it, arms extended. He grabbed both of them into a bear hug, turning his face to kiss Zach's cheek.

"You scared me, man."

"Dad, I'm so—"

"No." Gabe inched back and pointed a finger in his face. "I'm sorry, not you. I love you so much, Zachary." His voice caught as he hugged Zach again. "And I let you down, son. Not the other way around."

Zach stepped back, looking a little uncertain what he should say. "But, Dad, I..."

Gabe held up a hand. "Help Lizzie get these tulips in the van. I need to talk to your mother."

"Gabe." Rose stepped back, torn between the time needed to deliver the flowers and how much she just wanted to hold him and kiss him and hold him some more.

"This can't wait, Rosie," he said, tugging her into the store. "Somewhere...private. Fast. Now."

She blinked in astonishment, then let him pull her toward the cooler, yanking the door open and bringing her in.

"Gabe, I can't—"

"No, *I* can't," he said, cutting her off by pulling her close, searching her face like he was looking for the best place to land his first kiss. Normally, she'd show him. She'd take his gorgeous face in her hands, lost in his deep blue eyes, and kiss his mouth until neither one of them could breathe. But this was not the time or place.

"This can wait," she said on a half-laugh.

But he wasn't smiling. "No, Rose Wingate D'Angelo, it cannot wait. I was coming home this weekend to discuss a decision with you but I made it on the way up here."

She lifted a brow. "Another decision made without consulting me? We're not moving to Miami, if that's what you think the answer is."

"No, you are not. I'm coming home, Rose. I'm quitting school, I'm going back to work as an EMT, and I'm planting by backside right where it belongs—in our home, as the head of our family, living next to you every single day for the rest of our lives."

She just stared at him, stunned into silence.

"Yes," he continued, "I had a dream since I was a boy. But that same boy looked across a cafeteria one day, saw a gorgeous blonde named after a flower, and decided that she was my dream. And every day since then, you have made my dreams come true."

"Oh, Gabe." She shivered, but not from the cold. "But you wanted to be a doctor."

"I wanted to be a husband and father first. Rose, can

you ever forgive me for this...this...I don't know. Mid-life second-guessing?"

She angled her head, aware of her heart melting despite the chill. "If this was as bad as it got, yes. I forgive you. But I don't have to, Gabe. I love you and want you to be happy."

"I am. I was, anyway. And a month away from you and the kids and the fantastic, satisfying, meaningful life we built was all it took for me to realize everything I wanted was right here on Amelia Island. I'm not going back, Rose. I'm not transferring to another school, either. I already called Hutch and I can start my old job next week."

She tried to breathe but her exhale was nothing but a happy, happy sob. "Really? Because I can do this. I swear I can."

"No kidding!" he exclaimed on a laugh. "Better than anyone and with more grace and beauty than I could imagine. But this shouldn't have been a test of your parenting skills, Rose. You prove them every day. Babe, I love you and you *are* my dream and I never, ever want to spend another day or night away from you."

She looked up at him, feeling him pull her into his strong chest, knowing right down to her last cell that she loved him and would do anything for him...and that feeling was completely reciprocated.

"Now can I kiss you?" he asked.

"A million times."

As his lips touched hers, the cooler door popped open. "Seriously, you two?" Zach looked exasperated and amused. "Let's get these flowers to Hell Bride before the tulips wilt."

Laughing, they followed him out to the shop, just as Rose's phone rang. Bride trouble? She glanced at it, seeing Chloe's name on the screen as she stepped outside with Gabe and Zach.

"Hang on a sec," she said, tapping the speaker button. "Hey, Chloe, can I—"

"Mommy, Mommy! There are puppies!" Avery exclaimed.

"Four puppies!" Alyson added. "Aunt Chloe said we can have the one that looks like peanut butter and chocolate!"

"I want him, Mommy!" Avery exclaimed. "I want to name him Skippy!"

"I told her it's too much," Ethan chimed in, using his most grown-up voice. "With Dad gone and all..."

Rose looked up at Gabe, who couldn't wipe the smile from his face or the tears from his eyes. All he did was nod...rather enthusiastically.

"That sounds wonderful, honey!" Rose said. "Let's get Skippy!"

"She said yes!" Avery shrieked. "Aly! She said yes! It's the best day of our lives!"

Gabe lowered his face and gave her a light kiss, making it officially the best day of *all* their lives.

Chapter Twenty-three

Madeline

On the afternoon of the "surprise" vow renewal, there was a lot to coordinate so that Rex thought he was hosting a black tie event for one hundred, and Suze thought she was having a small beach gathering for family...and neither one knew what was really going on.

To keep the secret as long as possible, Madeline had suggested the "bridal party" all gather at her studio to dress, getting Suze out of the house so Rex could get ready at home.

"Close your eyes." Madeline issued the order as she and Suze reached the top step to her studio. All she'd told her mother was that she had a perfect dress for the perfect day.

"They're closed," Suze assured her.

"Stay right here," she said, guiding her mother into the studio.

Then she turned on her best spotlight to capture the glory of the dress she'd made and draped a few feet in the air on a satin hanger, warmed by the sunshine behind it.

"All right...you may look."

Suze lowered her hand and blinked into the light, a soft gasp stealing her breath. "Oh...my."

"I know it's a bit much for a beach—"

"It's perfect," she whispered, staring at the dress, her gaze roaming every exquisite inch. "That hem! It...dances."

"And so will you."

"At a beach wedding and a small dinner party."

"Metaphorically," Madeline corrected. "Do you want to try it on?"

"A little late for a fitting, isn't in?" Suze asked, taking a few steps closer. "We're renewing our vows in two hours."

"Yes, but I know your body as well as I know my own, so why don't you just dress here in my bride's room?"

"But...my makeup." She touched her unadorned face.

"Your bridesmaids will help you."

"Bridesmaids? This was supposed to be—"

"You've got seven of them, but we're not in matching dresses. We all picked shades of teal to match the ocean, and Rose has created small and breathtaking bouquets."

Suze turned as the first of the laughter floated up the stairs from Tori and Raina, who were cracking up as they rushed to the top of the stairs.

"I'm here!" Tori called. "Let the fun begin!"

"Tori!" Suze threw her arms out. "You made it!"

"For your special day!" Tori hugged her more petite mother so hard she nearly lifted her. As she did, she looked over Suze's shoulder and gasped. "Get out of town! That dress is fabulous!"

Suze laughed as she hugged Raina and touched her face. "You okay, sweet Raina? You look a little tired."

"I'm really pregnant and my darling sister's flight from Boston was delayed until midnight."

"I'm so sorry," Tori said as she turned and hugged Madeline, adding a big kiss on the cheek. "Are you kidding me with that dress? It's gorgeous!"

"It really is," Raina agreed, stepping closer to Madeline's creation. "I get what you said about the 1940s movie star vibe. Do you love it, Suze?"

She nodded slowly. "I was expecting something a little more understated, but I'm certainly not disappointed. I just...Madeline said you're all bridesmaids? For a little beach wedding?"

They had to work not to share a look and in that beat of silence, Madeline swooped in and lifted the dress. "Come on, Suze. Put it on. I can make any last-minute alterations."

"I'm sure it's perfect," she said, beaming at Madeline. "I'm in love with it, to be honest."

More voices from downstairs pulled their attention and, in a matter of seconds, Sadie and Chloe came up with Grace right behind them.

"It's Mom's wedding day!" Chloe sang out. "Now there's something most people don't get to say."

"It's a vow renewal," Suze said in the same musical voice. "But I feel like a bride."

Laughing, they all hugged and chatted as Rose came next, assisted by Gabe and Zach, who carried boxes of bouquets.

"You'll be a beautiful bride, Suze," Gabe said, giving her a kiss.

"That's so sweet," she said, looking a tad perplexed at all they'd done. "But I still thought this was a little...thing. A surprise for Rex."

Gabe just lifted a shoulder, deftly skipping the "surprise" part, since what Suze didn't know was that Rex had asked Gabe to be his best man.

"Your marriage wasn't a little thing," Gabe said. "Why should your re-marriage be one? By the way..." He looked at Rose. "Why don't we do this on our twentieth in a few years?"

She laughed and shook her head, but it was hard to wipe the smile from Rose's face since Gabe made the decision to move back and give up pursuing a medical degree.

"All right, Zach, let's scoot and let these ladies do the wedding thing." He planted a kiss on Rose's mouth and left them while Tori popped champagne and Chloe showed off pictures of her new home and business and Grace slipped over to peek at a rack of wedding dresses Madeline had recently finished.

"She's next," Suze whispered to Madeline as they watched her examine a lacy trim.

"No, you're next," Madeline responded, taking her mother's hand. "Who wants to do the makeup honors for the world's most beautiful mother?"

"I will!" Sadie jumped up from the sofa. "I learned some great tricks in Europe. Come on, let's get you in the hot seat."

Madeline's studio included a small lighted vanity, since so many brides wanted to have their wedding makeup tested the day of their final fitting. She'd prepared the area for today with all the makeup and brushes they'd need.

While the others sipped champagne and laid out their various teal dresses, Madeline and Sadie flanked Suze at the vanity, chatting about foundation and contour.

Settling into a chair to watch Sadie start the job, Madeline let out a sigh of pure happiness.

Sadie's secret had been hard to keep, and she was so happy it was over. True to her non-disclosure agreement, Sadie hadn't disclosed a thing. She'd never lied, but simply stuck to her story that she was tired of Brussels, needed a long break at home, and she'd be getting back into corporate marketing after the holidays.

And there'd been no other mention of Adam Carpenter, or whatever his real name was.

Madeline swallowed and worked to stuff him back into the compartment where he'd resided for twenty-five long years, but some days it was hard.

She longed to ask Sadie for more information, but knew she wouldn't get it. She'd done a little more searching online, but come up with nothing on the guy. All she could do was carry on and keep him locked away.

"Don't you think, Madeline?" Sadie asked brightly.

She shook her head and blinked. "Sorry, I was...lost for a moment."

Sadie gave a sad smile, something in her eyes telling

Madeline she knew exactly where she'd been. "I said a smoky eye is too much for someone as fair as Mom."

"Oh, definitely."

"Well, I'm officially the most pregnant bridesmaid," Raina joked, coming over to model her dress.

Susannah laughed and shook her head. "First of all, you're gorgeous. Second, this is a vow renewal, so why are there bridesmaids? And third..." As she talked, the others joined them, all waiting for her to finish. "Third is..." She wiped a tear and a few of them did the same. "Third..."

"You okay, Suze?" Tori asked.

She stood and pressed her hand to her chest, looking from one to the other. "Forty years ago, on this day, I wore a much more understated dress and went to a beach just south of where the Ritz-Carlton is now..."

They all fought smiles, knowing that was exactly where they were headed again.

"And I thought I had everything that day. Rex Wingate loved me," she said. "And with him came four little girls who..." She tried to swallow, her gaze landing on Madeline. "Who were just too perfect to actually be mine."

"We weren't perfect," Raina cracked. "Rose and I couldn't even make it down the aisle."

"You were both precious," Susannah said. "And you were electrifying..." She touched Tori's chin. "And you were well on your way to becoming my best friend," she said to Madeline. "And then..." She reached a hand to Sadie. "This wild angel burst on the scene, then sweet Grace, and finally..."

"Last but not least," Chloe joked as she fought the same tears they all had.

"Every one of you...perfect. A family of strong, amazing women."

"You made us that way, Mom," Sadie whispered and they all chimed in their agreement.

"I married your father," Susannah said, "but I won the jackpot of motherhood."

They fell into a group hug, crying out the tears before the mascara was applied and dresses were zipped.

An hour later, they reached the beach at Ocean Song, where the whole "surprise" started to fall apart when Susannah saw how many people were on the beach and Rex stood at the front in a tuxedo.

When some piped-in music started playing an instrumental melody, each sister walked down the short, sandy aisle and kissed their father. Madeline was last, waiting at the back with Suze.

She turned to her mother when it was time to walk. "Off I go, Suze. You start when I'm at the front."

But her mother was teary again.

"Be happy, Susannah Wingate! You get to marry Rex twice."

She put her hand on Madeline's face. "I love you. I can't help but wish I was the one going next and you were the one..." She swallowed. "I just love you so much, honey."

Madeline managed a smile. "Suze, I'm right where I'm supposed to be."

But with each step down that sandy aisle, she really

had to fight to keep Adam Carpenter locked away in her memory.

THE CEREMONY, dinner, and party flew by in a flurry of family and food, drinks and dancing. It was past eleven when the last of the invited guests left, but a large group of Wingates stayed gathered around one table, with chairs pulled up so they could be together.

The youngest kids had gone home with Kenzie and Zach to the beach house, but the sisters remained with Rex and Suze, plus Gabe, Travis, and Isaiah. Some sipped coffee, others nursed wine or champagne.

All of them glowed with the joy of being together and celebrating a marriage that served as a beacon of hope and light for everyone.

"That, dear Maddie, was everything I dreamed of and more." Rex leaned over and grinned at her. "I can't believe she had the same idea."

"The same but different," Madeline said as she glanced around the empty ballroom. "Wow, this zoomed by fast, didn't it?"

He nodded, following her gaze as if he was remembering the whole night. "I talked to every single person and it was glorious," he said, then he frowned and looked around the table. "Have you seen Raina? I haven't thanked her properly for securing us this amazing location."

"I think I saw her go toward the pool area, but she

looked wiped out. She might have been looking for a nice big chaise to take a nap, which, at seven months pregnant and nearly midnight, she deserves." Madeline glanced toward a hall that led to an outdoor exit where she'd seen Raina a few minutes ago. "Want me to look for her, Dad?"

"Just check on her, okay? She seems more exhausted than usual."

"I will." Madeline pushed up and walked to the back of the ballroom, turning the corner to a wide corridor that was designed to run from the kitchen to the lanai for pool food service. It was long and unlit, but she could see the pool lights glimmering on the other side of a glass door at the end.

As she was just about halfway there, a shadow darkened the door and it pushed open, and a man walked in.

In the dim light and distance, she couldn't make out who he was, but he was dressed too casually to be part of this event and not like any of the staff.

He slowed his step as he saw her, then stopped completely.

For a moment, her heart skipped as she realized she was essentially trapped in this hallway with him unless she pivoted and headed back to the main space.

She started to turn but something held her gaze on him. Everything about him was...familiar.

"Maddie? Is that you?"

She froze as all the blood in her body felt like it turned to ice. Only two people on Earth called her

Maddie and she'd just left one sitting in the ballroom. And the other one was—

"It's me, Adam," he said softly. "I need to see Sadie."

Adam. Adam Carpenter had just climbed out of his compartment and was suddenly in front of her...for real.

He took a few steps closer and she felt her whole body tremble with shock, with recognition, with a tsunami of emotions that she couldn't begin to understand or manage. Everything was a jumble of confusion, her pulse hammering so hard she could barely hear his words.

"What are you doing here?" she managed to whisper.

"I need to see Sadie, as soon as possible. She has to sign something."

She sucked in a soft breath, recoiling at how cold he seemed. That was how Adam said hello after twenty-five years? She braced her whole body as he slowly came closer, looking up at him, nearly speechless at how little he'd changed.

Yes, he was older, with a few lines around his eyes and gray in his hair. But his brown eyes were still warm, his slightly crooked nose still endearing, and the cleft in his chin still marking him as one of the most unique-looking men she'd ever met.

But she couldn't stand here and stare at the man she'd once loved. He wanted Sadie...and she wasn't entirely sure she wanted to give her sister up to him.

"She's already signed something," she finally managed to say. "Aren't you and that company finished with her?"

"Not quite. She's signed an NDA, but there is still one very important piece of paper that will end all this."

"All what?" she demanded.

Even in the dim light, she could see him swallow as he gave his head a shake. "I can't say. I have to—"

"You can't say? My, there's a lot you can't say, isn't there? Unlike twenty-five years ago, when you lied to me and made me think you were a loom operator with a good heart and kind words. But your heart wasn't good, was it? And your words weren't kind, were they? They were all lies so you could take down Elana Mau."

His hooded eyes shuttered. "Maddie, I'm sorry I disappeared. I worked for the FBI and I had a job to do."

"To charm a young woman to get access to her boss? And now you want access to my sister." She blocked his way toward the ballroom. "I don't think so."

"Please, you really don't know—or you shouldn't— what this is about. I'm not going to hurt her. I have a piece of paper to sign and when she does, her problems will be over. But I have until midnight and the deal ends."

"The deal? No, no. You either tell me what's going on with her, why you're here, and what she did or I'm going to scream bloody murder right now, and you'll be arrested for trespassing."

He huffed out a breath. "I have papers from the Saint Pierre family that, when signed, will free her and give her enough money to do whatever she wants for as long as she wants. Then I'll disappear."

"Just like you did last time."

"Maddie, I didn't want to—"

Behind him, the glass door shot open again. "Madeline?" Raina called with a question in her voice. "Is that you? Are you okay?"

For a moment, Madeline and Adam stared at each other, then he stepped to the side, as if to show he was no threat.

"This man is looking for Sadie."

Raina came closer, staring at him. "Yeah, I was by the pool and saw him come in here. Why do you need Sadie?"

"I represent the Saint Pierre family and they are requesting her signature on a form."

Raina choked softly. "Now? Here?"

He tilted his head as if to say, "Yes," and Raina looked at Madeline. "Isn't she in the ballroom?" Raina asked.

Madeline took a breath, searching his face again. "I just wanted to be sure this man is...legitimate."

"I assure you I am."

She gave a soft snort. "Fool me once..."

"Madeline?" Raina gave her a confused look. "Let's just take him to Sadie or go get her."

But she didn't move because...Sadie's secret. Whatever it was, taking him into that ballroom with her entire family could bring it out in the open and she still had to protect her sister. She'd *promised*.

"I'll get her." Just as she turned, the glass door opened once more, slamming against the wall as a man rushed in.

"Where is she?" he demanded, charging toward them.

Gasping, Madeline and Raina both backed up, but Adam went right to the man.

"Tristan, get out of here!"

Tristan? He must be—

"You son of a..." Tristan grabbed Adam's collar and pushed him against the wall, fire shooting from his eyes. "She's not signing it! She's not signing that paper."

With that, he shoved Adam out of the way and powered by them, running toward the ballroom.

"Tristan!" Adam cried, racing after him. "You'll screw up everything!"

Raina grabbed Madeline's arm. "Do you have any idea—"

"No! Let's go!"

They both ran in the same direction, turning into the ballroom right behind the two men, who marched toward the table of surprised people.

None more than Sadie, who turned snow white as the man called Tristan shot toward her.

"Sadie!"

Every single conversation came to a halt, and every person froze in shock. Everyone but Sadie, who stared at the man that Madeline could only see from behind. She stood very slowly, looking like she wasn't sure her legs would hold her.

"Tristan. What are you doing here?"

"Don't sign it, Sadie. Please, please don't sign it."

Rex stood next, not even using his cane. "Does someone want to tell us what's going on?"

For a long moment, no one said a word, but Madeline

couldn't help noticing that Gabe stood, too. Isaiah joined him, taking a few steps closer to Sadie. Travis was next—all of them ready to defend.

Sadie must have noticed, because she held up both hands as if to calm their fears. "He won't hurt me," she said softly. "At least, not the way you think."

"Sadie," Tristan said, inching closer. "You know I didn't mean to hurt you. That was my family. And I've left them. Well, I'm about to."

"I'll believe it when I see it," she said dryly.

Just then, Adam came around the table to her other side, holding out a piece of paper. "Sign it and be done," he said. "The money is ready to be transferred into your account."

The money? Madeline, not even realizing she held Raina's hand, walked to the table, somehow knowing she was about to get all the answers she'd wanted for weeks. But Sadie looked sad and broken, and she wasn't sure answers were worth her sister's misery.

"You don't want that money," Tristan said, taking a step closer to her other side. "You want me."

"Excuse me?" Rex said. "I'm still waiting for an explanation."

Sadie let out the longest, saddest sigh, her gaze locked on Tristan's blue eyes, his square jaw locked, his flaxen hair mussed from running.

"Dad, Mom, everyone," she said, her gaze moving around the whole family until it landed on Madeline with the tiniest, secret glimmer. "This is Tristan Saint Pierre."

"Tell them who I am, Sadie."

"I just did."

"Tell them, Sadie. Tell them *what* I am."

"He is..." She closed her eyes. "My husband."

As the room reacted with a rolling gasp, Adam took one step closer. "Not if you sign this paper and accept the payment Cecile and Gregoire have generously offered. You will be free from a foolish caper and Tristan can continue his life."

"Don't sign it, Sadie," Tristan ground out the words. "You are my wife. Please, I don't want to end this marriage."

"Tristan, we can't," she whispered. "It was a lark. A mistake. A moment of madness. And your family will disown you."

"I've disowned them."

Her eyes widened in shock.

"I'm not leaving you, Sadie. You think we were drunk and silly and danced our way into a Copenhagen wedding chapel because it was fun? No. I married you that night because I love you. I've loved you since the day you showed up in my kitchen and you know you feel the same way."

She stared at him, her whole face bloodless. "You make this decision and your family will make you miserable."

"I'm miserable without you."

"Then they'll make *me* miserable."

"Not if we're here."

"Here?" she scoffed. "You'd live on Amelia Island?"

"I've leased a storefront. I'm turning it into a chocolate shop."

Raina gasped and squeezed Madeline's hand and leaned close to whisper, "It's him! That's who rented the ice cream parlor."

Sadie looked just as stunned. "You did what?"

"You heard me. I need six weeks to undo my entire life in Brussels. Then I'm moving here with two goals: to make chocolate and to win you back."

Sadie blinked and a tear fell.

Adam cleared his throat, pulling all the attention from the riveted crowd. "Tris, you're willing to give up everything? The money, the name, the reputation? Are you sure? Because you have..." He glanced at his watch. "Fifteen seconds."

Tristan sighed, then looked at Sadie, reaching for her hand. "I'm sure," he said. "But you're not."

Sadie said nothing but her chest rose and fell with difficult breaths.

"I'll be back on the first of January," Tristan said. "Between now and then, you can think about us. And when I come back, you can either be my wife, or sign that paper. They'll still give you the payout. They'll do anything to get rid of you, and I'll do anything to keep you."

She looked at him, torn. Then, he closed the space between them and whispered something in her ear. Something that made her sigh and close her eyes with an emotion Madeline couldn't read.

With that, he gave a formal half-bow to Rex and

Susannah, then walked out the way he came. Adam was right behind him, but he slowed his step in front of Madeline, looking hard at her.

"If you love your sister, you'll talk her out of this madness. He was meant to be a Saint Pierre, in Brussels. And she was not meant to be his wife."

Madeline lifted her chin. "I'll let Sadie think for herself," she said. "We Wingate women are a lot smarter than you think."

He shuttered his eyes and followed Adam, leaving Madeline trembling in his wake.

But all eyes were on Sadie as they waited for her explanation.

"So...that was my husband," she said on a mirthless laugh. "I married him in a moment of alcohol-fueled madness, and his family really didn't like that, so it cost me my job and...and...I guess he's coming here." She bit her lip. "I hope you all love chocolate. And him."

"What about you?" Rex asked. "Do you love him?"

She sighed. "Well, since I just turned down a small fortune to end the marriage? I must feel something. I have a little time to figure it out."

Very slowly, Madeline walked toward Sadie, her arm outstretched. Sadie took the hand she offered, pulled her in, and hugged her.

"Whatever you decide," Madeline whispered, "we all love you and we'll help you through anything."

∽

DON'T MISS the next book in the Seven Sisters series, *The Chocolate Shop on Amelia Island.* Sadie faces the consequences of her clandestine marriage when Tristan opens his shop to tempt the town with truffles...and win back his wife. When Adam returns, Madeline learns the truth about the man she once loved and it rocks her whole perfectly structured world. Raina's babies are on the way and no matter how hard she tries to deny it, there's only one man she wants by her side...but is he gone forever? Step back into the world of the Wingates for sweet surprises, deep emotions, and a loving connection between seven sisters that carries them through every high and low in life.

Visit www.hopeholloway.com for release dates, covers, and sneak peeks into the series!

The Seven Sisters Series

The Carolina Christmas Trilogy

Do you need a little Christmas, right this very minute? Of course you do...brought to you by two beloved women's fiction authors, Hope Holloway and Cecelia Scott.

Introducing The Carolina Christmas Trilogy...a charming, heartwarming holiday trilogy that will whisk you away to a dreamy winter in the Blue Ridge Mountains. With sweet romance, strong family bonds, and an uplifting story of hope and joy, this is the perfect Christmas collaboration between two beloved women's fiction authors!

The Asheville Christmas Cabin – Book 1
The Asheville Christmas Gift – Book 2
The Asheville Christmas Wedding – Book 3

∾

Love Hope Holloway's books? If you haven't read her first two series, you're in for a treat! Chock full of family feels and beachy Florida settings, these sagas are for lovers of riveting and inspirational sagas about sisters, secrets, romance, mothers, and daughters...and the moments that make life worth living.

These series are complete, and available in e-book (also in Kindle Unlimited), paperback, and audio.

The Coconut Key Series

Set in the heart of the Florida Keys, these seven delightful novels will make you laugh out loud, wipe a happy tear, and believe in all the hope and happiness of a second chance at life.

A Secret in the Keys – Book 1
A Reunion in the Keys – Book 2
A Season in the Keys – Book 3
A Haven in the Keys – Book 4
A Return to the Keys – Book 5
A Wedding in the Keys – Book 6
A Promise in the Keys – Book 7

The Shellseeker Beach Series

Come to Shellseeker Beach and fall in love with a "found family" of unforgettable characters who face life's challenges with humor, heart, and hope.

About the Author

Hope Holloway is the author of charming, heartwarming women's fiction featuring unforgettable families and friends, and the emotional challenges they conquer. After more than twenty years in marketing, she launched a new career as an author of beach reads and feel-good fiction. A mother of two adult children, Hope and her husband of thirty years live in Florida. When not writing, she can be found walking the beach with her two rescue dogs, who beg her to include animals in every book. Visit her site at www.hopeholloway.com.